Bucket Nut

ALSO BY LIZA CODY

BACKHAND
RIFT
STALKER
UNDER CONTRACT
HEADCASE
BAD COMPANY
DUPE

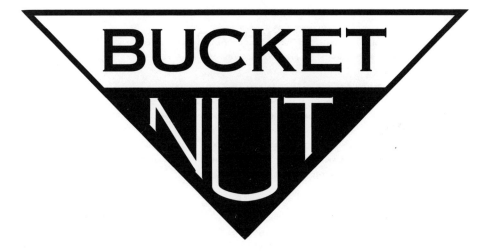

LIZA CODY

A PERFECT CRIME BOOK

DOUBLEDAY

NEW YORK LONDON TORONTO SYDNEY AUCKLAND

A Perfect Crime Book
Published by Doubleday
A Division of Bantam Doubleday Dell Publishing Group, Inc.
666 Fifth Avenue, New York, New York 10103

Doubleday is a Trademark of Doubleday,
a division of Bantam Doubleday Dell
Publishing Group, Inc.

Front matter designed by Cathy Braffet

Library of Congress Cataloging-in-Publication Data

Cody, Liza.
Bucket nut / by Liza Cody.
p.   cm.
I. Title.
PR6053.024788   1993
823'.914—dc20   92-30366
CIP

ISBN 0-385-46776-1

Printed in the United States of America

February 1993

1   3   5   7   9   10   8   6   4   2

First Edition in the United States of America

Chapter 1

THERE WAS A little bloke in the aisle screaming his head off. Quite sweet he looked in his grey mackintosh and muffler. His flat cap fell down over one eye.

'Bucket Nut!' he yelled.

I could hear him clearly over the screams and yells. The things they think of to say.

'Shut yer face!' I gave him the finger.

Out of the corner of my eye I saw the Blonde Bombshell stagger to her feet. I turned my back.

There was a little old lady in the second row bouncing up and down with rage.

'You big ugly bully,' she screeched. 'Big ugly . . . trollop!'

'Trollop yerself,' I shouted.

The Blonde Bombshell hit me in the back and I fell against the ropes. The front row came alive, bashing me with shoes, programmes and handbags. I rolled away to the middle of the ring.

The Blonde Bombshell crashed on top and twisted my arm behind my back.

The front row went wild.

'Kill 'er,' they howled. 'Have her rotten arm off.'

The Blonde Bombshell grabbed a handful of hair and pulled my head up off the canvas. She is such a wanker.

'Watchit,' I said. 'Mind me teeth.'

She knew I had the toothache. But she bashed my face into the floor. Silly cow.

I heaved myself up onto hands and knees with her on my back. She got an arm round my throat. She always gets it wrong: a sort of pinch rather than a lock. But they can't see that even

1

in the front row. And they were really going crazy in the front row.

'Ow-ow-ow,' I wailed to encourage them.

The Blonde Bombshell started to grind the other hand in my face. She really is a bitch. She knew about the toothache and it made me spitty with her.

I got the old quads bunched and then slowly I rose to my feet. She was clinging on. I could feel her breasts squashed against my shoulder blades and that wire-support bra she wears to give her extra cleavage dug into my spine.

She thought I was going to stand upright. She never learns.

Halfway up I went over in a forward roll and dumped her on her back. I twisted and at the last second crashed down on her shoulders. She was too winded to make a bridge. I had her.

The referee ambled over. He was taking his time because the crowd had gone all quiet.

'One . . . ' he said.

'Ooh, you bastard!' someone shouted. 'You cowardly filthy bastard!'

And the boos began. It sounds like a cattle market when I win a fight.

The Blonde Bombshell tensed to make a bridge. But I was so pissed off with her I wasn't going to let her up.

'Two,' the referee said reluctantly.

They booed me all the way to the dressing-room, and that made it a good night.

I'll give you some advice for free: if you set out to be a baddie in this life don't count on any applause. Count the boos. It's the only sure way to judge how well you're doing.

I was doing pretty well for a beginner.

We turned the corner in that chilly corridor at the back of the theatre, and I could still hear them booing. The wrong woman had won much too quickly.

'Ow, me bleedin' back,' the Blonde Bombshell complained. 'You might let up on those falls. I'll be black and blue in the morning.'

'And you might let up on my bleedin' teeth,' I said. 'I told you I had the toothache.'

'I forgot,' she said. Lying cow. She was losing sequins from off her fancy leotard, leaving a little trail of sparkle behind her. But I wasn't going to tell her that – not after what she did to my teeth. Having toothache does something nasty to your disposition.

And then there was her dip-brained boyfriend sitting in the dressing-room when we got there.

'Poor baby,' he said to the Bombshell, and he gave me a look. I was supposed to be nice to him because he was giving me a ride back to London after the show. That meant he thought I should let Poor Baby win.

'Have your arse out of here,' I said. 'I want to change.'

'I've seen more women's bodies than you've had hot dinners,' he said. Stupid git.

'Not mine, you haven't,' I said. 'And you're not going to.'

'Who says I want to?'

'Then move it,' I told him.

But he wanted to massage the Bombshell's shoulders with his big greasy hands. I almost felt sorry for her except she was purring and wiggling as if she enjoyed it.

Does everyone want to be wanted? Do all women want to be touched – even by a greasy-handed dip-brain? Well, I don't know the answer to that, but then, I'm different. Of course I don't like being big and ugly, but you have to admit that almost everything in this life can turn out to be an advantage. For one thing, it is definitely an advantage not to be fancied by the Bombshell's moronic boyfriend, in spite of his Ford Granada.

They don't heat the dressing-rooms in these old country theatres. It was probably a condemned building anyway. There is no shower. You are supposed to do the best you can with the wash basin in the corner.

I wouldn't mind that. The place wasn't designed for wrestling and these cruddy holes are the best I can expect at this stage of my career.

What I did mind was standing about in a draught, still sweating, with the toothache, while his poxy Lordship grabbed a feel.

Still, I had to be polite. The last train home from carrot country would have left hours ago. It's a fact of life, isn't it, that the further a place is from London the earlier the last train goes. I had to get back.

'Go on,' I said. 'Shift out of here.' I was trying to be friendly.

'Eva's shy,' the Bombshell said. Well, what would you expect from someone who wears a lipstick called Champagne Fizz in the ring?

'Eva?' Dip-brain said. 'Shy? Eva Wylie? 'Eave a bleeding beer barrel, more like.'

There is nothing more piddling than a dip-brain trying to be clever, and a Ford Granada doesn't give anyone the right to insult me. I stuffed his head in the wash basin and turned on the tap. Then I picked up my Puma sports bag, my jacket and shoes. It was best to leave before I got really narked.

In the corridor I was caught by Mr Deeds. He was looking a bit narked himself.

'When I ask for fifteen minutes,' he said, 'it's fifteen minutes I want. Not seven. Not ten. Not even twelve and a half.'

'Sorry Mr Deeds,' I said. Mr Deeds is the Governor.

'Get your act together, Eva,' he said. 'Little towns like this aren't too chuffed with women in the ring. I had a job getting you on the bill in the first place. You got to give the punters their money's worth.'

'I slipped,' I said. 'And Stella's got this bad back. We couldn't help it, Mr Deeds.'

'Slipped, my arse!' he said. 'I saw you flaming "slip". And I'm bleeding sure Stella's got a bad back – now.'

'Sorry Mr Deeds,' I said again. I was getting fed up standing in that draughty corridor apologising. I don't like apologising, especially when my teeth hurt, but there's not a lot else you can do when the man who pays you is narked.

'Play the sodding game, Eva, and you could make a few bob,' he went on. 'Piss us around and you're out. O-U-T. Got that?'

'Out.'

'Right,' he said. 'Next week it'll be a different story, right?'

'Right, Mr Deeds.'

He waddled away puffing on his cigar stump. Fat twat. It's always the fat twats who pay your wages. He's got a backside like an elephant. Trouble is, he's got a memory like an elephant too.

I was in a bit of a mood after talking to Mr Deeds, but I wanted to see Harsh before I left. If it hadn't been for Stella Bombshell, I'd have stayed to watch his bout. Harsh is good. He's an athlete, and I can't say better than that, can I?

I knocked on his dressing-room door. I was hoping he'd be alone but he wasn't. Not surprising, really. There aren't that many nice guys around, and everyone likes Harsh.

His girlfriend opened the door. I don't like her. Well, I say I don't like her, but actually I don't know her. She's tiny, and tonight she was wearing a kingfisher blue sari which made her look like a miniature princess. When she's around, I feel like a bloody haystack in a hurricane. I wished I'd had a wash.

'Hello, Eva,' Harsh said. He was against the wall stretching his achilles. He's one of the few who warms up properly before going on. That's why he doesn't have as many injuries as most. Also, he has beautiful balance. I warm up properly too. I'm working on the balance.

'Would you like a Coke, Eva?' Soraya said. She has lovely manners, but I still don't like her.

'I'm just on my way out,' I said. There was a slim chance he might ask me to stay and then give me a lift back to Town.

'I'll see you next week then,' he said.

'We're spending the night in Bath,' Soraya told me. And then I remembered that everyone except Stella Bombshell and me were booked at the Pavilion.

'Oh, well, ta-ta then,' I said, as if I hadn't a care in the world.

'Goodnight, Eva,' Soraya said. And Harsh smiled at me. He has a lovely smile, has Harsh. Shiny white teeth, all the right size.

5

If I can get enough fights, and if I do well enough in the Championships, I'm going to get my teeth fixed properly. I know a really good dentist and I'm saving up already, but it's expensive.

Chapter 2

YOU CAN'T WALK quietly on cinders.
    They call this old pile of parts the Grand Theatre, and even the car park at the back is as un-grand as you can possibly get. All the cars are parked any old how on hardcore and cinders. The Grand! Don't make me laugh.

Still, it wasn't lit. That's one good thing about rotten venues in carrot country – they don't light their car parks. It's like they're just asking you to borrow a car.

I found a Renault 12 that was really begging to be borrowed – the driver's door didn't even close properly, and the wiring panel was loose. When I started it I found the tank was nearly full.

I was doing the owner a favour really – provided he was insured.

Who needs a lift back to Town when there are so many carrot crunchers queuing up to lend you their motors?

It wasn't very late, but there was hardly anyone about on the streets of Frome as I drove out. It gave me a lonely sort of feeling. I like a bit of bustle, but you don't find it much in carrot country. Everyone goes to bed early after watching their Mary Poppins videos, I suppose. I couldn't even find a chipper open. What on earth do country people do for fun?

I was hungry. People my size need food after exercise. But another piece of advice I'll give you for free is – don't stop for nosh in a small town where you've just borrowed a car. Everyone is related to everyone else and someone's bound to see you and call the polizei.

I've learned a lot of self-control in the past couple of years.

So I drove straight past all the pubs and ignored my empty stomach.

There was a story Harsh told me once about the most famous wrestler in history. His name was Milo of Croton and he used to train by carrying a calf around on his shoulders for miles and miles. It was always the same calf. As the calf got bigger and heavier, Milo had to get stronger and stronger to lift it. Harsh said Milo was ahead of his time, and that story was about the basic principles of weight-training and how you have to train your muscles slowly against increasing resistance.

Milo won five Olympic titles, so I wouldn't sneer at his training methods if I were you. If Milo of Croton was anything like me, though, he would've ended up eating his calf with roast potatoes and lashings of gravy.

It isn't a good idea to think about roast potatoes when you're starving – not if you want to pass the next kebab house and get out of town without being caught in a borrowed motor.

I hate the country. When you get away from the town it's all dark and your headlights pick up corpses. You're always running over things that are already dead – hedgehogs, rabbits, foxes and things that have been squashed by so many cars you can't tell what they were. If it's got feathers, you know it was a bird, but otherwise it's anybody's guess.

Things stare at you with junky green eyes.

In the country, things are either dangerous or dead. People may not be much better than animals, but at least people don't leave other people dead on the roads. They take them away so that they don't have to get run over again and again. Just think what London would look like if everything that got run over was left where it lay.

And take the food.

I stopped at a chipper about thirty miles out of Frome. They were just shutting up shop when I got there and all they had left was a couple of mushy-pea fritters. Mushy-pea fritters! I ask you! I really do hate the country.

They tried to make me live in the country once. I was seven

years old, and it was one of those fostering deals. They sent me off to live with this weird couple who had a big house in Cambridgeshire where they kept dogs and ponies and about five other kids. It was the sort of deal that made all the social workers misty-eyed and damp-knickered.

'You'll love it, Eva,' they whinnied. 'All that space to run around in. All the lovely grass and trees.'

In my opinion, social workers don't know obbly-onkers about city kids. Everybody went to bed at nine o'clock. There was nothing to do. The ponies had evil tempers. The dogs farted and had fleas and crapped all over the 'lovely grass'. And the weird couple were religious freaks who expected all the kids to 'get along' with one another.

What makes people think that just because you're the same age as someone else you're going to get along? I mean the kind of kids who get fostered come from all over. They're nervous. Whatever kind of family you come from, you miss your home. There are kids who want to knock you about, kids who steal, kids who wet the bed, kids who set fires, kids who can't talk. And we're all supposed to get along, and be grateful for the grass and evil-tempered ponies.

Nature is supposed to be good for you. But it isn't. It bites, stings or poisons you at the drop of a hat. And besides, there are more birds in Trafalgar Square than ever I saw in the country – and that's counting all the dead ones in the road.

No. London's the place to be, and don't let anyone tell you different.

In London you can hustle. There's always a way to make a little biscuit – always somewhere to kip. It's best not to be too fussy about what or where, but if what you want is to get by, without too many folk asking questions, you can do it here.

If you're not stupid, that is. And I'm not stupid. A lot of people think I am – because I'm big. Big equals stupid, right? Well, anyone who thinks that is about as sharp as a golf ball.

And anyone who says it out loud to me gets a puffy kneecap.

I left the car at Waterloo and legged it home.

I had a home that year. And I had a proper job.

There was a chain-link fence with razor-wire curled in loops over the top of it. I got my keys out and undid the padlocks on the gate. As a precaution I whistled – wheee-yooooo. It was after midnight and the dogs would be hungry.

They hurled themselves out of the shadows, butting into my knees and thighs, slobbering.

'Hello, Ramses,' I said. 'Hello, Lineker.'

They were all right, as dogs go – but over-eager. They led the way to the shed, and I unlocked it. I mixed a couple of scoops of doggy-toast into the revolting meaty gunge they eat and stood back while they munched it up.

Then I picked up the torch and did my rounds.

It was a big place so a round took quite a long time. The best bit was the second-hand park because that was lit. All I had to do was check the fence and walk between the cars making sure no one was camping out on the back seats.

Then I walked round the sales room and offices, making sure all the doors were locked.

The worst part was the wrecker's yard. There was a big spot-light but the bulb was gone. I'd spoken to Mr Gambon about it three times, but he was a tight sod.

'You've got plant there,' I told him. 'Worth thousands. You've got parts and spares – mountains of them. A light bulb'd make my job easier.'

'Lazy cow,' he said. Me! But I should've known better than to ask for something on the grounds it'd make my job easier. That's like giving them a licence to say 'no'.

One of these days, I thought, I'd talk to the Owner about it. But since he moved out to Ongar I don't see much of him.

Lineker was snuffling in a pile of steel rods, but Ramses ran off to the perimeter fence. I took off after Ramses because he looked purposeful. I caught up in time to see him snap the hind-quarters off a big brown rat.

There were a couple of weak lights on the fence, and a sign which read Armour Protection. I don't know what Armour Protection is, or if it ever existed. The only protection that yard had, was me, Ramses and Lineker.

Chapter 3

M<small>Y HOUSE WAS</small> a Static Holiday Van.
Sometimes, along with used cars and commercial vehicles the Owner buys second-hand caravans and mobile homes. My Static had spent most of its life at Poole Harbour in Dorset, and when the weather is damp, you can still smell brine and sea-mould in the furnishings.

I would prefer something with its own wheels because then, if the worst happened, I could simply hitch it on to a car and move my whole home. If you want to move a Static you have to hoist it onto a flat-bed, and you can't do it quickly.

But when the Owner employed me, the Static was all he had. And I had to admit, smell or no, it beat dung out of a hostel.

At the time, everything I owned could be stuffed in a carrier bag. After six months in the Static my possessions have expanded, but I'm still proud of the fact that in the event of a disaster I could be out of there, fully packed and ready for anything in ten minutes flat.

In fact, I'll tell you a secret – out of the things I carry at all times is a two-ounce tobacco tin, and in that tin is everything I need to make light, heat, food and take care of minor ailments. There are tallow-protected matches, a flat shaved candle, scalpel blades, wire, a flexible saw, waterproof plasters, needle and thread, aspirins, tea bags and chicken stock cubes. It is really amazing what you can get into a two-ounce tobacco tin if you are scientific.

I got the idea out of an SAS Survival Handbook. It makes me feel better, and I'd recommend it to anyone who regularly wakes up in the middle of the night anxious about floods, fire, nuclear fallout or homelessness. Take a tip from me – be prepared for the worst and you'll sleep better.

Nighttime is the worst time. I like to be out and doing something rather than lying alone in the dark trying to sleep. That's why being a night-watch-woman is such an ace job for me. I'm not supposed to go to sleep, and if I want company there's always Ramses and Lineker, or a chat through the fence to some night-owl passerby.

I finished my rounds and then went to the Static for a little nosh. Someone had taped an envelope to the door. I opened it and, by torchlight, read the message. It was today's date, and the words – *Tomorrow, 6 p.m., Mr Cheng.*

Mr Cheng doesn't waste words. Mr Cheng doesn't waste anything. He probably thinks I can't read and he's doing me a favour by writing short letters. He thinks anyone who isn't Chinese is stupid, and compared to Mr Cheng perhaps they are. I could fold him up and put him in my knapsack. But I wouldn't, because Mr Cheng doesn't take too kindly to liberties.

I put the note in my pocket and unlocked the door.

I was well-pleased. Whatever Mr Cheng wanted me to do it meant extra ackers tomorrow. Extra ackers are always welcome. This job gives me the basic – a roof and food – but if I want a bit of a stash and to get my teeth fixed I need extra. That's where the wrestling and Mr Cheng come in.

I left the Static door open to clear the whiff of sea-mould. To tell the truth, I was a bit whiffy myself. Because of that argy-bargy with Bombshell's boyfriend I hadn't had a wash in Turnip Town.

Harsh says a fighter should always be one hundred per cent strict about personal hygiene, so I pumped up the water and put two kettles full on the gas stove.

There is a water heater, but it is electric powered and I don't use electricity in the Static. If you use electricity you get electricity bills. The Static is hooked up to the mains and metered, but the one who reads the meter and decides what I should pay is Mr Gambon. And the first couple of months after I moved in were such a rip-off I decided not to use the sodding stuff. I've got torches and I've got gas. When I run out of gas I buy a new bottle, and when a battery runs down I buy another.

I'm in control. Right?

I had a wash, and I put on a clean tracksuit. Then I made a pot of tea and warmed up a couple of cans of stew. Harsh says I should eat green vegetables, but there were potatoes and carrot in the stew. They may not be green but they are veg, so I reckoned they'd do. He also says I shouldn't eat white bread. But I don't like brown, especially the stuff with all the grain left in. Sometimes it hurts your teeth when you bite on it.

And sometimes I think Harsh is full of shit. Just about every-thing he tells me to do is hard work or tastes bad.

I compromised and ate two slices of white and two of brown.

While I ate I stared at my poster. The torch was propped so that the circle of light brought it up really nicely. 'Eva Wylie', it said, 'The London Lassassin.'

In the picture I was facing right with my head turned towards the camera. I was wearing black and making a bicep. It was a pretty good bicep, though I say it myself who shouldn't.

'Savage,' I said to myself, 'really savage.'

It made me feel as if I was getting somewhere. It made me feel real.

After a while, though, I looked down at the saucepan. I shouldn't eat out of the pan, I know, but it's only me, so I do. The remains of the stew had hardened at the bottom, and somehow it reminded me of those dead foxes on the road after they had been pounded and flayed by car after car after car.

I wondered where the time had gone and I didn't feel so good any more. Time is like that sometimes – it seems to leapfrog over itself. It leaves you feeling lost.

Lineker was barking, so I shook myself and went out to see what was up.

Lineker is beautiful. He's all muscle. His hair is so short and shiny it looks like someone coloured him with a spray can. But his bark . . . it's sort of falsetto and hysterical – like the voice of a small red-headed man.

Ramses, on the other hand, is bow-legged and short-necked. He rarely barks, but when he does it's like a bass guitar – quite musical really, but sinister.

There were a couple of kids outside the fence poking sticks at Lineker. Lineker was going ape. But Ramses just stood in the shadows waiting.

If you see two boys together you see two people up to no good. That's a fact of life. I'd bet you a week's wages three-quarters of the mischief in this world is done by males between the ages of eight and eighteen.

So what? As long as they don't do it on my patch I couldn't care less.

I said, 'You're out late.' Nothing hasty, see. I could have run them off straight away, but I kept my relaxed mental attitude. They were people to talk to after all.

The lad with the stick stepped back from the fence. His mate said, 'We was just talking to your dog.'

'You want to watch him,' I said. 'He's a bit vicious.'

'My brother's got a Doberman,' the lad with the stick told no one in particular. His mate was squinting at me with a funny look on his face.

'You ain't a man,' he said suddenly. 'You're a bleedin' tart.'

'Never!' his hoppo said.

'Straight up.'

'Godzilla!' He threw his stick at the fence, and they sprinted off into the night. Lineker went after them barking furiously.

'Fuck off, gob fart!' I yelled.

It was a pity really. Since the police moved the girls from Mandala Street it's been a bit quiet on this corner. I'd be lucky if I spoke to another soul till the men came at seven-thirty and I opened up the yard.

The fellers don't talk to me much but they do respect me. They respect me for two reasons. One – I can handle the dogs.

15

And two – there's been no thieving from the yard since I've been in charge. None at all.

   And that's all I ask from people. A little respect. Credit where it's due.

Chapter 4

I WOKE UP at about two in the afternoon. Sunlight squeezed through the orange curtains and made the Static look as if it was on fire.

The giant crusher was pounding away and there was the usual sound of crashing and wrenching and men shouting at each other.

It's never too quiet to sleep in a wrecker's yard.

I got up quickly and rushed through my suppling routine.

I was going to visit my mum, and I had to get there before three.

If you want to talk to my mum while she's sensible that's the time to do it. She doesn't get up before one, and she's a complete rat-bag until she has her first drink. Then she has a couple of good hours and after that it's downhill all the way till she goes to sleep at about four in the morning.

She's had a hard life, so you shouldn't blame her.

When you say someone has had a hard life you picture someone old. Don't you? Go on, admit it.

But actually, my mum isn't forty yet, and she'd look all right if she took care of herself. When she goes out in the evening all made up and dressed like a Christmas tree she looks pretty tasty – with the light behind her. You'd never know she was stoned out of her tiny mind and that within a couple of hours all the make-up would be smeared round her chin.

She lives on the second floor of a high rise – which is just as well as the lift never works and coming home in the state she does, if she lived any higher she'd spend most nights on the stairs.

Even so, the wind on the second floor walkway was something awful. I knocked on her door and waited.

When she came, she only opened the door a crack and peered out like a scared rabbit. She always looks scared when she opens the door, and, knowing the life she leads, I'm not surprised.

Kids whizzed behind me on skateboards and she flinched.

'I s'pose you'd better come in,' she said, and turned away.

As she passed the bedroom door she pulled it shut. That meant she had scored last night and he was still in there sleeping it off.

Like I said, you mustn't blame her – everybody's got to pay the rent somehow.

We went through to the kitchen.

Now, you might think the kitchen would be the worst room in this tip my ma calls home. But it isn't. It's the best. And the reason for that is that she never uses it except for making the occasional cup of instant coffee. Eating comes second to drinking in Ma's life. When she gets hungry she eats burgers.

The first thing she said when we got there was, 'If he comes in, you're my sister, right?'

I laughed, and she must have seen something in my face because she said, 'Scrub that – you're a neighbour.'

I said, 'Speaking of sisters . . . '

'Don't start all that again,' she interrupted. 'I've got the most awful head.'

I filled the kettle without saying anything, and made two cups of instant. She got a bottle from the cupboard under the sink and dumped some in her cup.

'Just to cool it down,' she said. She can't stop lying, Ma.

I waited a minute or so, and then I said, 'It's important, Ma. Have you heard anything?'

'It's the only reason you come here,' she said. 'Pestering me about her. You don't give a brass farthing about your poor old . . . '

'Mum,' I supplied for her. She can't bring herself to use the word.

'Don't call me that,' she snapped, looking over her shoulder at the door. She kicked it shut. Her feet were bare and dirty, and her big toes were strained over sideways from being squeezed into pointy shoes.

'What should I call you?' I asked. I was beginning to get a mood on.

'I've got a name.'

'I've got a sister!'

'Why don't you shut your face!' she yelled. 'She doesn't want to know you. Look at you!'

'How do you know?' I yelled back. 'We were close . . . '

'Years ago.'

'Not *that* many . . . '

Just then, in spite of the screaming, we both heard the toilet flush.

Ma got to her feet. She picked up her cup and the coffee I'd made for myself. She went off back to the bedroom.

'See yourself out,' she said as she left.

I wanted to break something.

But early training counts for a lot, and if there was one thing we learned as kids it was always to tiptoe around Ma's men. If Ma had a man in the house we either got out fast or we pretended we weren't there. Ma was never too choosy about who she brought home.

That was her downfall, really.

I went into the sitting-room. I was thinking that Ma should never've had kids.

But she did. And one of them was me.

The other one was Simone.

The sitting-room was a pit. It was thick with days of old smoke. The beer cans and ashtrays spilled off the coffee table and onto the floor. Someone had broken a bottle against the telly and a half eaten burger was mashed into the rug. All in all it looked like one of those country roads I don't go for.

If Ma had ever had a boyfriend like Harsh, I was thinking, things would've been a lot cleaner. Then Harsh might have been . . .

I stopped thinking about that.

What I wanted was behind the telly under the pile of Ma's old *True Love* magazines. She doesn't read that garbage any more – even Ma wises up sometimes – but, whenever she moves, she always carts the old ones along with her. She calls them her books.

Under Ma's books was an old photo album. Our nan left it to Ma when she died. There was a picture in the album I wanted to see. It was the last one ever taken of Simone and me together.

I turned the pages quickly. I didn't want to look at the ones of Ma when she was young. They always made me feel sort of choked, because Simone, when she was ten, and Ma, when she was ten, looked quite alike. Too alike for comfort.

I found the page. And there we were in our nan's front room.

I know exactly when that picture was taken. It was Simone's twelfth birthday – two days before they put a place of safety order on her and took her away. So it was two days before the last time I ever saw her.

Usually, when we got sent away, they'd send us away together. Or when we got back or bunked off we'd meet up at Ma's. Or, if we couldn't find Ma, we'd go to Nan's.

But that time, they split us up. And about a year after that Nan died.

Simone never came home again.

I heard later she got fostered out, and she must have liked the people because she stayed. Or, more likely, they liked her and persuaded her to stay.

It was hard not to like Simone, but I have to tell you, she was not a strong character. She could be persuaded. Especially if she didn't have me along to remind her of where we belonged.

I stared at her long-ago face. She was so pretty. Most people never knew we were sisters. I was taller than her even though I was a year younger. And I was never pretty.

The most important thing was to remember her face. Sometimes I have nightmares that I'm walking down the street and there's a beggar with her hand out. And I walk right by. I don't recognise Simone until she calls out to me. 'Eva,' she says, 'I'd've known you anywhere. But you've forgotten me.'

Well, I haven't forgotten. And one day I'll find her. It's got to happen because everyone says blood's thicker than water. For the same reason, I know that Simone is looking for me. She has to be. And she won't find me unless she finds Ma first, because a lot has happened to me since we last saw each other.

A lot has happened to Ma too, but at least she stayed in the same borough. That's what I'm counting on. And that's why I see Ma every couple of months. Apart, that is, from the fact that blood is thicker than water even where Ma is concerned.

Someone has to keep this family together.

Chapter 5

THE NOISES COMING from Ma's bedroom sounded like some-one having an asthma attack.

I knew I was safe to nose around in the sitting-room for a while. I didn't often get the chance. I closed the album on Simone's face and I started going through the rest of the pile of books looking for letters.

You see, with Ma, you never knew. She threw away unopened letters because she was afraid of bills and summonses.

'It's only trouble,' she'd say. 'It's trouble come with a stamp on the envelope.'

Sometimes, after she's had a few too many she'll just kick aside anything that comes through the door. She could have won half a million on the pools, or be up in court the next day for defrauding the Social Security. She'd never know.

I went to my nan's funeral with a social worker. They let me out for the occasion.

Ma wasn't there. She said she was too emotional, but if you ask me, she was too horizontal.

I went because I thought Simone would be there. And – you'll think I'm a right cow – I was quite grateful to Nan for providing a time for me to get out of Youth Custody and see Simone.

But Simone wasn't there either.

It was a big question to me, afterwards – why? Why hadn't Simone come?

Ma didn't know. She got really pissed off with me asking all the time.

Months later, when I finished my sentence and I was back at home, I found a letter. It was from Simone's social worker, and it said that after a great deal of consultation with Simone's new family it was felt it would not be in the best interests of the child to expose her to such a fraught occasion.

In other words they'd stopped her.

If Ma had told me that she'd have saved me months of worry and disappointment.

But Ma hadn't even opened the letter.

See what I mean?

'In the best interests of the child' – now there's a phrase. There was a joke that did the rounds when I was a kid. It went – What's the difference between a pit-bull terrier and a social worker? Answer – the pit-bull terrier gives the child back.

I had to stop myself thinking about the old days because I was getting a bit choked.

But thinking about social workers gave me an idea.

It was years since I last went to see Simone's foster family. Maybe I could find their address and pay them a visit. They wouldn't like it. They hadn't last time, but that was when I was still a kid and hadn't learned discipline and a relaxed mental attitude.

The asthma sounds from Ma's bedroom died away. In the silence that followed I got to my feet and went to the door.

Then a loud voice said, 'Where's me fuckin' wallet?'

I should have left earlier.

Ma said something I couldn't hear.

Then he said, 'Give us it back, slag!'

And then the trouble started.

Ma came storming into the sitting-room with her hair all over her face and nothing on. She went behind the sofa.

He came in, still pulling up his zip, with no shirt to hide his tattoos.

Ma said, 'You must've left it in the club, you must've dropped it in the club, you must've . . . '

But he wasn't quite that stupid. He said, 'I didn't drop nothing nowhere. Gi'ss it back, slag.'

'In the car then. On the stairs . . . '

'Shut it!'

'I'll help you look . . . '

He reached over the sofa and grabbed her wrist giving it a nasty twist.

'Bastard,' Ma screeched.

'You thieving mare!' he said and balled up his left fist.

I caught him by the hair with one hand and the seat of his strides with the other. I set my feet the way I do in the ring and then yanked and lifted at the same time.

He flew away from Ma and landed on his backside by the door.

Ma got pulled over the back of the sofa and fell in a heap on the cushions. The sofa tipped over.

She had obviously stuffed the bastard's wallet under one of the cushions, because, with the sofa on its side and the cushions all over the floor, I could see it clearly.

Ma could too, because she shut up screeching and sat on it.

I felt great.

The git on the floor said, 'Who the fuck're you?'

'On your bike, mister.'

He started to get up. But I kicked his arm and he went over again.

He didn't want to fight. Which was a pity because I really felt like it. He got out of the room sort of slithering on his arse. In the passage he scrambled to his feet and was out the front door like a hound out of the traps.

I went to the bedroom, took up the rest of his clothes and went after him.

He was shivering in the wind on the walkway. Tattoos aren't much good at keeping out the cold.

He said, 'She pinched my wad.'

'You heard her,' I said. 'You dropped it. Now move it before I go down and jump on your motor.'

You can always beat a man by threatening his car.

He picked up his clothes and went away.

When I got back in, Ma was still all of a heap on the floor.

She'd found a bottle somewhere and was tipping the contents down her throat.

She said, 'He hurt my arm. He really hurt my arm.' Whining like a little kid.

I said, 'Get some clothes on.'

I was pumped up, but I didn't like the fact that Ma was all undressed. She looked so weak and wobbly.

'Get dressed,' I repeated.

'My arm hurts,' she said, sucking the neck of her bottle. 'I think I'll go down the doctor's.' She just sat there.

I decided to leave, but as soon as I got outside and slammed the door I remembered about Simone's old address. I knocked and waited. Then I knocked again.

'What?' Ma yelled from behind the door.

'That family,' I yelled back. 'The ones that fostered Simone. Where do they live?'

'You're a pain in the bum,' she said through the letter box. 'You know what? You're a right pain in the bum.'

I waited, thinking that just this once she might do something for me. But nothing happened. So I went away.

Men have been hitting Ma ever since I can remember. Not that I blame them. Sometimes I feel like hitting her myself.

What I can't understand is why she never did anything about it.

All you have to do is go to the gym and get a bit stronger. If you are strong, men won't take liberties.

Nobody hits me any more – not unless I'm paid for it.

I hope Simone is strong. If anyone needs to be strong it's a pretty girl.

Of course, I was born with an advantage. I was born big. But big, in itself, isn't much use. Everybody knows big weak people.

No. Take a tip from me – if you want respect in this world – get rid of the wobbly bits.

Chapter 6

I SPENT THE next couple of hours at the gym lifting weights. Harsh uses Sam's gym too, only, that day he was still in cabbage country.

The best way to get out of a mood is to train hard. But it's easier to train if you're in company. Alone, you get bored and start skipping reps, and before you know it you stop checking your body position. If you stop that, you're in danger of lifting wrong and you could injure yourself.

Anyway, that day I had the place to myself, and time dragged, but I took a proper shower afterwards and washed my hair.

I used the phone to call the promoters and found they'd booked me to fight at the weekend. More lovely dosh.

Money worked where the weights failed that afternoon so I was in a much better mood when I showed up at Mr Cheng's restaurant at six o'clock.

The Beijing Garden used to be called the Peking Garden, but for some reason Mr Cheng changed it last year. The restaurant wasn't properly open when I got there, but it wasn't properly closed either. It was hardly ever closed because of all Mr Cheng's friends and relations and the gambling they do upstairs.

I was wearing my black leather jacket. Mr Cheng liked me to wear that jacket – he said it made me look like a gangster. It would have cost an arm and a leg, that jacket, if I'd paid for it.

Mr Cheng was in his shirtsleeves when I arrived. He was leaning on his counter punching his calculator and figuring things out. He is very clever with numbers. I think he likes them better than food or people.

He said, 'Lil job fewva.'

He meant, 'Little job for you Eva.' But he spoke so quickly I needed a second to translate.

'Colleckarntie,' he said.

Right, I thought – collect Auntie. That was easy enough.

'Later,' he went on, 'go tabnatroe fackountue.'

'What?'

He looked up. 'Wassamatter Eva? Defforsome'ing? I said, Later, go to Abernathy Road. There's an account due. I want you to collect.'

'Oh,' I said. 'OK, Mr Cheng, will do.'

He held out his hand. 'Key,' he said.

'Where?'

'Fristree.'

Which meant the Rover was in the Frith Street car park. I took the key and left. Mr Cheng talks too much.

I liked the Rover. It was big and black and people paid attention to it. And it made a change for me to drive a car with the owner's permission.

All the same, I wasn't quite legal, I'm never quite legal if you must know. The fact is that I don't have a driving licence. I'm a good driver and I never had an accident, but I never bothered with a licence. I would have to take the test. It would mean filling in forms and getting my name in the official computer. I wouldn't like that.

By rights, I should have told Mr Cheng about the licence. But he didn't ask, did he? And what they don't ask, I don't tell.

All he asked was, 'Drive, Eva?' Actually he said, 'Dry fever!'

And I said, 'Yes,' and that was that.

Mr Cheng asked me to drive for him because he wanted to talk business in the car on the way to the airport. It must have been dodgy business because he wanted someone who couldn't speak Chinese. I know as much about Chinese as he knows about wrestling so we suited perfectly.

I liked the Rover on the motorway. It felt dignified.

Driving across town to the Edgware Road after six o'clock

was a different matter. It was all stop-go-stop. I think sometimes that London is choking to death.

Auntie Lo lived in a big block of flats. There was a porter, and the lift worked, and no one sprayed pictures of private parts on the lobby walls.

The porter wouldn't let me in until he'd phoned up to Auntie Lo although he knew me well.

I have never been inside Auntie Lo's flat. The procedure is – I go up, ring her bell and wait. She looks at me through the spyhole, puts the chain on the door, says, 'That you, Eva?' through the crack. When she is absolutely sure it *is* me she comes tittuping out on her four-inch heels with her handbag clutched to her chest.

Auntie Lo is sixty-five if she's a day, but she always wears the most teenage shoes you ever saw. In other ways, from her little wool coat to her huge plastic handbag, she is Mr Cheng's Auntie. But those shoes!

She is a bit of a joker too – except it's always the same joke. And that evening was like every other time.

She said, 'When you getting married, Eva?' And burst into little huffs of laughter.

I said, 'Can't find a man big enough, Mrs Lo.' And waited while she locked all four locks on her door.

When she was ready we went down in the lift together, and she said, 'One of these days I write home – get you a big Chinese man.' And she huff-huff-huffed all the way to the ground floor.

I like Auntie Lo. She is a fixer. If anyone at the Beijing Garden has a problem, the standard response is, 'Ask Auntie Lo,' or if it's Mr Cheng talking, 'Ar skanti.'

On the way back to the restaurant we picked up two men. They were both a lot younger than Auntie Lo and they were waiting on the corner of Cabal Street.

'Big party tonight,' Auntie Lo said. And then as the two men got into the back of the Rover, she sniffed and said, 'Not big enough for you, Eva?'

'Not nearly.'

'Huff-huff-huff!'

Mr Cheng came out onto the pavement outside the Beijing Garden. He had put on his black jacket to help Auntie out of the car. With Auntie safely inside, he came back and handed me another key.

He said, 'Tay Kastra.' Which meant he did not want his precious Rover to go to Notting Hill Gate.

He also gave me a plain white envelope.

'Seesmee,' he said.

I parked the Rover and, as per instruction, took the Astra.

Mr Cheng's instructions may be a bit weird, but they are always precise. And if I follow them precisely – collect Auntie, see Smith, bring back the money – he will pay me precisely. There won't be any, 'Nice one, Eva, I'll owe you.' He won't even thank me. But it will be cash on the nail, and maybe more work next week.

You know where you are with Mr Cheng. What you won't know is what he's up to, or what he's thinking. And that suits me.

Bermuda Smith runs a cellar club – music, dancing, drink and food. A bit of everything. He books good bands.

White people go for the music and atmosphere but they aren't very comfortable.

The polizei go for the drugs.

Mr Cheng won't go there at all. He won't even let his Rover go.

I don't know what his business is with Bermuda Smith but whenever I turn up with a plain white envelope, which is about once every couple of months, Bermuda Smith gives me a carrier bag in return.

The carrier bag is always sealed with duct tape so I can't tell you what's inside. I think it's a lot of money.

Now you might think that I am well-placed to make a very big score here. But you would think wrong. And I will tell you for why. The first time I did a pick-up for Mr Cheng he had me followed. And the package I picked up was a dummy. I know, because he showed me. He didn't say anything. He just examined the package with a magnifying glass to see if I'd slit it with a razor blade. Then he opened it. It was full of cut-up newspaper. And a small incendiary device. It made me sweat just thinking about it.

Later, Auntie Lo said, 'To frighten the monkey, first let him see you kill the chicken.' She said it was Mr Cheng's philosophy of life.

Mr Cheng is a man who knows how to get respect.

It was too early for action at the club. Things don't really get going till after ten. But a few people were drinking at the bar or waiting for food. I went through to Bermuda Smith's office.

They say Bermuda Smith eats dog flesh to make himself fierce. They say he has four wives.

He looks like a wire coat-hanger. If he wants muscle he has to pay for it. He has plenty of gold – in his teeth.

'Hey, Eva!' he said. 'What's new?'

He pretends to be very friendly with me because of Mr Cheng.

I gave him the envelope and he stared at it.

'It's that time again,' he said. Then he brightened up. 'Hey, Eva, heard this one? What's the difference between a rabid dog and a woman with PMS?'

'Dunno, Mr Smith,' I said.

'Lipstick!' He cackled and then he shut his mouth like a clamp and said, 'Wait at the bar, Eva. Have yourself a drink.'

'I haven't got all day,' I said. I can be a bit snotty in a polite sort of way when I'm acting for Mr Cheng.

'Be cool,' he said. Then he scowled and pointed his finger at my belly button. 'You tell Cheng,' he said, 'you tell him I'm still taking pressure. I want action. You tell him. Now go.'

I went to the bar wishing that one day Bermuda Smith would invite me to wait in his office. His office is stuffed with toys – train sets, cars, fire engines, teddy bears – even dolls. They say he is making up for lost time.

The barman poured me a beer without asking what I wanted. While I drank I watched the band setting up on the platform at the other end of the cellar. It looked like an Ego Band. You know, black singer, black musicians and three white backing vocalists. They come the other way round too. I don't know why, but it always looks like a wank to me.

Anyway, there I was, watching the three white women trying to test their microphone, while the men plugged in the backline. I was minding my own business but I began to notice I was attracting attention.

This is not unusual. I am a very visible person. But it is annoying.

I looked down the bar and saw two white guys staring at me and talking to each other behind their hands. They saw that I had clocked them, but they didn't stop.

It makes me a bit spitty when people stare.

'It's five quid a look,' I said. 'Or go home and watch telly. I'm not the entertainment.'

That usually does one of two things – either they get embarrassed or they get narky themselves. Doesn't bother me which.

This time neither of those two things happened. The bloke who was staring the hardest got off his stool and came over. He took out his wallet and handed me a five pound note.

I thought I'd call his bluff, so I snatched the fiver and turned back to my drink without saying a word. He just stood there looking. Well, he'd paid for it so I suppose he was entitled. I was still narked, all the same.

After a while he said, 'Five quid an hour.'

'Get stuffed,' I said.

'No, seriously.'

'Get stuffed seriously,' I said. I didn't even look at him. He had a poncy accent. You can handle the middle classes quite easily by being a bit nasty. They aren't used to nasty.

This one wasn't put off. He said, 'I mean it.'

I said, 'Are you still here?' And gave him my best fuck-off look. It should have blown him away.

'I'm a sculptor,' he said.

'You're a tosser.'

31

'That too,' he said quite cheerfully. Say what you will about the middle classes – they know how to take an insult. Used to it, I suppose.

He went on, 'Look, I'm not joking. I'm a sculptor. All I'm interested in is form. Don't you know you'd make an absolutely splendid model?'

That really got up my nose.

I said, 'Don't you know you'd make an absolutely splendid corpse?'

He laughed.

What a sodding nerve!

'I know your sort,' I said, and stuck my fist up close to his mouth. 'Go on, have a laugh! Just do it somewhere else. I'll give you five seconds to get out of my face. After that you can kiss your teeth goodbye.'

He stepped back then, and looked a bit upset.

At that moment one of the backing singers came up to the bar and ordered a brandy and soda. She was stunning to look at – all hair and teeth.

I said, 'If you want a model, ask her. Maybe she'll believe you. Meantime why don't you crawl back under the bog seat where you belong.'

The 'sculptor' slunk away and rejoined his mate at the other end of the bar.

The backing singer gave me a vague smile and said, 'That's right, you tell him.' She had a poncy accent too.

The barman gave her the brandy and soda. She drank it in one go. It made her look less vague.

'I despise men,' she said in her cut-glass voice, and weaved her way back to the band.

I was so aggravated by what had happened that I left my beer and went to stand in the shadows near the fire exit. I don't mind people making fun of me so long as I get the chance to hit back. But I did not want to start anything while on business for Mr Cheng, because, sure as eggs is eggs, he would hear about it.

So I stood in the shadows and seethed.

Another thing which annoyed me was what I'd said — I told the 'sculptor' he could 'kiss his teeth goodbye.' I mean, how the freaking hell do you kiss your own teeth goodbye? It made me look like a pronk. He was probably having a giggle about it with his mate. I wished I could go and sort him out.

I was still brooding when Harry Richards came up with Bermuda Smith's carrier bag.

Harry used to be a light heavyweight boxer. But that was years ago. When I first came across him he was at the end of his second career as a heavyweight wrestler. He used to fight in a red mask because he had such a round, placid face no one could believe he was up to no good.

In those days I wasn't in the ring myself. I just followed the tour around helping with crowd-control and picking up the finer points of the game.

Harry is old — over fifty anyway — but he still trains now and then. He hasn't quite gone to seed. Certainly he still looks useful enough to work as one of Bermuda Smith's bouncers.

'Yo, Eva,' he said. He gave me the bag which was all done up with duct tape as usual. 'You look like you spittin' tintacks.'

'I'm in a mood, Harry,' I said.

'Yeah?' he said. 'You want to come back later and help out?'

'How?'

'New band. Big crowd comin' in. Could be trouble, so we gettin' in extra help tonight. You want a gig?'

'Depends what Mr Cheng wants me to do next.' I wasn't sure Mr Cheng would like me working for Bermuda Smith. But the offer was tempting. And it made me feel better to know that Harry Richards thought I was good enough.

'Tell you what, Harry,' I said after thinking about it. 'If I'm free I'll come.'

We walked to the door together.

I said, 'Who is that dweeg at the bar — the white one drinking red wine?'

'Who him?' Harry turned to look. 'He don't cause no hassle,

Eva. He just an artist. Lives in Holland Park. Gets drunk, likes to play saxophone with the band. If they let him.'

Harry grinned, and added, 'He play lousy sax, Eva.'

Chapter 7

M R CHENG IS like a spider at the centre of a web. He has contacts with people all over London, but he never goes anywhere himself.

There were three more envelopes to deliver that evening, three more bundles to collect.

It would be easier and quicker if Mr Cheng gave me all the envelopes at one time and let me go from one address to another. But that is not Mr Cheng's way. After each delivery and pick-up I had to return to the centre of the web.

You might think that Mr Cheng does not trust me because I am not Chinese. But most people who work for him are Chinese and they have to do the exact same thing. He is not a man to keep all his eggs in one basket.

When I was finished, at about eleven o'clock, one of the cooks sat me down in a corner and gave me a huge plateful of chicken, snow peas and rice. This is the other bonus about working for Mr Cheng. You always get fed. The cook gave me a spoon to eat with. He thinks I can't handle chopsticks and he is right.

I was halfway through my nosh when Mr Cheng came in with my own personal envelope. I laid down my spoon, slit open the envelope and counted the money while he stood waiting.

It looks like bad manners, doesn't it? But the reason I always count the money right then and there is because I do not want Mr Cheng to think I am a fool.

In fact, I am acting the same way he does. And I have always noticed that people only think you are stupid if you do things differently from them.

As soon as I saw the money was right, I said, 'Thanks Mr

Cheng,' and picked my spoon up. He grunted and left. That is the way it always goes and it gives me a nice comfortable feeling.

So there I was, with the night still young, and another job to do. I like to keep busy at night.

But I had responsibilities, so the first thing I did was borrow a car. This time it was a red Vauxhall Nova. I was in a hurry so I wanted a small car with a bit of poke and this one fairly whistled south to my side of the river.

Mr Gambon had released the dogs, as he always did, before locking up. He hates them, he says. Actually, he's afraid of them and he has a set of roller shutters fixed to their pen. The shutters are operated by a remote control switch, just like some people have on their garage doors, which he can work from outside the gate. Mr Gambon does not have much bottle.

I don't know what it is with attack dogs, but they always go for the crotch. Even when they're feeling friendly that is the place they butt you. I kneed Lineker in the chest to remind him to keep his distance. But both dogs were hungry and they followed me all around the yard as I inspected the fence for holes.

I wasn't going to feed them though. Not until I came back for good. Fed dogs go to sleep.

By rights I should have been there, on site, from the time Mr Gambon locked up to when the men arrived for work in the morning. But if I did that I wouldn't be able to pursue my career as a wrestler, would I? Or put in that extra hustle which will get my teeth fixed sooner rather than later.

With the inspection done I raced to the Static. It was time to stash my stash.

People who think I'm dumb are stupid. As a matter of fact, when it comes to hiding my savings I'm very clever. And when your bank or your building society has gone bust, and when your pretty little plastic card is only worth its own weight in plastic, you'll find out just how clever I am.

And if you think I'm going to tell you where I stash my stash, you're even stupider than I thought.

Look at it this way – my savings are protected by a razor-wire fence and by Ramses and Lineker. They are hidden in a place nobody knows about except me. And if by some outside chance you should stumble across them, there will still be a nasty surprise for you.

Can you say the same for *your* stash? I bet you can't.

Chapter 8

HARRY RICHARDS GATHERED his troops at the back of Bermuda Smith's cellar club. We kept to the shadows so as not to frighten the punters. We were ready for trouble. We were given free sandwiches but no booze. Harry is no fool.

Bermuda Smith went home early. He is no fool either.

The band played. The singers sang. The punters ate and drank and danced their little socks off.

Nothing happened.

It was just as well we were paid half in advance – cash.

I am a professional, which means that I don't work except for money. But being a professional has its responsibilities. So I stayed alert. I wasn't like some of the others who sat around their table playing cards. Those blokes, anyway, wouldn't play cards with a female. So I sat by myself and paid attention.

The so-called sculptor was at a table with three friends. He had this 'I am an artist, I can go and get drunk anywhere' pose. But his friends weren't quite so stupid. It looked as if they were trying to get him to slow down on the red plonk. This was sensible because in that club, if trouble came, he would be just another white dick-head – and not the man of the people he thought he was.

I hoped there would be trouble. If it came, maybe I would do something for him, just to show him who he had taken the piss out of. There again, maybe I wouldn't. That would show him too. Either way I was on to a winner.

I had this little daydream where I hauled his artistic white bum out of a hot spot, gave him back his sax and his wallet, and he said, 'Jesus, Eva, where did you learn to handle yourself like that? I'm really sorry I insulted you.' And in his ponciest voice he said, 'I do most humbly apologise.'

Most humbly apologise! – it made me laugh to myself.

I looked at the backing singer, the one who despised men, and I tried that out too.

'I despise men,' I said to the so-called sculptor as he stood before me in the gutter, all rumpled and forlorn.

'I most humbly apologise,' he replied.

Oh yeah! A woman can dream, can't she?

The lead singer was a strutter, a Lord of the Universe. He was all mouth and tight trousers. He had a voice, I'll say that for him, but all the rest was one great big wank. He'd belt out a line and then cock his pretty head as if listening for an echo. Sure enough, his adoring little harem of backing singers would give him back his own words in harmony. An ego trip if ever I saw one.

It wasn't perfect. The one who despised men looked as if she was being propped up between the other two. Her shiny gold hair was falling all over her face and her head was too heavy for her neck. She came in late on some of her lines.

And the punters were beginning to laugh at her. You could see everyone on stage getting narked. It spoiled the strutter's show.

He said something to her between numbers. It didn't look very nice because suddenly she tossed her hair out of her eyes and glared at him.

You could see his point. Boozers are a pain in the arse, especially if you have to rely on them for anything.

She was better in the next number, but she didn't look very reliable. I watched her closely. I was interested. What was a girl who despised men doing boosting the ego of a singer like that? She was small and a proper lovely with long legs and hair and long eyelashes. Everything long that should be long, just exactly what the magazines tell you a woman should look like.

She could afford to despise men, I thought.

It was just as I was thinking this, about how some women

could afford to despise men, when she fell off the platform. I suppose the other two got tired of holding her up because one of them stepped aside, and down she went.

There were a few oohs and ahs from the punters, and some of the dancers stopped to look. But the band scarcely missed a note. And she just lay on her back showing her knickers.

Harry Richards pushed his way to the front because that is the sort of disturbance he is paid to deal with. Except it is usually the punters who fall down stoned, not the entertainment.

He tried to pull her to her feet, but she wasn't having any of it. She started yelling, 'Get your filthy hands off me,' and, 'Bastards, you're all bastards.'

And then the polizei came boogieing in.

This was actually funny. There we all were, expecting trouble from the crowd, and what we got was the law.

That made the band stop playing. In the hush you could hear a sort of rustle and plop as packets of illegal substances hit the floor and got kicked aside. A couple of bloods got jammed in the door on the way to the Gents.

I think I was the only one laughing. I was clean as a hound's tooth. And I knew the back way out. This was important because, however pure I might have been right then and there, the polizei have a memory-bank and I have a record. And my record is not pure – mainly juvenile offences to be sure, but . . . it was best to move out sharpish.

This seemed to be the Thought Of The Day in Bermuda Smith's cellar club. Everyone was on the move – some in a rush, some ever so cool and casual – leaving their shit behind.

The only people not moving were a few tables full of white middle-class voyeurs who sat with their hands in front of them looking bewildered and a bit daft. What was it they hadn't been told?

And little Goldilocks. I saw someone step on her hand in his hurry to the Gents. She began to cry.

It was the way she cried which got my goat. She cried while staring vaguely around her, just like a little kid who wants everyone to know she's crying. She wants everyone to know she's crying because she is absolutely one hundred per cent sure some lovely, kind grown-up will come and save her, and dry her eyes and give her sweeties. It's the way nice kids with nice families cry. They're so confident, you see, even when they're miserable. But there are other kids who don't even bother to cry because it's just a waste of energy. They are a hundred per cent sure no one gives a fuck.

And who was Goldilocks crying for? Who did she want to dry her eyes? Well, I can tell you, because I saw her searching and I saw her reaching. She was crying for that twatty Lord of the Universe, him with the trousers and 1,000 horsepower strut. Dream on, Goldilocks.

I clocked all this while I was ever so casually ambling along to the concealed door which hid the passage to Bermuda Smith's office. The polizei were rampaging around trying to stop the stampede, and one of the oberleutnants was bellowing, 'Everybody, stay where you are!' Dream on, Fuehrer – some people *don't* automatically do what they're told, 'specially when shouted at.

The next thing that happened could've been a bit hairy. Someone lobbed a can of CS gas into the pack.

Well, you can imagine, can't you? Everyone screaming, and coughing and weeping and running every which way. Tables and chairs sent flying, broken glass. Now that's what I call anarchy.

'Nobody move!' the Fuehrer yelled at the seething mob. How stupid can you be?

But Fuehrers have one-track minds. Give them a job and they'll try to do it whatever else is happening.

And in this case *everything* else was happening – including the exit, hawking and spitting, of half the Fuehrer's force.

Laugh? I thought I'd never stop.

I blundered about quite happily. There are a lot of opportunities ripe for plucking in a bit of anarchy. People don't always watch out for their valuables in a crisis.

All the same, tear gas in an enclosed space gets to everyone eventually, and soon I was streaming from the eyes and nose like everyone else. Choking too, even with a table napkin protecting my face.

I don't know why I did it. Later I told myself it was because Goldilocks looked so pitiful. But that wasn't true.

Anyway, here's what happened.

I was choking. I had plucked enough chickens. I cut across the dance floor in front of the platform and I tripped over Goldilocks who was still there. She wasn't alone. A lady copper was trying to drag her to her feet. The lady cop was not in uniform but that's what she was, make no mistake. Who else would waste time trying to arrest some poor drunk in all that mess?

Goldilocks was in a dreadful state.

I said, 'Cock off, copper.' And I picked Goldilocks off the floor. I slung her over my shoulder and steamed out through Bermuda Smith's private door.

Like I say, I'll never know why I did it.

Chapter 9

FIRST, SHE SAID, 'Where's Calvin?' And then she threw up all over the pavement.

I was grateful to her. She could've thrown up down the back of my leather jacket, but she waited till we got outside. You can always recognise a lady.

Then she said, 'Where's my bag?'

Her bag, of course, was wherever she'd put it before going on stage. I told her so but she didn't seem interested any more.

She said, 'He's gone. He's broken my heart.'

'Bollocks,' I said. 'The heart is a muscle.'

And then she passed out.

Kindness is a lot of hard work. You can't borrow a motor with a passed out, pissed singer on your back, so I pulled her dress down as far as it would go and left her where she was.

I nearly left her completely because, what with it being Notting Hill and the polizei monging about all over the shop, suitable motors were pretty scarce. All I could find was a Fiat Panda, a real sardine tin I'd rather not be caught dead in.

Goldilocks probably lived in Hampstead or Highgate, I thought, somewhere totally out of my way. And then I thought, she's probably just got up and taken herself off home. She was the type who could get a taxi driver to take her all the way to Watford, and her without a penny in her pocket.

But I hadn't exactly left her at a bus stop, I'd left her in an out-of-the-way back street which wasn't very posh. So I thought the least I could do was go back and see if she'd gone home.

She was still there.

And that was how Goldilocks came to stay with me at the yard.

I had to fold her up to fit her into the Fiat Panda. I had to carry her through the yard. I had to put her in my own bed.

And as the night wore on I became more and more worried. She was not just drunk, she was ill. She kept on throwing up. She vibrated with chills. And she burned.

I didn't know what to do. Putting a drunk to bed is easy. But I've never been sick in my life so I didn't know what was wrong with her, and I didn't know whether to keep her warm or cool her down.

I found myself rushing around like a one-armed paper hanger.

She'd start shivering and moaning, so I covered her up. Then she'd practically toss the sleeping bag out the window. Then she'd say, 'Oh Jesus, give me water.' And then she'd throw it all up in the bucket.

Sick people are a pain in the arse.

I didn't like her eyes either. Sometimes they bugged out of her head as if she'd been electrocuted and sometimes they rolled around in their sockets like marbles in a cup.

Like I said, being kind is a lot of hard work, but the worst thing was that I was afraid she was going to die. I didn't know how I'd explain a stiff in my Static, so one of the reasons I rushed around like a rat with an itchy tail was so that she'd stay alive long enough for me to get rid of her in the morning.

But in the morning, just after I'd fed the dogs and put them back in their pen, Goldie drank some water, kept it down and dropped off to sleep. Before she went to sleep she looked at me as if she saw me for the first time, and she said, 'Thank you.'

Just thank you. But the way she said it, as if she really meant it, made me change my mind about getting shot of her.

I boiled water on my little gas ring and made tea. And then I sat on the end of the bed to look at her as she slept. I found that my hands had gone all trembly, and I had this ache at the back of my throat. I thought maybe I was going to get sick too.

In the end I threw all the sofa cushions on the floor in the main room and went to sleep there. It had been a busy day and I was tired.

I dreamed me and Simone were back at school – one of those 'approved' schools we kept being sent to in real life. And we decided to bunk off – the way we used to in real life. We came to a wall, and Simone said, 'No. I can't. It's too big. We'll get into trouble.' 'We're in trouble already,' I said. 'Come on, I'll give you a leg up.' She put one foot in my hands, and I noticed she was wearing white satin slippers with little red jewels in them. 'Where did you find the shoes?' I asked. And I gave her a leg up onto the wall. 'They're my glass slippers,' she said. And as I stood there the little red jewels started to fall like rain all around me and into my hair. I stooped to pick them up, because Simone was very particular about her shoes. But they turned to liquid. 'Hey!' I shouted, 'you're bleeding.' I looked up and saw for the first time that the top of the wall was covered with razor-wire. And Simone was caught in it. I tried to climb up to help her, but the wall had grown. There was no one to give me a leg up. So she stayed where she was, and I stayed where I was with blood in my hair.

I hate dreams.

It was weird waking up, knowing there was someone in my bedroom. In all the months I lived there no one but me had ever set foot in the Static. I looked in on her, but Goldie was out for the count. She could have been dead. That's how still she lay. But a wisp of goldie hair fluttered every time she breathed out. I was relieved.

I closed the bedroom door tight. There were things I had to do. Things I didn't want a stranger to see.

It was only a few wallets that had sort of fallen into my hands last night, but I didn't want anyone to get the wrong impression. I'm not a thief. Not really. It's just that sometimes I can't bear to pass up an opportunity, and people are so careless. You'll never believe how careless some people are. They leave their jackets hanging on the backs of their chairs with the wallet sticking out of a pocket. They leave their handbags on the floor where they can't keep an eye on them. They're mad. If you've got it and you want to keep it, for Christ's sake protect it. If you don't protect it, you're just telling people like me you don't want it. And if you don't want it, I'll take it. It's as simple as that.

If you want some of mine, you'll have to kill me to get it. That's simple too.

Sorting out the winnings was easy enough. I was only interested in the cash. Plastic just pisses me off. I know there's a market for it — that and driving licences — but I can't be bothered. It's enough bother getting rid of all the excess so it can't be traced back to me.

The cash went straight into my pocket. That left a little pile of wallets. Normally these would never have reached the Static. They'd have gone into a bin on the way home. But normally I don't rescue Goldies — it upsets my routine.

I was thinking about it when someone knocked on the door and made me half jump out of my skin. Nobody knocks on my door.

There were cushions all over the floor from where I'd slept and my first thought was to kick the wallets under there. But that reminded me of Ma and made me feel a bit sick. So I stuffed them in the back of the paraffin heater.

The knocking came again.

I should've sneaked a gander through the curtains but the knocking made me a bit narked and I did the wrong thing. I wrenched the door open and yelled, 'What?'

I shouldn't have opened the door at all because I found myself face to face with the lady copper from last night.

'Afternoon,' she said, and smiled — which really put me on my guard. If you want to survive in this life *never* trust the polizei when it smiles.

'Eva?' she said. 'Eva Wylie?'

'Wrong number,' I said, and slammed the door.

She knocked again. I ignored her.

I squinted through the curtains. She was standing a little way off just waiting. She looked relaxed and cheerful.

Keep it up a little longer, I thought, and I'll wipe that smile off for you. I'm a very patient person, but I was getting a mood on.

I daubed some margarine on a few slices of bread, and opened the jam pot. I hadn't had any breakfast and my blood sugar was probably low. That makes me moody too. Harsh says that an athlete should keep her blood sugar at a constant level, and I do try. But when you live on your own, you sometimes forget.

The lady copper knocked again. I ate three bits of bread and jam. I could wait her out, I thought, she wouldn't hang around all day.

Next time I looked through the curtains she was talking to a couple of yard men. They were having a laugh. That made me feel very narked.

I pulled the door open and stood on the step with my arms folded.

'Yeah?' I said, very cool. It would've looked better if I'd put the last slice of bread and jam down, but you can't remember everything in a crisis.

'Sorry to interrupt your tea,' she said, coming over.

'What's the time?' I said.

She looked a bit surprised but she said, 'Twenty past four.'

That brought me up short. I'd overslept. I thought it was only two-ish.

'I'm looking for Eleanor Crombie,' she said.

'Who?'

'Eleanor Crombie. You left that club with her last night.'

'Oh,' I said. So that was Goldie's real name. It figured. She looked like an Eleanor.

'Well?' the lady copper said.

'Well, what?'

'Where is she?'

'Who wants to know?' I was going to put my fists on my hips and look threatening but the bread and jam got in the way. I decided to eat it.

'Me. I want to know,' the lady copper said.

'Tough tiddles,' I said with my mouth full.

47

She flicked the crumbs off her shirt and began to look a bit impatient.

I was so pleased about the crumbs, even though it was an accident, that I decided to let up.

'I don't know where she went,' I said. 'I got her out of that mess, but that's as far as it went.'

'I thought she passed out.'

'All she needed was a breath of fresh air.'

'You didn't give her a lift anywhere?'

'No wheels,' I said virtuously.

'Did anyone pick her up?'

'Dunno.' I was getting fed up. I took another mouthful of bread, and she took another pace backwards. It's really nice when you make the polizei walk backwards.

'Do you go there regularly?' she asked.

'Where?'

'That club.'

They think they have the right to ask you anything, the polizei. They ask, you answer. If *you* want to know anything, go to the library.

'See that sign,' I said, pointing to the perimeter fence. 'That there sign says Armour Protection. That's me. I'm Armour Protection. There's been bugger all thieving off this yard in the last six months. And you want to know for why?'

'Why?'

'Because I'm up all night taking care of business. I don't go clubbing regular. Got it?'

'Okay, okay,' she said. 'No need to loose your rag.'

'You ain't seen nothing yet.' I went back into the Static and slammed the door.

This time she went away. I watched through the curtain. She had a very straight back. She'd probably look a treat in uniform, I thought. A back like that was wasted on plain clothes.

I was feeling pretty cheerful. It isn't often the polizei let you get the last word in. Maybe the lady copper was new at the job.

But cheerful or not I had to get rid of the wallets. I nearly got

48

caught in possession and it gave me quite a fright. So I stuck them into last night's empty stew cans and a couple of baked bean tins, collected all the rest of the rubbish and tied up the plastic bin bag. Then I took it all to the skip. It wasn't perfect, but it had to do.

The men in the yard watched me with more interest than usual. They were probably wondering what the polizei wanted. But as usual nobody spoke to me. It was a good thing none of them knew about Goldie or they would have told the lady copper.

As it was, I could imagine what they would have said to her. 'Nah,' they would've said, 'Eva lives on her own. No one goes to visit her.' That's what they would have said, because until last night that was the truth.

It is not a good thing to be talked about. In fact it's a bad thing. Someone from Bermuda Smith's club had talked about me and the result was a lady copper on my doorstep. It was funny for two reasons. The first is that not many folk from Bermuda Smith's talk to the polizei. Second – not many folk anywhere know my address.

It was not a lot of comfort to know that the polizei were looking for Goldie not me, because they had found me, not Goldie.

I thought back. All my old probation orders had run out, I was sure, and I didn't think there was anything outstanding they could nick me for. I'd lived a very righteous life for the past six months since I got a job and settled down. But you never knew. Once you've got a bad reputation you are never quite in the clear.

I decided to be extra careful about knocking off wallets and borrowing motors. And I checked all my survival kit just to make sure I could move out at a moment's notice.

That reminded me to check on Goldie. She was still sleeping which was a good thing because while she was asleep she couldn't ask for anything and I could calm down and do my exercises. All the same I wondered what she was wanted for.

Lying there in my old sleeping bag she looked as if butter wouldn't melt in her mouth.

She was a responsibility. She made me feel tied down. I did forty press-ups to relieve the tension. I wished I could do them on my knuckles like Harsh can but my hands aren't strong enough. After that I did squat-thrusts, and then bridges for my back. The worst bit was the sit-ups. I don't know why, but I find it really difficult to develop a good set of abdominal muscles. My shoulders, back and legs aren't bad, even though I do say it myself. But I sometimes despair of my abs. They just don't look right. Perhaps it's fluid retention. Perhaps I eat too much.

I looked at my London Lassassin poster. The abs didn't look too awful in that. It was just as well. You can't be heavyweight champion with a flabby gut. Well, you can, actually. You should see some of the men. But men and women are judged by different standards when it comes to looks. Don't ask me why, but it's so.

Chapter 10

GOLDIE WOKE UP at ten o'clock. She had slept fourteen straight hours barely moving a muscle. She was a mess – pale and shaky, that golden mop brown with sweat.

I made some tea and opened a tin of tomato soup. She wanted a shower and I tried to explain about the water-heater being electric but she didn't take it in.

'Can't you just turn the electricity on?' she asked.

I explained about Mr Gambon and the meter, but she just looked bewildered.

'Where am I?' she asked.

I told her. She looked bewildered and miserable.

'Why am I here?' she asked. She couldn't remember one single solitary thing about last night.

I told her about the raid, the tear gas and the lady copper.

She looked bewildered, miserable and frightened.

'Where's my handbag?' she asked.

I told her she left it at Bermuda Smith's club.

'Oh shit, shit, shit,' she said and looked as if, on top of everything else, she was going to cry.

'What's in it?' I asked.

She didn't answer. She just flopped back in the bed and stared at the ceiling, a picture of despair.

'What are the polizei after you for?' I asked.

'Oh Lord, I don't know,' she said to the ceiling.

'Come on!' I said. I was beginning to feel a bit miserable myself. I thought I'd done her a favour but she wasn't happy about anything.

'Don't shout at me,' she said. 'I feel awful.'

'Drink your tea,' I said and got up to go out. 'There's a bus stop at the bottom of the road. When you're ready I'll take you there.'

'Are you throwing me out?' she asked in a very small voice.

'Ain't you got a home to go to?' I asked, a bit sarcastic. 'My drum obviously ain't good enough for you.' I spoke rough just to show her I wasn't good enough for her either.

She stared at me.

'I got to protect myself,' I explained. 'I don't want the polizei glomming round here. And that's what you done. You brought them right to my doorstep and you don't have the decency to tell me for why.'

She burst into tears.

'Oh dry up,' I shouted.

I hate it when women cry. I never cry myself. I threw her a towel to blow her nose on and went out to make some more tea. Really, I wanted a beer, but someone who's having trouble with her abdominal muscles should lay off the beer. Beer and abs are deadly enemies.

The kettle was already steaming away. I'd put it on to heat water for Goldie to have a wash and then forgotten about it.

'Fuck it,' I said, and got a can of Hofmeister out of the cupboard. I opened it and plonked myself down on the sofa.

She came in a moment later. She was wrapped in a blanket and looked like one of those Help An Orphan posters.

She said, 'I'm sorry, Eva, really I am. I didn't know.'

'About what?'

'About the police.'

I said nothing, and she sat down beside me.

After a minute she said, 'I owe some money. I've got debts.'

'The polizei aren't interested in your debts.'

'No,' she said, 'but when you get into debt you get into other trouble too.'

That's the truth. 'Go on,' I said.

'I don't want to get you involved,' she said. 'All you did was help a stranger.'

That was the truth too. I was beginning to like her again.

'The real problem is that I lost my bag at the club,' she went on. 'The police will have found it.'

'Yeah?'

'Well, so they'll know who I am, where I live and what I was carrying.'

'What were you carrying?'

She sort of swayed. She was pale as milk.

She said, 'You don't want to know that, Eva. Look, if I could just use your phone, I could ask someone to pick me up. I can't go home, but I have friends who might help.'

'No phone.'

'What?'

'I don't have a phone,' I said.

She stared at me, open mouthed. Nothing had amazed her more than the fact that I didn't have a telephone.

'There's one near the post office on Kipling Street,' I said helpfully.

'I don't believe this,' she said. 'You can't really live by torch-light, with no hot water and no phone. No one lives like that.'

'Well, I do,' I said. 'You're the one in debt. You're the one can't pay her bills. You figure it out.' I was quite proud of myself really. She was so astounded.

'Why don't you eat your soup and have a wash?' I was feeling pretty kind by now. 'Then we'll work out what to do.'

She looked almost guilty.

'What's wrong?'

'Nothing.'

'Go on. What's wrong?'

'I hate tomato soup,' she muttered, looking at the floor. 'And your soap . . . well, it's the kind which irritates my skin. And the loo paper is hard.'

'Anything else?'

'I knew I'd hurt your feelings,' she said, looking mournful.

'I don't have feelings about "loo paper",' I said.

'Honestly, I didn't mean to hurt your feelings. It's just that I have this awful skin.'

Her skin looked like cream. But I supposed that was what made it different from mine.

'Make a list,' I said. 'I'll get what you need at Hanif's. He's open all night.'

'I've no money,' she told me, as if I didn't know. It made me feel good. She looked like a film star and talked poncy, but I had the dosh. I had the power to say yes or no.

She made a list, and I warned her not to go out because of the dogs.

Walking up the road though, I realised she hadn't told me diddly-eye-die about anything I wanted to know. I thought she did because she had this soft confiding manner. But she didn't. I would have to be a bit tough with her when I got back.

The light at Hanif's was dim and brown. Hanif does not like to spend money on electricity any more than I do, but he must. You never see his wife – she lurks somewhere in the storeroom – but you hear her. Their little boy follows customers round the aisles, his big eyes peeled for anyone boosting the odd packet of biscuits. He is almost as good a watchdog as Ramses.

I was embarrassed. Soft bog rolls, clear soap and cream of asparagus soup were not what Hanif expected to see in my basket. I threw in a few batteries so he wouldn't think I'd gone bonkers. He never says much to me anyway. The first time I went in there he called me 'sir', and he has never quite recovered.

It started to rain while I was in Hanif's and the little boy only followed me as far as the door. Sometimes he follows me fifty yards down the street before his father calls him back. I don't know why.

I walked quickly. After a long dry spell the rubbish on the pavement was turning mushy and the rain gave the road a ripe smell like a meat pie on the turn.

At the corner where the yard fence began I saw a motorbike propped in the gutter. It was a Kawasaki, a big one. I went across to look. It was wet, but the saddle was nearly dry. The rider had only just dismounted, but there was no one in the street.

I let myself into the yard. To my surprise the dogs did not come to greet me. But as I got closer to the Static I heard them – Ramses' bass wo-wo-wo, and Lineker's rap-rap-rap. I dropped the shopping on the Static steps, grabbed the torch and a crowbar and ran to the far side fence to join them.

I was just in time to see a feller in motorcycle gear pull away from the wire and run down the street. The dogs hared off after him. I followed the dogs. We were all running parallel – him on his side of the fence, us on ours. I made as much noise as they did, yelling, 'Oi, ball-bonce,' and banging on the fence with the crowbar. Silent and deadly is not my way at all. I always make a big production, and it seems to work.

Because of the dark and piles of car parts I was slower than the man and the dogs so I didn't get too close. But I heard the Kawasaki start up – varoom – and I saw its tail-light disappear round the corner.

The dogs were excited. They crowded me against the fence, jumping up and snatching at my jacket. I shouted them down. But when they were calmer I made a fuss of them. They had done their job.

We went back to the place where the bother had begun. The fence was in perfect nick, but the man had dropped a set of wire-cutters on the pavement outside. I brought them in. I was pleased with myself. Chalk up one more success to Armour Protection.

There was music coming from the Static. I had forgotten about Goldie, but I picked up the shopping and went in.

'Haven't you got anything but Metalica and Bonnie Raitt?' she said. 'What was all the noise about?'

She was playing Real Man and she'd nicked one of my black Guns N' Roses sweatshirts. It came nearly down to her knees and looked nice.

'Intruder,' I said and started to unpack the shopping on the counter. 'We saw him off.'

I found myself wanting to tell her about it but she took the soap and shampoo and shimmied away to the bathroom.

When she was all clean and shiny she came back and made asparagus soup, and it was really nice sitting there by torchlight, just the two of us. I fixed a new gas cylinder to the fire so that she could dry her hair. She did not seem inclined to talk, so I had to prod her.

'It's a long story,' she said.

'I don't mind,' I said, and it's true. I like stories.

'I left home about this time last year,' she told me. 'I was having trouble with my father. Well, you know what fathers are like.'

Actually, I don't. If there's one thing I know nothing about, it's fathers, but I didn't say anything.

'I was sharing a flat with a couple of other girls. I wanted to be a model, and I did get some work, you know, catalogues and things but it was never enough. So I did waitressing and reception, all that stuff where they just need a face. But I was always behind with the rent. The other girls were the same. It's awful. By the time you've bought the clothes and make-up you need, there's never enough for the electricity bill. In the end they cut off the phone and the power and the landlord got really nasty. So we did a flit.'

She sighed. 'The other two gave up and went home,' she said. 'But I was too proud or something.' She sighed again. 'Too stupid I suppose. While I was in that reception job, I met a guy who worked for a record company. So I moved in with him. And he got me a couple of gigs on pop promos. But I couldn't really sing or dance. Just a face again. So I thought I'd better get some lessons.

'It was okay for a couple of months. But the guy I was living with, he was in the music business, and there were lots of parties. And there were the lessons. I was supposed to be sharing the rent, and I did give him something, I really did. But he chucked me out.'

She looked ever so sad. I said, 'Did you love him?'

'It's not that. It's just funny. You live with a guy, and you sleep with him and all that, and then he chucks you out because you're behind with the rent.'

I didn't know what to say. She seemed such a baby. But it was weird too, listening to her story. I mean, I never would have thought girls like her had to pay the rent. Someone always looked after them. Right? And why not? Beauty is something you pay for, isn't it?

'How old are you?' I asked.

'Twenty.'

'What happened then?' I asked. 'How did you get mixed up with the Lord of the Trousers, whatsisname, Calvin?'

'Who?'

'Calvin?'

'He's really going to be somebody,' she said proudly. 'You saw him. Isn't he gorgeous?'

And then her face fell. 'Oh God,' she said, 'Calvin. You'll never guess what I did for him last night.'

'What?'

That was when we heard the dogs start up again.

'What now?' I said, narked. Talking to Goldie was an education. I didn't want to go out. But the dogs kept on and on, so I put on my coat and went.

There was an Astra parked under a street lamp, and when I got closer I saw it was Mr Cheng's Astra. I shushed the dogs and waited by the wire. A man got out. It wasn't Mr Cheng. Well, I knew it wouldn't be because Mr Cheng never went anywhere. It was one of the guys who worked at the Beijing Garden. I couldn't remember his name.

'Eva?' he called.

'Yeah?'

'Got to ask you a question.'

'Yeah?'

'Come out.'

'Nah,' I said. 'I don't want to mess around with all the locks again. Come over here.'

But he wouldn't. Scared of the dogs, I suppose.

'Mr Cheng wants to know if you went back to Bermuda Smith's club last night,' he called from his side of the street.

'Why?'

'Someone said they saw you.'

'So?' I yelled. I was a bit choked. People at Bermuda Smith's had been dobbing on me right, left and centre.

'Were you there?'

'What if I was?'

'Mr Cheng says come and see him.'

'When?'

'Tomorrow.'

'Okay.'

He got into the Astra and drove away. I went back to the Static. I was not pleased.

'Farkin' Bermuda Smith,' I said, shaking the rain off my coat. 'If I never do him a favour again it'll be too soon. Last night was nothing but trouble.'

Goldie looked up. She was sitting on the floor by the fire combing her hair.

She said, 'Do you work for him?'

'Was helping out.' I told her about how I got involved, and about how Harry Richards used to be a wrestler.

She looked astounded all over again. 'I never knew.'

'What?'

'About you working for Mr Smith . . . about women doing that sort of thing.'

'If you're big enough, and strong enough, and ugly enough.'

'You aren't ugly,' she said. 'You're just . . . unusual.'

'That's me,' I said. 'Unusual.'

I was so pleased I had to get up and make us both a cup of tea. She sat there combing her hair, looking very thoughtful and I guessed she was thinking about Calvin.

But she said, 'That intruder – the one on the motorbike. Do you think he was looking for me?'

I hadn't thought of that. I should have, because people thieving for motor parts don't usually come on bikes. They come with vans. And, I had to admit, I'd never had so many visitors before Goldie came along. And that made me think of the lady copper again.

So I said, 'You'd better tell me what you did last night.'

And she said, 'Can I trust you?'

Now you may or may not know it, but this is a very big question. People ask it and answer it without much thought. But they shouldn't. Also, have you noticed, hardly anyone ever says, 'No, you can't trust me.' But really that's what just about everyone *should* say.

So I said, 'I dunno. Depends on what you want to trust me with.'

She stared at me.

I tried to explain. 'Maybe I could dob on you and get you into bother if I know your secrets. But you could land me in the shit if I don't. See what I mean?'

She looked confused.

I said, 'It's a responsibility, knowing other people's secrets. But, like, what about the polizei coming here? I'm not exactly Snow White myself and I can't take the heat. You've got to make up your own mind.'

'All right,' she said. 'I'll tell you.'

I suddenly felt very weird. I didn't understand her at all. I'd more or less told her she couldn't trust me, but it hadn't made a blind bit of difference.

'You know I was sick last night?' she began.

'Yeah.'

'Well, I think I was suffering from narcotic poisoning.' She paused to see how I would react.

'I thought you were rat-arsed,' I said, frowning.

'I'd had a couple of drinks, but that wasn't it.'

'I don't like druggies,' I said, feeling even more upset.

'I'm not a druggy. I've never taken heroin before in my life. I want you to believe that.' She stopped and looked at me and I noticed that her eyes had black borders around the blue which made her look very deep and mysterious.

'Do you believe me?'

'All right,' I said, because it seemed important.

'Calvin was Peter Pan,' she said, 'and I was Tinkerbell.'

'What?'

'Peter Pan,' she said. 'You know. The book by J. M. Barrie.'

'I can read books,' I said. I thought it was about time I checked on the dogs. It was awfully hot in the Static.

'Don't be like that,' she said.

'Like what?'

'Cross,' she said. 'I only meant that there's a passage in *Peter Pan* where Captain Hook poisons Peter's medicine. Wendy leaves medicine for Peter in a spoon. Captain Hook puts poison in it. And Tinkerbell can't get Peter to believe it's poison. So in order to show him she drinks the poison herself and nearly dies.'

'That's stupid,' I said.

'Yes? Then I was stupid too.'

'I don't mean *you're* stupid.'

She sighed. 'What happened was that I found out Calvin was taking drugs. I found out last night because he put them in my bag. I expect he thought it was safer that way. Black guys are stopped and searched for no reason whereas white girls never are.'

I knew what she was talking about there and I felt better.

'We had an awful row about it. I said he was destroying himself. He said it was only fools who couldn't control it. So I took some myself – just to show him. And also so that there would be less for him to take.'

'You must be barking mad,' I told her.

'But think about it,' she cried. 'See it from my point of view. I was so upset that he took smack. I thought if I took some he'd be upset for me too – that he'd look at what he was doing with different eyes.'

'And did he?'

'He couldn't have cared less. And when I started to get ill on stage he came over and fired me.'

It was beginning to make sense to me now – what I'd seen

60

last night, and the way she'd said he broke her heart. She had sacrificed herself for him and he had kicked her in the teeth. I felt quite sorry for her, but all the same she was an awful fool.

'You've got to promise me something,' I said.

'What?'

'That you'll never do any of that shit again. It's a fuck-up. It's the stupidest fuck-up I know.'

'Yes,' she said. 'But you see what's happened, don't you? Calvin's drugs and Calvin's syringe are in my handbag. And I can't get it back, and I can't go home.'

'You don't have to draw me pictures,' I said. 'I won't kick you out, and I won't dob on you. But you have to swear you won't do that stuff again.'

'You don't have to worry about that. It was revolting. It wasn't nice at all. It made me really sick and now it's twenty-four hours later and I still don't feel right.'

'You were lucky,' I told her. 'You might have liked it.' And that was that.

Chapter 11

THE NEXT DAY I took Goldie to Sam's Gym. After what she had told me the night before I thought she could do with some healthy exercise, and besides, we had run out of milk for breakfast. Also I was hoping to see Harsh.

Goldie caused quite a kerfuffle at Sam's Gym. Suddenly everyone was coming over to me helloing and how-you-doing. Anyone would have thought I was popular. Gruff Gordon was there and Pete Carver and Danny Julio who is half a father and son tagteam. The son, Flying Phil, was there too. He's called Flying Phil because of the work he does off the ropes and corners.

I could tell Goldie was a bit nervous because, even while she smiled and said hello, she had her thumbs tucked into fists. People think I don't notice details, but I do. And one thing I've noticed is that anxious women clutch their own thumbs. Don't ask me why.

Gruff Gordon and Pete Carver are very big men and enough to make anyone nervous who isn't accustomed. So I gave Goldie some dosh to make phone calls and buy herself some clobber. She couldn't go around in my Guns N' Roses sweatshirt for ever.

'Who's the doll? Who's the chick?' The fellers kept asking, and I lied to them.

We had decided, Goldie and me, that as so many people were taking an unhealthy interest in her we'd better keep her real name to ourselves. And since I already called her Goldie and she liked it we would call her Goldie Green.

'Fancy you having a friend like her!' Pete Carver said.

'Why shouldn't she?' Gruff Gordon asked. Which was nice of him, except that Gruff Gordon could bullshit for Britain and whenever he's nice to me I wonder what he wants.

I ignored them both and went to the mat to warm up. Always warm up properly before lifting. Some of the fellers, especially the young ones, think it's macho not to. But they're just asking for it.

After that I moved onto the machines and Danny and Phil Julio took over the mat to work out some new moves. I was doing leg curls when Harsh came in and started to warm up in the corner. I watched him, ticking off all his exercises, making sure I had done everything he was doing. I hadn't forgotten a single one, and I was well chuffed.

Then Goldie came back. She had bought herself some pretty Lycra gear and looked a treat. But she had a glum expression on her face.

'I can't get hold of anyone,' she whispered. 'I phoned everyone and no one answers. You'd think all my friends had been wiped off the face of the earth.'

I stopped what I was doing. Goldie talking made me lose count of my repetitions. But my femoral muscles were hurting so I thought I'd done enough.

'Never mind,' I said. 'Try again later.'

'But . . . ' she said, and stopped. She looked as if the end of the world was nigh.

'But what?' I had quite a glow on from all the physical stuff. It always cheers me up no end.

'Christ, Eva,' she whispered, 'I'm stony broke, I'm wanted by the you know who, my boyfriend dumped me, I can't even go home to change clothes and now I'm in debt to you too.'

'I don't mind subbing you,' I said, and it was true because it wouldn't be for long. Nice middle-class girls always have nice middle-class families to bail them out. It was, I thought, only a matter of time before she tapped them, and then she'd be in the clear. If I'd been her I would've done it months ago. Then she would pay me back. True, she was in debt to British Gas, British Telecom, the South Eastern Electricity Board, three landlords and Putney Borough Council. But those weren't people. I was people.

'You'll pay me back,' I said.

'You're a pal, Eva,' she said, and that was all I wanted to hear.

I turned over and lay face down, fitting my feet under the bar again. That way I raised the weights on the back of my ankles, one, two, three, four . . . and this time the muscles at the back of my thighs took the strain.

Lying there and looking past Goldie I saw that Mr Deeds had come in. He was talking to Gruff Gordon. While they talked they sauntered across the gym in my direction.

Gruff Gordon stopped in front of Goldie. He said, 'Got time for a natter, Girlie?'

'My name's Goldie Green,' Goldie said. She had a lot of dignity, I will say.

'Miss Green to you,' I said, and lost count of my reps again.

'No slacking now, Eva,' Mr Deeds said. 'You only managed to tear Bombshell's muscles in Frome. If you keep up the good work you could break her back on Saturday.'

He winked at Gruff Gordon who snorted.

I pulled my feet out from under the bar and rolled over. I did not want to talk to these people lying on my face. But Mr Deeds took Goldie's arm and walked her over to the window. I followed.

'Piss off, Eva,' Gruff said and tried to elbow me out. 'This is private.'

'Not from me it ain't,' I said. 'I know your sort.'

'Piss off,' he said again.

Mr Deeds came back and said, 'Take it easy, Eva. This is business, right? Get on with your work.'

Goldie had her arms folded across her chest and I was sure she was clutching her thumbs, but she held her head high. There wasn't anything I could do about it once Mr Deeds had spoken to me.

I started work on another machine where I could watch them talking by the window. This one was for the back and shoulders.

You grip a bar above your head and pull it down behind your shoulders. I was feeling so choked I didn't bother to count.

After a while Goldie came over and said, 'They've offered me a job, Eva. Isn't that wonderful?'

I was sweating like a pig and I said nothing.

'They want me to be Gruff's valet. Starting Saturday. Cash in hand. Isn't that great?'

'No,' I said. I let go and the bar shot up. The weights fell with an almighty clang. You're not supposed to do that because it damages the equipment. But I didn't care.

I got up and went over to Gruff and Mr Deeds.

'If she's going to be anybody's valet,' I said, 'she's going to be mine.'

I wished I'd thought of it before them – Goldie holding my robe and standing in my corner. Goldie cheering me on.

Gruff starting laughing. 'Beauty and the Beast,' he said. 'Don't be so bleeding thick, Eva. Girls don't have valets.'

'Why not?'

We were standing toe to toe. I could have punched him in his fat belly. I pictured my fist sinking in up to the wrist.

Mr Deeds pushed Gruff away. He said, 'Calm down, Eva. It's all settled. I was looking for a new heavyweight gimmick, and your friend is like a gift from heaven.'

'No!'

'Be sensible. She can't be your valet, and that's final. The punters might have bad thoughts about that.'

'More than they do already?' Gruff asked.

'Shut yer face!' I yelled. He was really winding me up.

Goldie put a hand on my arm. 'It's just a job,' she said.

'Fuck off,' I said. 'It's not just a job.'

I turned away from them and went back to the machines. The one I chose is like a rowing boat. You sit facing it and pull the bar back hard until you're almost stretched out backwards and then you let it in slowly, feeling the resistance all the way. It's a very good machine for the abs. And I needed to work on my abs.

I worked on my abs.

Harsh said, 'You're pulling too much weight, Eva. Stop.'

I stopped. I hadn't seen him coming. He took several kilos off and I started pulling again. He watched.

'How many?' he asked.

'Dunno,' I said. 'I lost count.'

'Stop.'

I stopped.

'You're pulling too much weight. You aren't counting. Do you wish to hurt yourself?'

'No.'

'I think you do wish to hurt yourself.'

'I don't.'

'Get up.'

I got up, and Harsh took my place at the machine. He pulled back slowly and smoothly.

'Watch.'

He pulled and released slowly, rhythmically, one, two, three, four, five, up to ten. The machine made scarcely any sound. His abs were hard and even. He stopped.

'Bad technique is worse than no technique at all.'

'I know,' I said.

'Your anger hurts only yourself,' he said.

'I'm not angry.'

'Why not? You have been slighted.'

'By those squelch-bags? Don't make me laugh.'

'Good,' he said. He gave me his place and went away. I started pulling again. Properly. I began to feel better. It's funny but I often don't know when I'm doing something wrong. It takes someone like Harsh to point it out.

Harsh is a purist. He is a wrestler's wrestler. He may not be a star heavyweight or a crowd puller or a top biller, and maybe he's the guy they put on first after the interval when half the punters are still in the bar, but sometimes when he's fighting, other wrestlers will leave their dressing-rooms to watch. And

66

sometimes they even clap. Harsh is a straight shooter. And I can't say fairer than that.

Afterwards I took a breather, lying back on one of the benches. Gruff Gordon and Pete Carver were on the mat showing off, and Goldie was standing by being told what to do by Mr Deeds. Mr Deeds had his fat hand on her shoulder, but I didn't watch. I shut my eyes and breathed deeply.

Sam's Gym is a noisy smelly place, but I like it. Or I would do if persons like Gruff Gordon went elsewhere.

I packed it in early that afternoon. I was sore all over, and my teeth were beginning to hurt again. It was a relief to stand under a heavy stream of hot water and let it massage my neck and shoulders.

As I stood there I found myself thinking about Ma and the way she wouldn't help me find Simone. You'd have thought she'd want us all together again. Simone was her favourite when she remembered about us – which wasn't often. And I thought of the way she said, 'Simone doesn't want to know you.'

Doesn't. Like she had just that minute talked to Simone and Simone had said, 'I don't want to know Eva.'

It couldn't be true. Simone would never say that. And the only reason we were apart was because we couldn't find each other.

But suppose Ma was *keeping* us apart. I know it sounds stupid, but suppose she was?

Standing there under the hot water I tried to think about it. It seemed so stupid, but I couldn't help feeling suspicious. Ma was always against me. Ever since I could remember she called me a thorn in her flesh. It would be just like her to keep me away from the one thing I wanted. It's amazing, when you think about it, that I've got so much family feeling, considering the example she sets.

And another thing – Ma would do anything for money. Suppose Simone's foster family paid Ma to keep away – to keep me away. I only ever went to see them once, and that wasn't very nice.

In the shower, with the water beating on my head, I nearly

remembered what hadn't been nice about the time I went to find Simone. But my teeth were hurting something cruel so I turned off the taps.

I decided I had to find a dentist quickly. I got dressed and left the changing room.

Amazing things were happening in the gym. I was just in time to see Pete Carver throw Gruff arse-over-tit across the mat. Then he picked Goldie up and slung her over his back. Goldie struggled and squirmed.

'It's a little pantomime,' Harsh told me. He was standing with the Julios, watching.

'I want some screaming,' Mr Deeds told Goldie, 'but otherwise it's shaping up fine.'

'Special,' Flying Phil said. 'You got Gruff with one fall against him, which makes Pete really cocky. And then Pete kidnaps Gruff's valet because he fancies her and he's jealous of Gruff.'

'Okay,' Mr Deeds said. 'Gruff, you're all fuddled and concussed, right? You get up. You look for Pete but he's gone from the ring, right? You look for your Girl. Where is she?'

Gruff got to his feet looking fuddled and concussed – not unlike his normal expression if you ask me.

'Give him an Oscar,' I said.

Gruff gave me a look.

'If you can't take this serious, Eva,' Mr Deeds said, 'Fuck off out of it.'

'It's entertainment,' Harsh said quietly. Harsh is so philosophical about everything that sometimes he really pisses me off.

'It's pitiful,' I said. But I said it out of the corner of my mouth so that no one could hear except Harsh. 'They're so old and fat they can't fight straight any more. If they were proper heavyweights they wouldn't be seen dead doing this shit.'

Harsh didn't answer, but Danny Julio said, 'You should've seen Gruff a few years ago. He was a big man. But that was when we were on telly and there was money in the game.'

When Danny Julio starts gobbing off about how many times

68

he was on telly in the dear old days you know it's time to get on your bike. I made for the door.

Mr Deeds was saying, 'Okay Gruff, you see your Girl. Pete's got her. I want real fury here. I want a real howl, a *roar*. Like the Incredible Hulk, right?'

I pushed through the door and out into the corridor. I didn't even look at Goldie. What did I care? It wasn't as if she was family or anything.

She came running after me. 'Where are you going, Eva? Wait.'

I stopped but I didn't turn round.

She said, 'Why are you doing this?'

'What?'

'This.'

'You're making a fool of yourself.'

'It's money,' she said. 'I've got nothing.'

'You've got me.'

'*You've* got nothing.'

'I've got everything,' I said. 'I've got everything I need.'

'I didn't mean to hurt you. If I'd known you would be like this I would've turned them down. But I've got to earn some money. I can't keep sponging off you.'

'All right,' I said. She always came up with the right thing to say.

'Really?'

'I *said* "all right".'

'Yes, but where are you going?'

'To the dentist,' I said.

Just then we heard this horrible noise from inside the gym. It was Gruff Gordon practising his roar.

Goldie looked at me, and I looked at her, and we both cracked up. When I recovered I said, 'I'll come back and pick you up in an hour or two.'

'You won't forget?'

'Nah,' I said.

'Do you really have toothache?' she asked. 'You look a bit pale.'

69

'Yeah.'

'Well, take care,' she said. 'Toothache's horrid.' And she went back into the gym. That was Goldie all right. She always thought of the right thing to say.

So I walked along, looking for a dentist, not thinking about anything very much. I didn't have an appointment but I thought, if I found one, they might take me in as an emergency. But I sort of lost track of time and I found myself just round the corner from my mum's block of flats. I hate it when that happens, because I'm never exactly sure how I got where I get to. But, look on the bright side, the toothache was gone. I don't know where that went either but I wasn't grumbling.

Ma might just as well live in a yard like me. There are so many piles of rubbish and motors up on bricks that her block looks as if it is growing out of a garbage tip.

I climbed the stairs to her flat and knocked on the door. She didn't answer, but I could hear the telly blaring away inside. I knocked again.

Of course it was a daft time to go and see Ma. She would either be totally slobbed out or in the boozer.

The woman next door poked her head out and said, 'What's all the racket?'

'I'm looking for my ma.'

'She your mum?' The woman looked me up and down, sort of surprised. 'I didn't know she had kids.'

Well, she wouldn't, would she? Ma doesn't admit to much.

'She's gone out,' the woman said. 'Left her bleedin' telly on again.'

'Got a spare key?' I asked.

'These walls are paper thin,' she said. 'She ought to have more consideration, your mum.' Her lips were all thin and pinched with blame. I knew that look.

'She's had a hard life,' I said. The way I always do.

'Ain't we all?' she said. 'Hang on a tick.'

She came back quickly with a pink plastic spatula.

'Try this,' she said. 'It works on next door but one.'

The spatula had some old egg on it but it fitted between door and jamb.

'Give it a shove,' the woman said.

I gave it a shove and the lock came open.

'The way they build these places,' the woman said, 'we're none of us safe in our beds.' She held out her hand and I gave her back her spatula.

'Ta,' I said and I went in.

'And turn that bleedin' noise off,' she shouted after me.

When I turned off Ma's telly I could hear the woman's telly through the wall. And her kids screaming. It's the only way to survive in these places. You make so much din yourself you can't hear anything else. I'm glad I don't have neighbours.

I went into Ma's bedroom. Now, believe me or believe me not, I had never before been in Ma's bedroom – not in this present flat, I hadn't. And it gave me quite a turn, because there on her clatty old dressing table was a picture of Simone in an oval silver frame. And, what is more, it was a picture of Simone as I had never seen her. It was a picture of Simone grown up.

'Piss on a pudding!' I said, and I had to sit down on Ma's rumply sweaty bed. I felt hot and cold and wobbly all at the same time. And then I found I couldn't really look at the picture. I looked everywhere else and it was as if I didn't want to see it.

It meant that all my suspicions about Ma were true, and it made me feel hollow inside.

'You're a mean, lying, crafty, old witch,' I said to Ma, who wasn't there. And then I got up and pulled open all the drawers of her dressing table and her chest of drawers one by one. And I threw everything onto the floor and stamped on the heaps of her clothes. And I ripped one of her dresses to shreds with my bare hands.

It was while I was doing this that I saw her old jewellery case, and in it were her beads and earrings and bangles. And I remembered how Simone and I used to dress up in Ma's clothes when Ma was out, and how Simone would deck herself out with all Ma's beads and pretend to be a princess.

71

Then I felt a bit sorry for the mess I'd made and I started to put everything away again. Because, when all was said and done, Ma was just being Ma, and she *did* have a hard life.

It was while I was tidying up that I found the letter. There was only the one and it came from a solicitor in Braintree, Essex. It was at the back of the drawer where Ma put her underwear when she remembered. I just glanced at the top of it, but it was enough to know that the letter talked about 'the child,' and 'our clients'. I stuffed it into my jacket pocket for later.

It was time to look grown-up Simone straight in the face. I stared at her and she looked back at me from over her shoulder. She was wearing a gold and black ball gown but her shoulders were bare, and funnily enough she did look a bit like a princess. Only it was a real princess she looked like, and that was because the dress and hairstyle were copies of what Princess Di wore a few years back. And she gazed out from under her eyelashes just the way the real princess did.

I was disappointed, but I could see why Ma would want the picture on her dressing table. Then I thought it was just the good-girlie sort of crap foster parents would want her to wear, and it made me feel better to know that Simone hadn't chosen her own clothes. But all the same I didn't like the picture.

The one I liked was the old one on Simone's twelfth birthday. Ma didn't deserve it any more so I went into the sitting-room and stole the album. Ma wouldn't notice. She had about as much family feeling as a fly who lays her eggs on a piece of rotten meat and then buzzes off.

Chapter 12

I T WAS A seesaw day – up, down, up, down. As I walked away
from Ma's place I found something I have never before found
in all my life – a Ford Cortina, door open, keys in ignition,
engine warm. A bleeding Christmas present. Nobody, in my
experience, ever leaves a motor in that condition. Ever. I have
always had to put some work in for my motors, because nobody
made it easy for me. Nobody.

What a day!

I got back to Sam's Gym in double quick time, and when I
got there I saw Harsh sitting on one of the benches in a funny
position and, behind him, that artist dweeg from Bermuda
Smith's bar was drawing his picture.

I was very surprised, but I said, 'Where's my friend Goldie?'
Because Goldie was why I'd come and I couldn't see her anywhere.

Harsh said, 'Showers.'

And the artist said, 'Don't move, please.'

'What the fuck you doing here?' I asked.

'I'll tell you in a minute,' he said. He looked at Harsh and he
looked at his picture but not at me. His fingers were black with
charcoal and his hands moved like terriers on the paper.

I looked at the picture, and you could tell it was Harsh, even
though it was only his back, because of the shape of his trapezius
muscles. I was surprised again. At least he knew enough to
recognise a good trapezius when he saw it.

'He's done your trapezius proud,' I told Harsh, in case he was
worried. 'And the lats aren't half bad either.'

Harsh said nothing, so I went into the showers to find Goldie.
She was fluffing up her hair under the hand drier and she had a

sort of shine on. I was pleased because I'd thought some exercise would do her good, and I was right.

'Phew!' she said when she noticed me. 'That Gruff Gordon smells like a circus bear when he sweats, and Pete's not much better.'

'They're out of shape,' I said. 'If you're out of shape your sweat smells bad.'

'I never knew that.'

'Yeah,' I told her. 'It's all the grease and poisons coming out through the pores.'

'Really?'

'If you're fit it's just salt and water. And that don't pong hardly at all.'

'The things you find out!' Goldie said, brushing away at her hair.

'You can tell how healthy a person is just from the way their sweat smells.'

'No kidding.'

'Yeah. I wouldn't be amazed if Gruff Gordon dropped dead tomorrow – the way he stinks.'

'Not till after Saturday, please,' she said, straightening up and turning towards the mirror. 'If he doesn't fight, Mr Deeds won't give me the other half of my money.'

I wanted to tell her about Simone and the solicitor's letter. I thought, with her education, she might be able to explain what it was all about. But she was doing something to her eyes, and you can't expect any sense out of someone who's drawing lines round her eyes, can you?

She smudged the corners with her little finger and as if by magic her eyes became big and mysterious. I've never understood how that happens. I tried it once and it looked like someone had bopped me.

She stared at herself and sighed, although I couldn't for the life of me see what she had to sigh about.

'Let's go,' she said, and started to collect up loads of bags and packages. She really had been shopping, and I was quite worried until I remembered that Mr Deeds had given her an advance.

'He's changing all the posters,' she said. 'For Saturday.'

'Who?'

'Mr Deeds.'

'Why?'

'He wants my name on them. "Gruff Gordon and Goldie".'

'Yeah?'

I couldn't help it – I was choked. Because Gruff and Pete, being heavyweights, got top billing. So that meant her name would be at the top of the bill too. And in bigger letters than mine. And it wasn't as if she could fight.

'What's the matter?' she asked. She had this way of knowing something was wrong when all I said was 'Yeah.' It really pissed me off.

'Look,' she said, facing me, 'don't worry.'

'I'm not worried.'

'I'm just a face again,' she said. 'I can't actually *do* anything. No one takes me seriously. I'm a prop. Y'know, a puppet or a mascot. Like George says, a gimmick.'

'Who's George?'

'Mr Deeds. George Deeds.'

Well, I never knew that. I'd been working for him for months and he never told *me* his name was George.

'Nobody knows me,' she said. 'Nobody knows who I am. Only you. I'm just a face.'

She looked so sad I said, 'Your legs aren't bad either.' Just to cheer her up. And she started laughing so hard I thought she'd choke. It made me laugh too, except I wasn't sure what was funny.

We were still in pieces when we went through to the gym. The artist bloke had stopped drawing and was talking to Harsh.

Harsh said, 'Don't bite his head off, Eva. Give him a hearing.' And he went to the men's showers.

'Interesting chap,' the artist said, watching him go.

'Well?' I said. 'How'd you find this place?'

'Harry Richards told me you trained here,' he said. 'Don't look like that. He didn't tell me your address or anything. And I really had to twist his arm to get this far. He knows me, and he knows I'm all right.'

'Silly old fool,' I said. I was wondering who else Harry told. But Harry wouldn't dob on me to the polizei. Not Harry.

'Just a minute,' he said. He patted his pockets. Then he shook his drawing book, and a small, glossy book fell on the floor. He picked it up and gave it to me. On the front it said, *'Shrodinger Gallery. An Exhibition of Sculpture by Dave de Lysle R.A.'*

'That's me,' he said, 'Dave de Lysle.'

'R.A.' I said. 'I can read.'

'I'm giving you the catalogue to prove that I'm genuine.'

'Oh you're genuine all right.'

'I'd better talk fast,' he said. 'Because I can see you aren't going to give me much time. There's a new sports complex being built near Winnipeg, in Canada. They ran this competition, which I won, to do a relief frieze, or rather, friezes, over the main doorways. Also a free standing group in a fountain setting. The theme of the work, or rather, works, is of course, to be sport, physical fitness, strength, energy etcetera. The style is to be figurative. I need models. You'd be perfect. I would pay by the hour. Standard rates. You could fit it in with your other activities, to suit yourself.'

'How much?' I asked, and then I had a thought. 'Would I have to take my clothes off?'

'Well . . . '

'Fuck *off*!' I said. I grabbed Goldie's elbow and made for the door.

She said, 'I knew a sculptor once. He talked too much too.'

'Sport!' I said. 'Physical fitness! It's all bums and tits to them. Ever seen anyone train without their clothes on?'

'No.'

'There you are then. He's just another grimy old perve.'

He caught up with us on the street.

'At least come and see my studio,' he said, gasping for breath.

For a guy interested in physical fitness he had a lot to learn.
'Come with Harsh. He's thinking about it.'

'He is?' I stopped.

'Bring your friend if you're worried.'

'I'm not worried,' I said. 'I could throw a guy like you over a
number 3 bus.'

'I don't doubt it,' he said, and I thought he looked sincere.

'I'll consult my advisor,' I said, feeling a bit pleased. I walked
off fast. Goldie had to trot to keep up.

'Slow down,' she said. 'Who's your advisor?'

'You are.'

She burst out laughing. 'You really do speak your mind,' she
said.

'I can't speak anyone else's.'

I still had Dave de Lysle's catalogue in my hand so I gave it
to Goldie. We turned the corner into a side street, and I had a
good look up and down. There was no one interested so I
unlocked the Cortina and got in. Goldie got in beside me.

She said, 'That's weird.'

'What?'

'I sort of remember your car as smaller.'

That gave me a bit of a jolt. I thought she was completely
brain-dead in the Fiat Panda the night I rescued her.

'Why didn't we drive to the gym in this?' she asked.

'I only just picked it up,' I said. 'There was someone else
driving it.' I believe in telling the truth. Especially when lying
my head off.

'Where are we going?'

'Home. I've got to see to the dogs. And if you're staying with
me you'd better get to know them.'

She liked the dogs. I made her wear my jacket so that she
smelled like me as well as like her, and after a while they seemed
to accept her. She fed them some of their biscuits out of her
hand.

'They're not bleeding pets,' I said. 'You got to be careful.'

'I know,' she said. 'My father has working dogs too.'

Lineker was nuzzling up to her and she stroked his head. I've always had my doubts about Lineker. Given half a chance he'd lick your hand and fetch sticks. He's a bit young and he needs Ramses to keep him up to the mark.

You can't afford to let a dog go soft – not if he's got a job to do. That goes for humans too. Take it from me. It's a tough old world but you'll get by if you don't weaken.

'You won't bite me, will you?' Goldie said to Lineker.

'It's not you I'm worried about,' I said. 'It's him. Don't pet him.'

'But he likes me.'

'So what? If he goes soft he gets put down. Because he'd be no use on the job. But no one in their right mind would want him for anything else. See?'

'You're so hard, Eva,' she said.

'No,' I said. 'I'm softer than you. You *want* him to like you. You aren't thinking about him at all.'

She looked at me and her eyes filled with tears. Which made me feel dead choked so I went and emptied the chemical toilet because that needed to be done, and I was right and she was wrong.

When I got back to the Static she had lit the torches and the fire and it was warm and cosy in there. All the same, it felt as if we had quarrelled. I was uneasy.

But she said, 'What do you do alone at night? I don't suppose . . . no you can't have.'

'What?'

'Television.'

'Hum,' I said, thinking about it. I wanted to give her a telly because I didn't like feeling we'd quarrelled.

'I can rig one up,' I said. 'A little one. Black and white.'

'How?'

'Car battery.' As I thought about it I remembered that the Owner had a really little one which he could plug into the cigarette lighter of his motor. He took it to the races with him so he could watch the golf while he was at the track.

Outside, it was cold enough to see your breath. I was thinking about how I could get into the main office without breaking anything when all at once I thought about the artist bloke and how he said I would be 'perfect'. It was such a queer notion that I stopped dead. I couldn't think why he said it, and I couldn't think why Harsh was taking him seriously. Maybe I was missing something.

I wondered how much 'standard rates' was and whether it was worth associating with such a grimbo for the sake of my teeth. I am a martyr to my teeth, and sooner or later I will have to do something proper about them.

I want to have the front ones capped because they are a bit chipped and uneven which means I can't smile in photographs. When I was getting my London Lassassin poster done the photographer told me to keep my mouth shut. He was a bit rude about it in the end because I kept forgetting. That was what decided me. If I was going to have a career I ought to have a good set of gnashers, like Harsh.

The main office doors were locked tighter than a fish's arse. But someone had left the window to the ladies' lavatory ajar. It was Mr Gambon's job to lock up the main office and he'd cocked it up. I was pleased for two reasons. One – I could get in without smashing a window. Two – Mr Gambon was such a snotty bastard it would give me great pleasure to tell him he'd cocked up.

I pinched the little telly with no trouble at all. The trouble came with the battery. You wouldn't think, in a place chock full of cars and car parts, I'd have trouble finding a battery but I did. The good ones were all shut away in a shed which had no windows. No one had forgotten to lock that.

I could have nicked one out of one of the second-hand motors on the lot, but that was too risky. You never knew which were going to be taken out and driven.

In the end I let myself out of the yard and went to find a battery on the street.

I don't know about you, but I make it a rule not to get up to anything hooky too close to home. But it was a cold night, and rules are made to be broken. I wanted to get back to the Static quick. I wanted to see Goldie's face when I presented her with her own little telly.

It's when you are thinking too far ahead that trouble creeps up on you.

I found a nice Volkswagen not a hundred yards from the main gate, and it only took a couple of minutes to get inside and unlatch the bonnet. I took the terminals off the battery and I was just lifting it out when a hand landed on my shoulder and a voice said, 'You're coming with me.'

I swear my heart stopped, I was that scared. I whipped round. I was still holding the battery. There was this dark figure of a man with his arm raised.

I threw the battery at him.

Well, I wasn't to know, was I? A person shouldn't scare the brown stuff out of another person late at night, should they?

You probably already know it, but a car battery is a big hard heavy thing and not many people, male or female, can throw one far. This one landed somewhere between the knot of his tie and his trousers. He went down like a shot deer, and just lay there.

'Eva?' he said in a funny woozy way. 'What you done, Eva?'

He was Chinese. That was all I could see in the dark. So I said, 'You from Mr Cheng?'

He didn't say anything at all. His eyes were closed and his breathing was all wispy.

'Shit in the shallow end,' I said. Because I'd forgotten I'd promised to go and see Mr Cheng. I was beginning to feel really bad about it.

I thought the man would die and I didn't know what to do. He shouldn't have come up behind me in the dark, but I shouldn't have thrown a battery at him without checking whether he was someone I knew.

I picked the battery off his chest and I knelt down beside him. 'I'm sorry,' I said. 'I didn't know it was you.'

But having said that, I realised I didn't actually know his name. He might have been the bloke who came the night before, but on the other hand he might have been someone else entirely. And really, if you're going to kill someone you ought to know his name. It's a matter of respect.

One way or another it seemed best not to let him die on the pavement, so I picked him up and put him on the back seat of the Volkswagen. Then I picked up the battery and fitted it back in the motor. I wired it, started it, and drove away.

I drove him to St Thomas's Hospital on Lambeth Palace Road. It was the only one I could think of with a big accident department. While I was driving I worried about him dying, and I worried about Goldie all by herself in the Static, and I worried about what Mr Cheng would think. I mean, he wouldn't take too kindly to me clobbering one of his waiters with a car battery. It was a good thing the battery was all right or we'd never have got to St Thomas's.

I decided I'd better go and sort it out with Mr Cheng.

The Beijing Garden was closed but someone came down to let me in. Everyone was upstairs in a private parlour. Some of them were playing that weird Chinese domino game and a lot of money was going round.

As soon as she saw me, Auntie Lo left her game and came over.

'Mr Cheng is waiting for you, Eva,' she said. 'You are very late.'

'I've got a problem, Mrs Lo,' I said. 'The man Mr Cheng sent to fetch me is at St Thomas's Hospital. He had a bit of an accident.'

'Accident? With a car?'

'Well,' I said, breaking it to her gently, 'it was a bit of an accident with a bit of a car. But I took him to the hospital and they're looking after him ever so well.'

'Oh dear, dear, dear,' Auntie Lo said. She turned away, beckoned over two thin young men and spoke to them. Then, in English she said, 'Say again where Kenny is.'

I told them. The two men looked at each other and at Auntie Lo. All three of them left the room. I stood by the door twiddling my thumbs, feeling pronkish.

After a while Auntie Lo came back and led me to Mr Cheng's office. He was sitting behind his desk, and with him were the two men I had picked up in the Rover with Auntie Lo three days ago.

The first thing Mr Cheng said was, 'Where zastra?'

'I don't know, Mr Cheng.' I was relieved he was asking about the car and not Kenny. 'It's probably near my place.'

'Yoogetastra,' Mr Cheng said.

'Now?' I said.

'Now,' Auntie Lo said. 'Straight away.'

'Whatew see Smees?' Mr Cheng asked. 'Whygo there?'

So I explained about Harry Richards expecting trouble and how he'd asked me to help.

'I'd finished all my jobs for you, Mr Cheng,' I said finally.

'Ha!' said Mr Cheng.

'What happened?' Auntie Lo asked.

I told her about the police and the tear gas.

'Did you see who threw gas?'

'No.'

'No?'

I shook my head. They seemed to expect something more and I began to feel awkward. They weren't exactly unfriendly but nobody was smiling.

There was a silence that went on for ages, with everyone looking at me. Then Auntie Lo said, 'Go get the Astra, Eva. Come straight back.'

'Couldn't it wait for tomorrow?' I asked.

'Gotta lil job fewva,' Mr Cheng said.

'You need money, don't you Eva?' said Auntie Lo.

Suddenly Mr Cheng pointed a bony finger at me and rattled off something which started, 'few din cummy nastra . . . '

It took me a minute to work it out, and then I said, 'I didn't even *see* the Astra. I came in another car which . . . belongs to someone else.'

Mr Cheng seemed to be obsessed with his Astra.

'Anyway,' I went on, because I'd had a thought. 'Your bloke Kenny must still have the keys, so unless you've got a spare set I can't very well pick the Astra up.'

'Hah!' said Mr Cheng.

All four of them chewed on some more silence and I shifted from one foot to the other. I was tired. I wanted to go home. I didn't want to explain about Kenny or the VW. I thought I'd got out of it rather well, but I didn't want to be at the Beijing Garden when the two skinny guys came back from the hospital.

All at once Mr Cheng, Auntie Lo and the other two started talking to each other. They talked for about ten minutes while I just stood there. It wasn't very polite.

Then Mr Cheng said, 'Way touside, Eva.'

And Auntie Lo said, 'Don't go away, Eva. We'll need you in a minute.'

So I went outside and sat on a chair in the passage. After a while a bloke came up from downstairs and brought me a cup of green tea and a bowl of prawn crackers which made me feel a bit better. But I still wasn't very happy about being there. I should have been back at the yard with Goldie and the dogs. I was afraid Goldie would be worried.

Chapter 13

'LISTEN TO ME, Eva,' said Auntie Lo. 'This is important.'
She was alone in Mr Cheng's office, which was surprising because I hadn't seen Mr Cheng and the other two come out.

'Where's Mr Cheng?' I asked.

'Eva!' said Auntie Lo. 'You must listen.'

'OK.' But I was puzzled because I couldn't see a door except the one I had used.

'This is a very important little job,' she said. 'It's because Kenny is in hospital. If not, he would do it. See?'

'Yeah.' I did feel bad about Kenny. The nurse in Casualty told me he had several cracked ribs, and I think she said he had a bruised lung, but I couldn't be quite sure. Anyway it sounded painful.

'It wasn't my fault,' I said.

'Don't you want to help Mr Cheng?' Auntie Lo asked. She looked so Auntyish in her pleated skirt and grey woolly. I looked at her feet and sure enough she was wearing pink dancing shoes.

'Of course I want to help,' I said.

'Good,' she said. 'Mr Cheng wants you to deliver a package.'

'OK.'

'It is important. It is important that nobody sees. For your protection.'

'Mine?' I said. Auntie Lo was not smiling, and I wished she would make her joke about finding me a husband instead of talking about how important it all was.

'I like you, Eva,' she said. 'Mr Cheng trusts you. We do not wish to get you into trouble.'

'I don't mind a bit of trouble.' I suddenly felt very happy.

'We mind. So you must be very careful. The package is for

84

Mr Aycliffe. He is expecting it. But there are two things.' She held up two fingers. 'Two important things. One – you must *not* be seen giving it to him. Two – you must not see his face.'

'Why?'

'Mr Aycliffe is being watched by the police. They wish to catch him and put him in prison. We do not want this to happen. Mr Aycliffe is a good man who has made some mistakes but he does not deserve prison. This arrangement will protect you, and it will protect Mr Aycliffe.'

'Oh,' I said. She gave me a moment to think about it. Then I said, 'How can I give Mr Aycliffe a package if I can't see him?'

'We have thought a lot about this, Eva. And we have a plan. Mr Aycliffe works at a club near the Harrow Road. You know the Harrow Road, Eva?'

'Yeah.'

'There is a front entrance – which you do *not* use. You do not use front door, Eva. Right?'

'Right.'

'You use kitchen door.'

'Kitchen door. Right.'

'The door will be open, but there will be no one in the kitchen.'

'How do you know there won't be anyone in the kitchen.'

Auntie Lo looked at her watch. 'Too late,' she said. 'Kitchen closed. Only drinks served from bar. Mr Aycliffe has told us this.'

I should have thought of that. By most people's reckoning it was nearly morning. Late night clubs were different.

'This package,' Auntie Lo went on, 'is in a Safeway carrier bag. To look like rubbish, Eva. You walk into kitchen. You will see another door. Through that door is passage. In passage is where they put the empties. All crates, bottles, other rubbish. You put the Safeway bag with this other rubbish, Eva. You got that?'

'Yeah.'

'Then you walk out. When club closes it is Mr Aycliffe's job to take out rubbish. See?'

85

'Oh, I get it,' I said. 'He takes out the rubbish and takes the package at the same time. And no one will know a thing about it.'

'That is correct. I see you got brains too, Eva. Not just a pretty face.' Auntie Lo suddenly started her huff-huff laughter. And that made me laugh too. It was one of her jokes. I know for a fact that neither Auntie Lo nor Mr Cheng think I'm very smart. It's because they are Chinese, and as everyone knows Chinese people are very smart indeed.

So I didn't mind very much when Auntie Lo went through all her instructions again. She practically drew me a map of how to get to the kitchen of Mr Aycliffe's place. Then she let me go.

It was a funny time of night – not many people on the streets. Just one or two rolling home, one or two still looking for somewhere to score and one or two off to work on the early shift. Normally I like being out and about when it's halfway between late and early. But this time I was a bit strung out. I was worried about Goldie and I was worried about Auntie Lo's package. Also, I was being followed. I drove in the VW but I noticed two Chinese blokes not far behind in Mr Cheng's Rover.

It was just like Mr Cheng to give me a job and then send someone along to make sure I did it right. But it made me tense all the same.

Mostly, when people give you instructions about how to get somewhere they make a mistake or they leave something out. Auntie Lo made no mistakes and she left nothing out. That's how smart she is – everything was exactly the way she said it would be.

The place looked like a shebeen from the front. It was in a broken down row of buildings and there was music coming from the open door. I drove past and turned the corner.

The kitchen door was old and wooden, but it was covered with locks and bolts. The back street looked as if it needed all the locks and bolts you could throw at it. There were broken windows and doors with kicked in panels and houses I knew without looking were filled with dossers.

But inside the kitchen it smelled of onions and chillis and it wasn't all that dirty even though they had left a lot of washing up in the sink.

The music was very loud so nobody could have heard me come in. I went over to the door opposite and opened it slowly. The passage was just what I was expecting. It wasn't lit, but coloured lights spilled through the doors to the bar and dance floor. I saw all the empty bottles and crates stacked to one side. I put the Safeway carrier bag on top of them.

I should have left straight away but I couldn't resist having a gander through the bar door to see if I could spot Mr Aycliffe.

I pushed the door open just a crack. The music was deafening. At first all I could see was a few people dancing and a few people drinking. And then I noticed that one of the dancers was Calvin. Goldie's loverboy, the Lord of the Trousers. He was dancing with an absolutely gorgeous lady. She looked totally wigged-out and she was hanging round his neck like a garland of flowers, but you could see from the shape of her and the way other men watched her that she was absolutely gorgeous.

Poor Goldie. It made me want to hang the bleeding snot-gobbler from the light bulb and swing on his feet. I mean, what right did a little turd like that have to mess with a nice woman's affections? Especially when she was a friend of mine.

Another time I might have steamed in and sorted him out. But now I was under orders to be invisible – although why anyone would pick me for that when I'm one of the most visible women I know, was a mystery. When I thought about it I realised that, of course, it wasn't me they'd picked. They had picked Kenny. And Kenny, if my experience of not seeing him was anything to go by, was about as visible as the Holy Ghost.

I sneaked a last quick look at Calvin and his luscious lady. If he was a woman, I thought, they'd probably call him a slag. As it was they would call her a slag and him a stud and it just wasn't fair. All that man-woman stuff really gets up my nose. I'm glad I'm not involved.

Leaving the music and the coloured lights behind I crossed the passage and went back into the kitchen. It was time to make a quick exit. But when I got to the kitchen door I found I couldn't open it.

I pushed, and I rattled the handle, and I put my shoulder to it but the door was stuck fast.

'Shit a bus,' I said out loud. Because if I couldn't get through the kitchen door I would have to go out through the bar and then everyone would see me – including Calvin who might recognise me from Bermuda Smith's club. And then Mr Cheng and Auntie Lo would be peeved and perhaps they wouldn't give me any more work. You have to do what you are told and be reliable or they don't trust you.

There was one small window, but there were bars across it. The bars wouldn't budge an inch when I heaved on them. The only hope was the door.

I went back to it and tried again. I hauled up on the handle in case the bottom was jammed. It wasn't.

I was sweating like live pork in a sauna. I couldn't understand what was happening. The door had opened so easily when I went in. Everything had gone according to plan. How could such a cock-up happen at the last minute?

It was stupid. It was only a door.

I backed away. Took a run. And hit the door near the lock with a drop-kick. This was a dodgy move. With flying kicks you can land on your arse if you get it wrong. But I heard something splinter.

I picked myself up and tried the handle again. This time it felt looser.

I backed off again and took a longer run. I hit the door perfectly just below the handle. There was a tearing sound of rotten wood splitting, and the door popped open. Thank the Lord for a good pair of boots.

Outside, I closed the door as best I could. And . . . well . . . it is hard to describe what happened next. It was like a dream.

You see, I had just found out why the door wouldn't open, when this thing happened.

The kitchen wall exploded.

It did.

It just flew outwards. One minute it was a wall, and the next minute it was bricks and mortar flying through the air.

The door fell on me.

I remember thinking what a waste of effort it was kicking it open, when it was going to fall over anyway.

I swear I didn't black out, but when I opened my eyes, both me and the door were in the middle of the road yards away from the kitchen and I couldn't remember how we got there.

The funny thing was that I did not hear a thing.

I just saw the wall come apart. And the door fell on me. That's all.

It was like a dream.

It was so weird I actually thought I *was* dreaming. Really dreaming.

You know those dreams where you have to get home? You *must* get home but you don't know the way because you don't know where you are now.

Well it was like that.

I got up. There was rubble all over the street. There were flames and smoke. There were one or two people moving very slowly.

I walked away. I thought, 'I'm dreaming about the war.'

I remember seeing a car bent in half. And another one with a table poking through the windscreen.

But I just walked away because I thought I was dreaming about the war and I had to get home. I couldn't hear anything, so it had to be a dream. Right?

I just sort of floated away. I couldn't hear anything and I couldn't feel anything. I couldn't even feel my feet on the pavement. That is what dreams are like.

There was a woman in the gutter, stark naked and covered in blood. She had bits of glass sticking out of her skin. Her mouth was wide open, as if she was screaming. But I couldn't hear her so I floated on by.

Because it was a dream, see, a dream about the war, and I had to go home.

Chapter 14

WAKING UP HURT. There was a ditch with a clay bottom. It was all wet. I was in the ditch. I was all wet and cold.

It was dawn.

I thought, 'This isn't home.'

But in a way it *was* home. Or rather, it was a place I lived in about a year ago. Actually, it was a place I slept in when I was living rough. But they tore it down. They were going to build luxury flats there but the money ran out and all they had done was dig the foundations.

I was lying in the foundations. My head hurt. My teeth hurt. My skin hurt.

My lovely leather jacket was in tatters and I only had half a T-shirt. My jeans were shredded from the crotch down, and one boot was missing.

I sort of remembered what had happened, but only in the way you remember dreams. Bits of it kept slipping away.

But I was in a real ditch. I was real. And I can tell you for free I had a real earache.

'Chin up, Eva,' I said out loud.

I heaved myself out of the ditch, and I felt very weak and wobbly. Everything hurt so much I nearly threw up. But I am big and strong and mean and tough – well, I was before that door fell on me – so I started to hobble off home.

Borrowing a car was out because my survival tin was gone and all the bits of wire and things I needed were gone too. So I just hobbled on keeping close to walls and things I could lean on.

It was very embarrassing because bits of me were poking through my clothes and it was dawn and people could see me.

Not that there were many people looking. It was too early for that.

I'm used to people staring at me. But usually they stare because I'm big and strong and mean and tough. I'm not used to being stared at when I'm weak and feeble and not dressed properly. It wasn't nice. I felt sort of naked. Well, if you must know, I *was* sort of naked. So I hung on to my rags and limped as fast as I could.

It all goes to show – basic strength and fitness do count for something. Getting home without falling down or going to sleep every ten steps of the way was something a feebler person just could not have done. But I did it. So stick that up your nose and blow it out your ear. I bet you've been having a bit of a giggle at me all this time – a big woman making herself bigger and tougher. Well, let me tell you, I'm never sick, I don't get head-aches, and when I get hurt I can always tough it out. What can you say about yourself? Eh? Go on, how would you manage if you'd been blown half way across a road with a door on top of you?

I know you think I'm stupid. Don't try to tell me different, because I know, see. And maybe I'd done a stupid thing. All right. But even clever people can do stupid things. You don't have to be all-round stupid to be conned. Clever people can be fooled too. Hasn't anyone ever taken you for a sucker? Well okay. I'm not judging you, so don't you sit there and judge me!

So I got home when ninety-nine people out of a hundred would've given up or collapsed. I'm proud of that. I even fed the dogs and penned them. I'm proud of that too. There wasn't a lot to be proud of that morning but I always try to look on the positive side. Well, you must, mustn't you, when the negative side is too horrible to think about.

I tried to be quiet, going into the Static, but I was stumbling around like a blind camel in a bowling-alley.

Goldie came out of the bedroom tangled and tousled and rubbing her eyes. I remember seeing the little telly on the floor where I'd left it before going out to find a battery to run it off. It seemed a long, long time ago.

I said, 'I'll find another battery tomorrow.' And then I was sitting on the floor with Goldie holding my hand, making little cooing sounds. My face was all wet.

'Don't cry,' Goldie was saying, 'don't cry.'

And I said, 'Fuck off. I *never* cry.'

She said, 'You just never came back. You went out to get a battery and you didn't come back. I've been worried sick.'

And she said, 'I'll make some tea.' And, 'Don't move, I'll help.'

And she brought a bowl of warm water, soap and a towel. And although I could only hear out of one ear I began to feel ever so much better.

You just can't imagine how bloody terrific, magic, it is to have a friend when you're in lumber. Just try it, and you'll see.

Goldie was wonderful – just like a mother, really. Someone's mother – not mine of course – I should be so lucky. She cleaned up all the burns and scrapes I never knew I'd got and dabbed on antiseptic cream, and put me to bed in the bed she'd just got out of. Well, it was my own bed, actually, but it smelled of her so it seemed like her bed.

I said, 'I've done a terrible thing.'

'Sleep,' she said.

'No – I think I've killed a load of people.'

'What?' she said. 'Don't be silly.'

'It was a bomb. I put it there.'

She looked at me, and one eyebrow went up.

'Sleep,' she said. 'Tell me about it later. It won't seem so bad when you wake up.'

She thought I was raving. I was quite glad, because I didn't want to tell her about Calvin. For all I knew Calvin had been blown to smithereens like everything else in the shebeen, and I didn't want to tell her.

And I couldn't keep my eyes open. I didn't want to go to sleep because I was afraid I might have dreams, but my lids kept acting like cat-flaps.

Of course there were dreams, but I kept on top of them. I'd see those bricks floating silently out of that kitchen wall and I'd say to myself, 'Hey-up, it's a dream,' and then I'd come half awake. Not properly awake – I couldn't quite manage that – but just enough to stop those bricks. Then I would hear voices – Goldie's voice, men's voices – and I struggled to open my eyes. But I couldn't, and I'd sink back into the bricks and the burning.

Hours later, I woke up. It was afternoon and there were voices coming from the main room.

I squinted through a crack in the door because I always like to see who is there before going into company. Goldie was by herself watching telly.

I said, 'Where did you get the battery?'

'Didn't need a battery,' she said. 'I'm using mains electricity.'

'Cocking Caspar!' I said. 'I told you about that! Do you want to beggar me?'

'Don't shout at me. It won't cost you a penny. I got one of the guys in the yard to hook us up to the mains, and he did this awfully clever thing with a piece of cable. He's by-passed the meter. So we can have all the power we need and no electricity bill.'

'You talked to the blokes in the yard? You're stupid. Know what? You're really stupid. Now what happens if the polizei come back? The only reason you got away with it last time was because I lied for you and the blokes didn't know you were here.'

'Don't shout at me!' Goldie shouted. She stood up. She had her hands on her hips and she looked really spitty. 'I can't live here and not be seen for eight hours a day. I can't live here and not talk to a soul except for you. I feel like a hostage or something. And this business of heating every drop of water and not being able to have a shower even though there's a perfectly good one in the bathroom – well, it may be all right for you but it isn't for me. It's *primitive*, if you must know.'

'Fuck off then,' I said. 'If I'm too primitive for you, why don't you fuck off out of it?'

94

'Okay!' she said. 'I will. If you want me to go I'll go.'

'Go on then!'

'I will.'

'What you waiting for?'

'Nothing,' she said. 'Nothing, nothing, nothing.'

She pushed past me into the bedroom and started clattering around with all her carrier bags.

I looked around the main room. It was warm. The fire glowed. There was tea in the pot. The telly mumbled away in the corner.

Goldie came to the doorway. She said, 'Can I borrow one of your sports bags?'

''Course,' I said. I went over and put my hands round the warm teapot. 'What's mine is yours. You know that.'

'Yes,' she said. 'I'm sorry about the electricity. But you were so cut up and bruised. I thought you might benefit from a nice hot shower. I thought you'd be pleased.'

She'd done it for me! I poured the tea into two mugs and handed her one. We sat down side by side on the sofa.

'Who did you talk to in the yard?' I asked.

'His name is Rob,' she said. But it didn't mean sod all to me. I didn't know any of their names.

'So long as it wasn't Mr Gambon,' I said.

'Oh no. Rob says he's a mean git.'

'Too right.'

'Listen Eva,' she said. 'I told Rob the bailiffs were after me. For tax evasion. And you were helping out. He understood completely.'

'Oh yeah?'

'He was very sympathetic.'

'I bet.'

'He was! He won't tell anyone. Honestly.'

'Yeah,' I said. 'And when is he taking you out "for a drink"?'

She sipped her tea like a lady and looked at me over the rim of her mug.

'Tonight?' I asked.

'What could I do?'

'Kick him in the nob,' I said. 'Nothing. Everybody got to pay the rent. You pay your way, I'll pay mine.'

'He's got to get home to his wife. I won't be gone long,' she said.

We looked at each other. She laughed. I didn't feel like laughing.

'Don't let's argue,' Goldie said.

'We ain't arguing. We both know the score.' But I wasn't sure that she did know the score. Not the way I know it.

'Tell me what happened last night?' she asked. She settled back in the sofa all curled up like a kitten. How do you tell a kitten you just blasted her ex-boyfriend to buggery? Go on, you tell me.

'What happened?' she asked again. 'This morning you were babbling about a bomb or something.'

'Did I say that? There was an explosion. I was all shook up.'

'You can say that again,' she said seriously. 'You looked like a corpse.'

'I still can't hear out of my left ear hole,' I said. It was true. I could hear everything she said because she was sitting on my right. But my left ear had gone dead. It was like having water in it, only worse.

'There *was* an explosion!' she said, amazed.

'Gas main,' I said. 'I can't quite remember but it must've been a gas main.'

She sat there waiting for me to go on, but I didn't know how.

After a bit she said, 'You left here at about midnight. You said you were going to find a battery. You came home at seven in the morning looking like leukaemia on two legs. What happened in between? Seven hours, Eva. You must remember *something*.'

'I don't know,' I said. 'I must've slept in that ditch but I don't remember how I got there. It's hard to think. I've got a toothache.'

'And that's another thing, Eva. You said you were going to the dentist yesterday. But you didn't.'

'What are you – the polizei?' I was a bit narked.

'Oh Eva!' she said, looking hurt. 'I was worried sick about you. You might've been killed. I just want to know what's going on.'

'Nothing's going on. It was one cock-up after another.' I told her about forgetting to go and see Mr Cheng. I told her about him sending Kenny. I told her about me taking Kenny to St Thomas's. But I was a bit careful what I said. I didn't want her to think I was some sort of villain, because I'm not. Not really. Things just happen.

What I said was that Kenny had collapsed on the street – which he had. I didn't want her to know that I'd sort of helped him collapse.

She said I must be accident prone, and I agreed with her. All the same it was funny how much I wanted to tell her the real story. I wanted to get it off my chest. It was funny, because never in all my life have I actually wanted to tell someone something I was ashamed of. Well you don't, do you? If you do something dodgy you keep it to yourself. Otherwise people can dob off on you. You're in someone else's power if you talk too much.

But this time I wanted to talk. It was too big to keep to myself.

Also I wanted someone to understand why I was going to wring Auntie Lo's plump little neck like a dirty dish rag. And why I was going to lob bricks through the Beijing Garden window and duff up Mr Cheng till he looked like Chicken Chop Suey. I wanted Goldie to know why I was going to do these things. I didn't want her to think I was mean with no reason.

'Eva!' Goldie said suddenly.

'What?'

'What are you doing? You'll cut your hand.'

I looked down and saw that somehow I had broken the handle off my mug.

'Don't know me own strength,' I said. But it had me worried. How do you do a thing like that without knowing you've done it?

'Go back to bed,' she said. 'You look dreadful.'

Just then her friend Rob came tap-tapping at the door and she went to answer it. I realised that the men were leaving for the night and soon I would have to lock up and let the dogs out.

I heard Goldie say, 'Just a minute, I'll get my coat.'

She came back saying, 'He's here. Will you be all right, Eva? I won't be gone long.'

I was feeling so rough I didn't even answer.

'I'll be back soon, honestly,' she said, shrugging on her jacket.

I mean, how could she? If she was worried enough to ask me how I felt shouldn't she be worried enough to stop in with me?

So I said nothing, and she went out with that bum-drop, Rob, from the yard. All for a few units of free electricity. Power on the cheap. Shocking! Ha-bloody-ha.

I turned off the light and sat in the dark watching telly, not thinking.

It was on the local news.

It really did look like old films of the war.

The newsreader was saying, 'An explosion in the early hours of this morning in a North London drinking club . . . the emergency services searching through the rubble . . . it is still not known how many . . . the police have issued an appeal for anyone in the vicinity of Harrow Road at approximately 3 a.m. this morning . . .'

I was so amazed I stood up to watch. You'll think I'm bleeding daft but it seemed more real on telly. I expect it was the lights – it was all so clear and bright on the bricks and beams and glass. When I was there the dust hadn't settled. There had been loads of dust and smoke and I suppose that was what made it seem like a dream.

I just stood there gawping. There was hardly a wall left standing. That whole shebeen was a heap of bricks and burnt timber. The only people you could see were firemen in their yellow helmets. I was half expecting to see the screaming woman and

98

I was glad she was gone. I didn't want to see her again. Because she would look more real on telly too, and she was bad enough in a dream.

I turned the telly off and went to find my jacket. It wasn't there, and then I remembered that it was ruined too. So I unearthed the old padded one I used to wear before I got into leather. I put it on and went out.

The yard was silent and empty. I let the dogs out of their pen and they went rushing off into the dark. I followed them slowly. There was still work to be done – doors and windows to check, cars to count, fences to mend. The trouble was that I felt too heavy to do it. Really, I felt as if I weighed a ton.

Then I thought about my leather jacket again and I hurried back to the Static to see if I could find it. It was important because of what I had put in the pocket.

By the steps to the Static I found a plastic bin bag. Goldie had shoved all my old clothes inside. I took my jacket out and sat down on the steps. The lovely soft leather was shredded and it smelled of smoke. I laid it on my knees. The pockets were torn and the letter from the solicitor in Braintree, Essex – the letter about Simone – was gone. So I just sat there and stared into the dark.

The dogs came snuffling up. Lineker made a grab for my jacket. At first I tried to pull it back off him. Then I let him have it.

'Kill!' I said.

He worried at it and tossed it around and snarled and tore. Why not? It was good practice for him. Ramses sat still a little way off and stared at me with his evil yellow eyes.

'Look at something else,' I said, and I got up and walked to the gate. Ramses followed at a distance. He growled deep down in his throat. He did not like me that evening. He did not like me at all.

When I got to the gate I climbed up on it and looked down the street. There was no sign of Goldie coming home. There was no sign of anyone. To tell you the truth I wasn't expecting Goldie. I didn't think I'd ever see her again.

Ramses crouched and snarled when I got off the gate.

I snarled back at him. 'You evil bastard, you,' I said. I walked towards him, and he backed off.

'You're bad,' I said. 'You're rotten wicked.'

He backed off further. He did not go for me, but I almost wished he would. I'd give him such a pounding . . . but he didn't go for me.

I went back to the Static, flung myself down on the sofa and went to sleep.

The dogs woke me up at around midnight. I went to the gate to let Goldie in. She was bright and giggly and loaded down with Selfridges bags.

'You're pissed,' I said.

'Hello to you too,' she said. 'We went late night Christmas shopping in the West End.'

'Where did you get the money?'

'I bought you a present.'

'Stuff it,' I said. 'Selfridges doesn't stay open till midnight. Even I know that.'

'Want to see your present?' she asked, holding one of the bags behind her back, squirming like a little kid.

'Go to bed,' I said. '*He* may respect you in the morning, but I won't.'

So she went to bed. In my bed. And I lay down on the sofa again. I could've throttled her. But she'd have probably enjoyed it – the mood she was in – all tiddly and smelling like a cat.

CHAPTER 15

NEXT MORNING, WHILE Goldie was still asleep, I penned the
dogs, opened the yard and went out to the Mandala Street
Market. I bought some bread, milk and bananas. I thought about
boosting another leather jacket off one of the clothes stalls, but
I didn't feel lucky. You have got to feel lucky when you go out
on the boost. If you don't, you're just asking to be nicked. I felt
a lot better that morning but not lucky enough.

The men had started work in the yard when I got back so I
decided to put in a few more hours sleep. But Goldie woke up
at eleven.

'Ooh,' she moaned, 'my head!'

'Serves you right,' I said and made her a cup of tea. Which
was pretty nice of me considering all the trouble she'd put me
to.

She had two mugs of tea and two bananas. She didn't say
much. After breakfast she had a shower. And I didn't say much
either. Well, what did she expect, the dirty mare, leaving me all
alone when I was blue and aching for a bit of company.

But she looked so cross-eyed and forlorn that I forgave her
and we went up to Sam's Gym for a workout. She didn't want
to go, but I told her she'd feel better if she sweated the poison
out of her system. She said she'd rather have a sauna. I said she
was a lazy cow, and that's how we made it up – although we'd
never actually fought.

We were the only two there to begin with. I showed her how
to warm up properly. She was very supple so those dancing
lessons must have been good for something. Then I showed her
how to use a couple of the simpler machines with not much
weight attached.

After a while, Sam himself came down to talk to us. Sam is a legend, but he hardly ever comes out of his office.

Goldie said she thought weight-training would be easier if it could be done to music.

'It's not meant to be easy,' Sam said, but he put on the tape the evening class used for aerobics. And time fairly zipped by.

I was not pulling much weight myself, to tell you the honest truth. I was sore and heavy and sweating pure manure. If we hadn't had the music I'd have given up after half an hour.

'Do you think you'll be all right for tomorrow?' Goldie asked.

'Tomorrow?'

'Yes,' Goldie said anxiously. 'It's tomorrow. Saturday.'

'I know it's Saturday,' I said. But I didn't, and it came as quite a shock. I thought I still had days to prepare. Life had been jumping up and biting back in the past few days. Somewhere, somehow, I'd lost a chunk of time.

It was just as well I was only fighting Bombshell again. I could handle Bombshell blindfold with one arm amputated.

Goldie was sitting on one of the bikes. She was pedalling slowly, warming down.

'I feel great,' she said. 'You were right, Eva. I needed that. I wouldn't want to weight-train as a regular thing though. I don't want to get big.'

'Myth,' Sam said.

'What?'

'Myth. You can train for shape and definition. You don't have to train for bulk. I could design you a programme.'

'Really?'

'Take him up on it,' I said. Blokes are always on at Sam to design them programmes, but he hardly ever does. 'Work it out for yourself,' he says, 'like I did.' Now here he was, offering Goldie one for free.

'I don't want to get stiff,' she said. 'I'm a dancer.'

'Dancers do weights,' he said. 'You won't get big or stiff. You'll see.' He went back to his office just as Mr Deeds came in.

'Morning, girls,' he said.

'Good morning, George,' Goldie said.

'Have I got news for you!' He put his briefcase down on one of the benches.

'We were just going for a shower,' I said. I didn't like the way he was eyeing Goldie's wet leotard.

'Hang about. I want to show you the posters. And I'll need you, Goldie, for rehearsal. Where's Gruff and Pete?'

'Dunno, Mr Deeds.'

'They should've been here twenty minutes ago.' He looked at his watch. Then he pulled a poster out of his briefcase, unfolded it and held it across his chest.

There it was in big black letters – 'BATTLE OF THE TITANS – THE CARVER VERSUS GRUFF GORDON – featuring his valet The One and Only Glamour Girl Goldie'.

I had to admit it looked pretty good. But what caught my eye was further down the bill. It said, 'Star of the East, ROCKIN' SHERRY-LEE LEWIS V THE LONDON LASSASSIN'.

'What?' I said, my mouth dropping open.

'Glamour Girl Goldie,' Goldie said.

'Knew you'd like it,' Mr Deeds said, beaming so wide you could see his gums.

'Jesus!' said Goldie.

'But . . . ' I said.

'You can have your shower now,' Mr Deeds said, fondling Goldie's elbow. 'Can't have you getting chilled, can we. Want me to come in and scrub your back? Ha-ha-ha.'

'I think I can manage, thank you, George,' Goldie said. She gave him a stunning smile and walked away to the showers.

'Class,' Mr Deeds sighed. 'That kid's got real class.'

'But, Mr Deeds . . . ' I said pointing to where it said Star of the East, ROCKIN' SHERRY-LEE LEWIS.

'Oh, you noticed,' he said, and he looked at me for the first time. 'What's up with you, Eva? Lost an argument with an armoured car? Yeah, we had a change of plan. I got a sick note

103

from Bombshell's physio. She's out. Sherry's manager owes me one, so she's in.'

'But . . .'

'We could of dropped you off the bill,' he said and folded up the poster. 'But I thought, Nah, give the girl a chance. 'Bout time you had some opposition. She wants to win, of course. It's in her contract. But it's a step up for you, Eva. A real step up.'

'Yeah,' I said very sincerely. I won't say Sherry-Lee Lewis is Klondyke Kate, exactly. But she *is* a contender. And she is *big*.

'Say, "Thank you Mr Deeds",' Mr Deeds said.

'Thanks boss,' I said. And I meant it.

I saw Sherry-Lee Lewis fight once in Newcastle. She's popular, for a woman, in Newcastle. She was very athletic, very useful. She never said anything to me — well she wouldn't — I was just there to help with equipment and stuff. But she smiled once as she walked past. I liked her.

'Run along,' Mr Deeds said. 'You pong something awful.'

Isn't that typical? Just when you think life is a total write-off you get a sparkler. All the grind you put in on something which is beginning to look like a waste of time suddenly pays. Your slot machine spits coins! Whango! Zippety-doo-dah!

It was a shame I wasn't a hundred per cent physically. But you can't have everything. And even if I wasn't in peak condition I could still make a good fight of it. If Sherry-Lee Lewis wanted one. And I thought she would. She didn't look like a woman who went through the motions. She looked like a woman who enjoyed her own strength — who would like to test it every now and then. There are women like that. Believe me.

Bombshell isn't like that. She likes prancing round the ring in her glitter tights and lipstick. The only way she can beat me is on a technicality. Even the punters know that. Which is why I have to get myself disqualified sometimes — just to please the crowd.

I walked on springs to the changing-room. Goldie was in the shower washing her hair. I stepped in beside her. I couldn't contain myself.

I said, 'Sherry-Lee Lewis. I'm fighting the Star of the East tomorrow.'

'Is that good?'

'Good? It's solid platinum.'

'Great,' Goldie said. 'I'm pleased for you. Do you want my shampoo?'

She gave me her shampoo and got out to dry. Well, she wouldn't understand, would she? She'd only been around for a few days.

I washed all over in her shampoo because I'd forgotten the soap. It smelled brilliant.

'Glamour Girl Goldie,' she shouted over the noise of the water. 'Did you see that?'

'Don't you like it?' I was surprised.

'Goldie's all right. Glamour Girl is plain tacky.'

'Oh.' I turned off the water and got out.

She was putting on a brand new leotard. It was a soft green colour and had stripy leggings to match.

She saw me watching and said, 'Eva? I've got a bit of a confession to make.'

'What?'

'Don't be angry.'

'Why should I be angry?'

'I borrowed a bit more money.'

'Who from?'

'You.'

'Me?'

'It was in the clothes I threw away. I went through all the pockets and I found this roll of notes. So I put it aside for you, and when Rob came to collect me last night I thought I'd better not go out without any money at all. You know, in case he got rough and I had to take a taxi home. But I was in a hurry and I picked it *all* up by mistake. And somehow, last night, it all got spent.'

'What else?'

'What do you mean?'

'In my pockets. *What else did you find in my pockets?*' I was practically dancing up and down on the tiled floor.

'Nothing,' she said, alarmed, 'Just a letter. I put it under the jam jar. Eva! What're you doing?'

I had picked her up and swung her round.

'Goldie, you are bloody magic,' I said. I put her down. I was getting her all wet again.

'You don't mind about the money?'

'It's only money,' I said, ecstatic. 'That letter is my sister.'

'What?'

So, while I dried and changed, and while she did her hair and make-up, I told her about Simone and the foster parents. And then I got to the bit I've never told anyone – the bit I don't like to remember – about when I was thirteen and I went to their house. Simone was shut in the bedroom, I know she was, and they wouldn't let me see her and they called the polizei to take me away.

When I got to that bit Goldie stopped doing her make-up and just sat and listened. I mean she really listened.

People don't, you know. You can see them sitting there thinking about what *they* are going to say next and waiting till they can interrupt.

But Goldie sat and listened. She never took her eyes off me till I finished.

Then she said, 'But Eva, if you've already been to the foster parents' house why do you need the solicitors to tell you their address?'

Which was a good question. The answer is that something went wrong with my head after that and I was shut away for quite a few months in a sort of hospital. When I came out I couldn't find the house again. I thought I found the street but all the houses looked alike.

I did not tell Goldie this. People do not like to hear about things going wrong with other people's heads. Even when it's years and years ago.

I said, 'They moved. Ma said they moved but she didn't know where.'

'So what are you going to do? How are you going to get a firm of solicitors to tell you where a client lives?'

'I'm grown up now,' I said. 'No one shoves me around any more. I do the shoving.'

'Mmm.'

'What do you mean, "Mmm"?'

Goldie looked at me with a funny expression on her face.

'What?' I asked.

'Eva,' she said, very quietly. 'Eva, they are middle class.'

'So what?'

'If you go in like a raging bull, they'll get frightened. When the middle classes get frightened you'd better watch out. That is when they're most dangerous.'

'They don't scare me.'

'They should. These are solicitors. They are there to protect the middle classes. So are the police. You tried it before. Remember what happened then?'

'I was only thirteen then.'

'No difference. It'd be better if you tried a little subterfuge.'

'What's that?'

'It's going the long way round. It's ringing up and pretending to be . . . another solicitor . . . or an insurance agent – one of their own kind. Someone they would tell things to.'

'Shit,' I said. 'I'd rather bang heads.'

'I know,' she said. 'Let me think about it.'

Just then Gruff Gordon came barging in. He said, 'What're you girls doing in here – perming your eyelashes?'

Can you believe the nerve of the man? I shoulder-charged him, right in the soft bit under his ribcage. And when he was outside I said, 'See what it says on the door, bollock-drip? It says "Ladies". Ladies is us, not you, so bugger off till we're ready.'

When I got back Goldie was laughing so hard there were tears in her eyes.

'His face,' she said, 'did you see his face?'

I hadn't looked at his face but I guessed it must've been pretty funny, the way she was carrying on.

She wiped her eyes and started to put on more eyeliner.

'Will you really?' I asked.

'What?'

'Think about the solicitors.'

'Okay,' she said, looking at me in the mirror. 'If you want.'

I did want. She was right. I don't know how to talk to people. I always rub them up the wrong way. I don't know why – I only say what I think.

And looking at her I realised why she knew so much more than I did about solicitors and things. Really and truly, she was one of them. Which made me feel weird, because she was broke and homeless, and I wasn't.

But now I felt light and easy when only an hour before I had felt blue and heavy. I didn't care about Gruff Gordon and Pete Carver and the silly pantomime they were rehearsing with Goldie. I didn't care that she was Gruff Gordon's valet and not mine. Who needs a valet when they've got a friend to talk to?

And besides, I wasn't fighting Bombshell at the bottom of the bill any more. I was fighting Sherry-Lee Lewis, the Star of the East, who knew how to get a bit of respect. I was on my way.

I don't know about your life, but mine is a bit like a coin. Flip it once and it comes down heads, flip it again and it comes down tails. Heads, tails – I never know which side I'm going to land.

I wasn't exactly thinking about this. I was minding my own business, watching Gruff and Pete go through their moves – battle of the Titans, my arse! Battle of the bellies more like. Maybe I was enjoying feeling so good when last night I was feeling so bad, when in walked Harry Richards with his Adidas bag and my coin took another flip.

I wish I knew who was doing the flipping – I'd have a word with him about it if I could.

Anyway, in walked Harry Richards, with his smiley moon-face. He used to have to fight in a mask because he looked so harmless. He always has a pleasant word for everyone.

He walked in saying, 'Yo, Mr Deeds. Yo, Gruff, Pete. What's happenin'?'

And then he saw me, and his moon-face just froze. He stood stone-still staring at me. And then he saw Goldie. His mouth dropped open and his chewing gum fell out onto the floor.

'For fuck-sake, Eva,' he said. 'I thought you was dead.'

If I'd had any chewing gum in my mouth it would've dropped out too. I mean, what a thing to say.

'Watcher, Harry,' Mr Deeds said. 'You come to work out? When you going to put your mask back on and fight for me again?'

'I don't feel so good,' Harry said. 'Think I'll go off home and rest.' And he turned round and went out the door.

I caught him in the hall.

'What's up, Harry?' I said.

'Don't talk to me, Eva,' he said, pulling his arm away. 'If you not dead you in big trouble, and I don't want no trouble.'

'What you talking about?' I stood between him and the street and every time he tried to go around me I stood in his way.

'You fuck me up, Eva,' he said. 'They give me hell about you an' that little girl from the band. I didn't know you was friends with her.'

'How did I fuck you up?' I asked. 'You said "help out", and I helped out. There wasn't bugger all I could do after the polizei came except leg it.'

'Don't give me that,' he said. 'I wouldn't have asked you to help out except I thought you was workin' for the Chengs. And what else for does Bermuda Smith pay Mr Cheng?'

'I don't know. What does Bermuda Smith pay Mr Cheng for, Harry?'

Harry gave me the nearest thing he had to a dirty look.

'You tellin' me you don't know?' he said. 'You come draggin' your arse in every month, bad mouthin' all, like you was Mr Cheng himself. What you talkin' about, girl?'

I was shocked. I couldn't believe that was how Harry Richards saw me. I always thought we got along.

'Listen, haemorrhoid,' I said, 'I don't bad mouth anyone. I'm just trying to make the rent and get by. I run errands for Mr Cheng — or I used to — but he never tells me dipsy-doodle about nothing. I'm just a round-eyed chunk of muscle to him, like you are to Bermuda Smith.'

'There you go, calling folk names again,' Harry said sadly. 'At least I work for my own kind.'

'Well, what is *my* own kind Harry? Tell me that. I don't have a "kind". So I work for anyone who pays.'

'Then you should be loyal to who pays. Not go shack up with the enemy. Not bite the feedin' hand.'

'I don't!' I shouted. I was really shocked now. 'I've *never* done that, Harry.'

'Then what you doin' with that little girl from Count Suckle band? I saw you, Eva. I saw you take her away. An' she's here now. That band. They throw gas, they wreck our club.'

'What?' I said. 'What?' And I sat down on the cold floor. I didn't know what to think and I wanted to lie down and go to sleep.

Harry said, 'What you think Bermuda Smith give you to take to Mr Cheng, Eva? Every month you come, what you think you carrying? Hair oil? Bananas?'

'Money, Harry,' I said. 'I thought I was carrying money.'

'Yeah, money,' Harry said. 'And what sort of money was that, Eva? You think Bermuda Smith pay Mr Cheng instalments on his wife's fridge-freezer?'

He looked at me with pity and then walked slowly out onto the street. He stood there for a minute watching the traffic. Then he turned round and walked slowly back.

He said, 'Maybe you not bad, Eva. Maybe you just very, very stupid.'

I couldn't look him in the face. I just looked at his poor old flat feet. 'You don't understand, do you?'

'No,' I said. 'I don't understand anything.'

He squatted down so that his face was level with mine.

'Cheng send you to Count Suckle's place with a bomb, Eva. And you still don't understand. You supposed to be dead.'

'I know that,' I said. 'And someone locked me in. I couldn't open the door so I broke it and I saw it had been locked. Then the wall exploded.'

'I'm sorry for you, Eva,' Harry said. 'You work for people you don't know. You supposed to be inside Count Suckle's place under all them bricks. You supposed to be two birds killed with one stone.'

'Why, Harry? Why did they do that to me?'

'Protection war,' Harry said. 'Everyone think you on the other side. Count Suckle, he want Bermuda Smith's account. He say Bermuda Smith should stick to his own kind, not pay good money to bad Chinese. Mr Cheng say Count Suckle messing around on Cheng territory. Bermuda Smith pay Chengs for protection. Bermuda Smith stupid too. He book that band without checking where it come from.'

'Who is Count Suckle, Harry?' I asked.

'Just another bad man who take in weaker folk's dirty linen,' he said. 'Like Mr Cheng. Big man in community relations. Big man in entertainment, Eva. Got accounts in half the clubs in North West London. Got his own little place – but you saw that, Eva.'

I nodded.

'That little place like his home, Eva. That where he started out. Count Suckle sentimental about that little place. Cheng know that.'

Harry was tired of squatting so he sat on the floor too.

'Bermuda Smith's club is closed,' he said. 'I got no job no more.'

'I'm sorry.'

'Three people dead at Count Suckle's place.'

I covered my face with my hands. I did not want to hear.

'Three, Eva.'

'Why?' I said. 'I don't understand.'

'That band. They from Count Suckle. He sent them. They bring in tear gas. It was all behind the stage, Eva. The roadie threw the first can. You don't use your eyes, Eva? Other folk use their eyes. They see you take up that little girl and go.'

'But it wasn't her, Harry. She was rat-arsed.'

'Her foolishness. She had the cans in her bag. She's that pretty-boy singer's woman, Eva. That singer, he Count Suckle's man.'

'No,' I said.

'Your foolishness, Eva,' Harry said. He straightened up and rubbed his thighs. 'You just a dumb fighter like me. Got no brain in your head.'

I said, 'What am I going to do?'

Harry looked away. 'I don't know what you going to do. Me, I'd get rid of that little girl pretty damn quick. And I take a plane somewhere. See, nobody owe you nothin' but evil, girl. Not Bermuda Smith, not Cheng, not Count Suckle people. Lucky for you everybody think you dead.'

Harry walked away to the street. He did not look at me. It was like he said – I was dead. I did not exist.

But then, like the first time, he turned round and came back.

'Dumb as you, Eva,' he said. 'I come to talk to Mr Deeds – ask him for a job.' And he walked past me into the gym.

I sat on the floor in the hall. I couldn't have moved if I'd tried.

Chapter 16

I KNOW HOW to build a house in the snow. You can make trenches, caves or igloos. You make three levels: the top one for the fire, the middle one to sleep on and the bottom one for storage and to trap cold air.

If I was alone in the arctic I could survive for ages. I read about it in my SAS Survival Handbook.

'Mark out a circle on the ground about 4m (13 1/2ft) in diameter and tramp it down to consolidate the floor as you proceed . . . '

I could do that, easy.

Harsh walked in with a couple of blokes I know. The others went straight into the gym without saying hello, but Harsh stopped and said, 'What are you doing out here in the cold?'

'Waiting for Goldie,' I said. 'Harsh?'

'Yes.'

'Can I talk to you? I've got a bit of a problem.'

'Later, Eva,' he said. 'I've got work to do.'

He followed the other two into the gym.

The bola is a weapon Eskimos use to bring down birds. You wrap stones in circles of cloth and you knot lengths of string round each bit of cloth. Then you tie the other ends of the strings together and, shazam, you've got a bola. I like the bola. You don't have to be clever to make one and you don't have to be a great shot to aim it right. You just whirl it round your head and let fly in the general direction of what you want to hit.

I could make a spear or a bow and arrow, but really the bola is best. I had a brilliant thought – suppose I use ball bearings? There were loads of ball bearings back at the yard.

I got up. Harsh was right. It was pretty cold in the hall. Perhaps that was why I was thinking about Eskimos.

You think I'm stupid. Go on – you can be straight with me. You think I don't know what you're thinking. You think I don't know what's going on.

Well let me tell you something – Harry Richards did not say much I didn't know already. Even while he was talking I kept saying to myself – 'I *knew* that.' Except about the band. I didn't know about the band.

And as for Goldie, well, she practically told me, didn't she? She was going to tell me what was in the bag she was so worried about. She *was*. But we were interrupted and later, when she knew I was working for Mr Cheng she said it was drugs in her bag. She told me it was drugs but if she hadn't been frightened of the Chengs she would have told me about the cans of gas. She *would*.

Anyway, what she told me about the drugs was probably true too. She *was* sick, very sick, and it wasn't just booze. I know about booze.

Goldie didn't lie to me. She just left a few things out. You can't blame her for that. I left a few things out too. People leave a few things out all the time. What are you going to do about it – shoot us?

I went back to the yard.

I should have told Goldie where I was going but I didn't. I didn't because I wanted to think about what to do.

You think I was wasting my time sitting around in the cold thinking about Eskimos. Well, that's how much you know. I wasn't wasting my time at all.

If you suddenly hear that you are in danger you think about protecting yourself. If you don't think about protecting yourself then you really are wasting your time. I am not as stupid as you think.

On my way back to the yard I stopped off and bought a ball of nice strong string. And when I was home at the yard I collected a lot of heavy stones and handfuls of ball bearings.

Now do you get it? A weapon the Eskimos use to catch birds in the Arctic is also used by gauchos in South America to bring down larger animals. The bola gets tangled in their legs and they fall over. And what is a human being if it isn't a larger animal? Tell me that, or do I have to explain everything?

I did not make one bola. I made three. Because it wasn't as if I was only in trouble with one person. I was in trouble with just about everyone. Of course everyone that counted thought I was dead, but that wouldn't last.

Because I was going to be famous, wasn't I? I was fighting Rockin' Sherry-Lee Lewis, Star of the East. And after that, who knows. You can't be a famous wrestler if everyone thinks you are dead. Nobody gives a wet fart about a dead wrestler unless you are someone like Milo of Croton.

I like working with my hands. It takes your mind off your troubles. You think about what you are doing instead of about what you are thinking. But when you've finished what you are doing, you often find that your brain has been carrying on without you. Which is nice of it really – it gets its own work done without upsetting you.

Brains are funny things. You'd think a brain would do what you tell it, like an arm or a leg. But it doesn't. Sometimes it does the opposite. I don't know about yours, but *my* brain has a mind of its own.

If you don't believe me, listen to this. When I finished making my three bolas I found I had made them about a foot shorter than the SAS Survival Handbook says. I was quite pleased with myself about that because bolas are supposed to be used in wide open spaces and there aren't many of those in London. In fact, when I pictured Mr Cheng all tangled up and falling bum-over-bonce, it was always in his own restaurant.

That was all right, but the funny thing was that I found I had solved the problem of how to get Simone's address out of the solicitor. It was simple. I would get that artist dweeg, Dave de Lysle, to do it for me. He had exactly the right sort of voice. He could pronk-off to a solicitor for hours without breaking wind.

All I had to do was to let him draw a couple of drawings of me. After all he did say I was 'perfect'. And perfection has a price.

Just to prove that some things are fated – when I went to look for the solicitor's letter I found that Goldie had put it with Dave de Lysle's catalogue. They were one on top of the other under the jam pot just like she said. Which went to prove that Goldie was straight with me.

Right then and there, the thought that popped into my head was, 'Golf balls'. First – I bet myself that Dave de Lysle and the solicitors were golfing types. Second – you could make a super-de luxe model bola with golf balls. Now tell me the brain isn't a peculiar thing.

All this time I had been feeling quite safe and comfortable. But I was getting prepared. I packed a bag. I replaced everything I had kept in my survival tin. And I added some tins of stew, beans and soup. Because in my head were two pictures. In one picture I was camping in a derelict house eating the stew. In the other picture I was swinging the bag with amazing force and hitting someone over the head with it. Tins of stew are good for that.

I kept looking at my London Lassassin poster. It was me, and it was not me. I am the villain – the one in the black costume – the one they love to hate. That's me, but it's not me. An assassin is a paid killer. I'm not. But I am. Three people dead at Count Suckle's. I did it. And I did not do it.

To tell you the truth I was not sure what I was. I can't expect you to understand, so there's no point talking about it. It made me feel bad – bad like a villain, and bad like angry and sad. But there's no point talking about it so I won't.

All I wanted was to be ready.

Someone knocked on my door and I was ready for that. I went to answer it with a bola in one hand and a tin of soup in the other. You never know who you're going to find behind a door.

But it was only that tart-raker, Rob from the yard, looking for Goldie. The nerve of him!

'Eleanor here?' he said.

'No.'

'I thought she'd want a drink later.'

Blokes like him take it for granted women will want what they want.

'She ain't here,' I said.

'Tell her I asked,' he said, without a please or thank you. Which is typical.

'Tell her yourself,' I said and shut the door.

He knocked again.

'Listen,' he said, when I opened up, 'I asked you nice . . . '

'And I told you nice. She's out.'

'When's she coming back? Only someone's been sniffing round. I didn't say nothing, but she'll want to know.'

'Who?'

'I'll tell her myself.'

'Then you won't tell her at all,' I said. ''Cos unless I know who to look out for she'll find another place to stay.'

He thought about it. You could hear the gears grinding. Then he said, 'Couple of sammies. Big bastards. None of us here'd give them the time of day.'

'When?'

'Hour or so ago.'

'Right,' I said. 'Thanks. I'll warn her.'

It gave me belly-ache to thank him, but I did. *That* is mental discipline and Harsh would've been proud of me. But the other thing which gave me gut-ache was the fact that someone, probably from Count Suckle's or Bermuda Smith's was looking for Goldie. It made sense. Bermuda could be after her because of the CS gas, and Count Suckle because of me. If you are seen in the wrong company when the smelly stuff's flying you are in bad trouble. I'm used to bad trouble – I didn't mind. But Goldie might.

I had to look after her.

I left the Static. Everything I needed was in an army surplus knapsack. If everyone is gunning for you, really you should do a little more than crawl underground with a few cans of stew for company. But if push comes to shove you should be ready to do that too.

The only trouble was I wanted to be famous.

The only trouble was Goldie.

The only trouble was that when I left the yard and went to find my Cortina I saw two black guys camped out in a white Maestro van just round the corner where they could spy on the gate.

They did not see me — well maybe they did, but they were looking for Goldie and reading the *Racing News*.

They were a bit of a problem because my Cortina was parked just behind them. I ducked out of sight and went the long way round the block coming up on the Cortina from behind.

All the time, I was wondering if I should stuff a hamburger up their exhaust pipe and lob a breezeblock through their windscreen just to show them who they were dealing with. But by the time I got to the Cortina I decided that if everyone thought I was dead I might as well stay dead till after Sherry-Lee Lewis. After that it wouldn't matter. After that I'd be a contender too and they'd have to think twice before messing with me. Everyone would know I was alive and kicking.

I started the motor, U-turned and drove off before they'd had time to pick a winner in the 3.30 at Newmarket. No flies on me — a cloud of dust with the speed of light, hi-ho, Silver — and away I went. Lovely. I'd show Harry Richards how dumb I was! I'd show everyone.

But when I got to the gym there was nobody there. Not a soul, and I suddenly felt flat and a bit shivery. You can't show everyone if no one's there.

And I had to warn Goldie about the two guys in the Maestro van. I could just see her going home to the yard to find me and those two phlegm-blobs jumping on her from behind. She had to be told, but she wasn't there.

I'd never thought about it before, but a gym without any bodies in it is a sad place. It smells of old sweat and all the machines stand idle like a factory gone bust. There's none of that clanking and thudding and grunting that make it human.

While I was standing there, wondering which way to turn, Sam came in with a spanner and an oil can, so I said, 'Where's everyone gone?'

He looked at the clock on the wall. It was two-thirty.

He said, 'The lunchtime trade came in. Your mob went to the pub.'

I should have thought of that, except I had been too busy to think about the time. Us professionals don't mix much with the recreationals. Too many plump office workers spoil the atmosphere so we move over the road to the Prince of Wales for a beer and a meat pie.

I went straight away.

The Prince of Wales is a gloomy pub. They don't waste much money on bright lights and video games. The only extra they have is a snooker table in the back. Otherwise it is just a pub.

When I went in I couldn't see anyone and it worried the life out of me. But I went through and found them all in the snooker room.

Mr Deeds was showing Goldie how to play, dirty old tosser, and he was leaning over her, saying, 'You've got to keep the bridge hand steady, darlin'!'

Gruff Gordon said, 'Give it some deep screw, girlie.' He was nudging Pete and leering like the brainless tub of lard he was.

'I think I'd do better, George, if you didn't crowd me so much,' Goldie said. You couldn't fault her on her manners. I'd've nailed his willie to the floor if he'd rubbed it up against me the way he was rubbing up against her.

The Julios were playing cribbage in a corner and Harsh was sitting by himself reading the *Independent*.

Goldie looked up when I came in. She looked up and smiled at me. The snooker lights which hung over the table caught her hair and gave her a halo. She seemed to be glowing – all gold. Even her skin looked like honey.

She looked up and smiled at me.

'Hello, Eva,' she said. Just that. My friend. Mine.

'Got to talk to you,' I said. I must've sounded a bit croaky because there seemed to be something caught in my throat.

'Something's come up,' I said.

'What's come up?' Pete asked, elbowing Gruff Gordon.

'Ask George Deeds,' Gruff said, falling about laughing.

I think that's what I hate most about some men – they really do know how to spoil a lovely thing.

'Smutty sods,' Mr Deeds said, looking flattered.

Goldie straightened up. She laid the cue down and came round the table to me.

'Somewhere private,' I said. I did not want to be in the same room as Gruff Gordon, Pete Carver and Mr Deeds.

We went through to the bar. I bought myself a beer and a vodka and orange for her. We sat at a table in a corner where we couldn't be overheard.

I said, 'Someone has been asking questions about you at the yard. And when I left there were two blokes waiting outside in a van.'

'Who?' she asked, looking at me, very clear-eyed, very steady.

'I don't know. Two black guys.'

She said nothing. She just kept on looking at me.

I said, 'They could be from Bermuda Smith, or they could be from Count Suckle.'

Her eyes widened, just a fraction.

'You know about Count Suckle,' she said. It was not a question. She sighed. 'I would have told you. I was going to tell you. But I didn't know how things stood with you and Bermuda Smith and the Chengs.'

'Yeah,' I said. 'What I thought.'

'But I don't understand why anyone from Count Suckle's Club would want to see me. I wasn't important.'

'Because of me,' I said. 'Each of us was all right on our own. But when we teamed up we were trouble. You got me into lumber with the Chengs and Bermuda Smith, and I got you in lumber with Count Suckle. 'Specially now, with the bomb and everything.'

'What bomb?'

'The bomb,' I said, 'you know, I told you about an explosion.'

'You said it was a gas main.' She was staring at me. Her face had gone all white and wooden.

'Yeah . . . well . . . '

'A bomb, where?' she asked. 'Where, Eva?'

I couldn't look at her any more.

'*Where?*'

I said, 'Count Suckle sent CS gas. Mr Cheng sent a bomb.'

'The club?' she said. 'You bombed the club?'

'No!'

'What do you mean? You said Mr Cheng sent a bomb.'

'Yes. Mr Cheng sent it.'

She put her hand on my arm.

'Look at me, Eva,' she said.

I looked and saw that she was quite steady again.

'Tell me about it, Eva,' she said. 'Just tell me.'

'They were trying to kill me too,' I said. 'I didn't know it was a bomb.'

'You took a bomb to the club?'

'In a Safeway carrier bag. They said it was money for Mr Aycliffe.'

'Who?'

'Mr Aycliffe.'

She shook her head. She didn't know the name.

'Who was there?' she asked.

'I don't know,' I said. 'I wasn't supposed to see anyone.'

'Calvin,' she said. 'Was Calvin there?'

'I didn't see.'

'You saw,' she said. 'Was he there?'

'I *didn't* see. They tried to kill me too.'

She stood up.

'Where are you going?' I grabbed her sleeve.

121

She shook me off and went to the bar. The barman pointed to the phone. She went to it and dialled a number.

I got up and hurried over. I put my hand on the phone to cut her call off.

'Don't,' I said. 'Don't. It's too late.'

She hit my hand with the receiver.

'Go away,' she said, very steady, very clear.

I backed off.

'*Go away!*'

I went to our table and watched from there. She had the receiver to her ear. She didn't talk. After a bit she dialled another number. Then another. This time she talked.

She turned her back on me and talked to someone. Then she stopped talking. Her arms hung down by her sides, the receiver was still in her hand.

I counted to fifty while I watched her. She stood with her arms by her sides and her back to me while I counted up to fifty.

Then she put the receiver back in its cradle and came over to me.

'I thought you'd like to know,' she said, very steady, very clear, 'Calvin is alive. He was crushed, under the rubble for three hours. He has lost one eye, and half of his face, but he is alive. I thought you'd like to know the result of what you did.'

It was worse than I'd ever imagined it would be. There was absolutely nothing in her eyes. It was horrible. It was like looking at a dead animal.

She stood in front of me with her hands by her sides and said, 'Marsha's dead. Val's dead. Micky's dead. They were friends of mine. You know that, Eva?'

I could only shake my head.

'But you did know Calvin,' she went on, very steady, very clear. 'You saw him. You saw he was beautiful. You heard him sing. You watched him dance.'

'They tried to kill me too,' I said uselessly. 'The bomb was supposed to kill me too.'

'But it didn't, did it, Eva? You got away with a few scrapes and bruises. Do you think that makes up for Val, Micky and Marsha? Do you think that makes up for Calvin's eye? You'd have to die several times over to make up for that, Eva.'

She never even raised her voice. She turned away and walked out of the pub.

At first I couldn't move. It felt like she'd kicked the guts out of me. Then I got up and ran after her. Well, I had to try, didn't I?

I caught her just as she was going to cross the road. She wasn't looking right or left.

'*Goldie!*' I shouted. 'You'll get yourself run over.'

I grabbed her arm.

'Listen to me,' I shouted. 'You've got to listen. You know I wouldn't do what I did on purpose. You *must* know. We're friends.'

She didn't look at me. She said, 'I wouldn't be friends with you if you were the last person on earth.'

And she set off across the road looking neither right nor left. Cars screeched to a stop, bikes swerved, drivers leaned on their horns. She walked straight across the road and disappeared into the crowd of shoppers on the other side.

I tried to follow her, but none of the traffic stopped for me so by the time I got to the other side she was gone and I didn't even know which way she had gone. First I ran one way, and then the other. I searched at the bus stops, I even went down the tube to see if she was catching a train. But London had just opened its great big mouth and swallowed her.

In the end I went back to Sam's Gym. Mr Deeds was there, the Julios were there, and another tag-team called the Icemen, but, even though I looked in the showers and the ladies' lavatories, Goldie was not there.

By then, I didn't expect she would be. It was as if something that had happened before was happening again. I knew I wouldn't find her. Don't ask me how. I just knew it.

I had to keep trying. Well, you do, don't you? But I knew I'd lost her. I was racing my motor. I was scrabbling around like a rat in a trap, but I had to keep going because there was nothing else to do.

There was nothing for it but to go back to the yard. I thought, maybe she'll go back there too. Then I thought, of course she'll go back there. After all, everything she owned was in the Static – all that new clobber she'd bought. For certain she would go back to the yard.

So I ran out of Sam's Gym. But I couldn't for the life of me remember where I had parked the Cortina. While I stood dithering on the pavement I saw Harsh go by, walking towards the tube station and I remembered that I wanted to talk to him. Now more than ever, except I couldn't quite remember what I wanted to say. So I watched him walk by.

He walked so easily. He carried his kit in a cricket bag slung across his shoulder. He did not dawdle. He did not hurry. He covered the ground perfectly balanced and ever so graceful. And I thought how astonishing it was that you could tell just what he was like by watching him walk.

I raced after him.

'Harsh!' I yelled. 'Harsh – wait.'

He stopped and turned back.

'Harsh,' I said. I was out of breath, sweating. 'Harsh,' I said, 'I've lost Goldie. I can't find her. She's gone.'

'Yes?' he said politely. He did not know how much it mattered.

'She's gone, Harsh, really gone. She won't forgive me because of the bomb. And there won't be anyone to look after her. They'll try to kill her the way they tried to kill me.'

'Eva,' he said. 'I do not understand what you are saying. Nor do I understand why you have chosen to say it to me. But if you will listen for a moment and stop jumping up and down. I will tell you something which may help.'

He was so totally calm that I did stop jumping up and down.

'Eva,' he said, 'again you are allowing your emotions to hurt you. You are like a thing blown in the wind. At the moment the wind is blowing you against a wall. The wall is hard. It will not

124

be broken. You will not break the wall. The wall will break you.'

I knew it was important because he spoke very seriously. But I didn't understand a single word. Or rather I understood every single word, but I didn't know what he meant.

'But what about Goldie?' I asked. 'I've got to find Goldie.'

'No,' he said. 'You do not have to find Goldie. What you have to find is peace. When you have found that you will no longer be blown in the wind. Then you will find Goldie or you will not find Goldie. Either way, you will not hurt yourself because trivial things will not matter.'

Did I ever tell you that Harsh has the thickest, most beautiful black eyelashes in the world? And that sometimes, although he is very dark, he reminds me of an angel? I'm telling you this because just then it seemed as if he was talking from a long way away and very high up.

He went on down to the tube station and left me standing like a wattock on the pavement. I didn't know what to think, but I found myself wondering if he talked like that to Soraya. And if he did, how had he lived so long? But maybe Soraya understood him. Sure as eggs I didn't. I wished I did because I had the feeling that he had said something very helpful, but I didn't know what.

Harsh is awfully wise, but there's not much point being wise if no one understands you.

Chapter 17

Back in nineteen eighty-something Simone and I were at a place called Burlington House. It was a short-stay home. Because it was nearly Christmas there was no school, so the girls there spent all day raking leaves, mopping floors and polishing windows. There was a bell to get up with, a bell to tell you it was breakfast and a bell for however the bastards who ran the place decided to break up the day. You said grace before and after every meal. The only time you got out was on a Sunday morning to go to church. You could watch telly for an hour at night if you had been good. If you were bad you were refused privileges, which included telly, margarine on your bread, sugar in your tea, a proper bed.

Small punishments which added up.

Somehow, I was never good enough. We'd only been there a couple of months when I was eating dry bread, drinking sugarless tea and sleeping on the floor in the hall with no telly for comfort. It was a way of life, and it really pissed me off.

Simone never toed the line any more than I did but she always looked as if she did. It was a talent, a real talent. If it was bottled, I'd spend a fortune trying to buy it.

But one day, one of the screws found some cigarette butts on the ground outside Simone's dormitory window. I don't think it was actually Simone smoking. She always said it wasn't. She said she always shredded her butts and flushed them down the bog, and I believe her – she wasn't careless.

But the other slags in Simone's dorm fingered her, and she found herself sleeping out in the hall with me. It was very cold that year. In the mornings you found ice formed *inside* the windows. Simone wasn't used to it and she was very upset and uncomfortable that night. Even worse, because smoking was such a sin and a crime at Burlington House she was going to get the strap in the morning. It had never happened to her before, and she was scared stiff.

I told her it wasn't too bad, but she was shivering and crying so much that I couldn't comfort her.

'It wasn't me,' she kept saying. And I felt really bad for her.

The funny thing was that I was always being fitted up. Well, not even fitted up. If something happened, the screws always looked at me first. I'll never know why. Probably I've just got that sort of face. But anyway I was done as many times for stuff I didn't do as I was for stuff I did do. It didn't matter much. Like I say, it was a way of life.

But Simone was different. She was pretty and delicate. People liked her. She was used to being treated well – or as well as anyone got treated in places like Burlington House. She expected it. I expected it. So it was almost as bad for me as it was for her when she was fingered and made to sleep on the floor knowing she would be strapped in the morning.

I couldn't understand why she'd been fingered. As I said, people liked her. So I asked her why. And it turned out that there was this girl called Rosie Price and her special friend was called Sheena. You have to be a bit careful about people with special friends in places like Burlington House. Special friends are rather like married couples. I never had one myself – except for Simone – but a sister doesn't count. Well, anyway, Sheena liked Simone. Simone liked Sheena. Simone liked nearly everyone and nearly everyone liked her.

But Sheena spent too much time with Simone and Rosie Price got choked. She thought Sheena was going to leave her. Probably this was not true because Rosie Price was a big girl, and there were advantages to having a big special friend in a place like Burlington House.

According to Simone, this was what was behind it all. She

127

told me that when the screws found the fag ends and busted the dormitory, Rosie Price stood straight up and pointed the finger at Simone. Simone said that while Rosie Price was doing this she was staring at Sheena, facing her down, daring her, making her choose there and then. Sheena didn't dare choose Simone. She backed up Rosie Price. And then the other girls in the dorm backed *her* up because, as I say, Rosie Price was a big girl for her age.

You can't blame them. Stuff like that happens all the time at places like Burlington House.

I tell a lie. I say, now, you can't blame them. Now, I have a relaxed mental attitude and loads of self-discipline. But then, I blamed them and I was really bitter against Rosie Price. Really bitter.

I told Simone. I told her we should go in there to Rosie Price's dorm and duff her over. But that made Simone cry even harder. She said if we did that Rosie Price would get her alone and make her pay for it. She said all she wanted was to get back in the dorm, like normal, and show Rosie Price how nice she was. She didn't want anyone to hate her, see.

But I knew different. I knew girls like Rosie Price. They never let up. Once they've got you down they keep kicking. And the trouble with places like Burlington House is that you can't get away from girls like Rosie Price.

So I did it by myself. I filled a jug with cold water and I went along to Rosie Price's dorm, and I tiptoed up to her bed. I threw the water all over her and her bed and when she woke up screaming I shoved the wet pillow over her face and hit her with the jug. I hit her three times, as hard as I could, and then I tried to leg it before the others could get up and turn the light on.

But one of them did manage to turn the light on before I could get out of the door, so they all saw that it was me. And I saw that I'd got the wrong bed. I'd poured water all over Sheena by mistake. Rosie Price was bone dry and madder than a wasp's nest.

So I did a runner. I grabbed Simone and we went and hid in the boiler-room in the basement. Which wasn't a bad idea, because as I say it was nearly Christmas and very cold, and it was warmer in the basement than it was in the hall.

Rosie Price didn't find us.

I suppose we were reported missing at morning roll call but it didn't much matter. We went over the wall while everyone else was at breakfast.

I told Simone it meant we'd be home for Christmas, and so we were. But Ma wasn't too pleased to see us, and Nan thought we'd only get ourselves into more trouble. Simone never said anything much but she must've been pleased because when they caught up with us they didn't send us back to Burlington House. They sent us somewhere more secure and it wasn't any better than Burlington House but at least Rosie Price wasn't there. And at least we'd got home for Christmas even if we weren't very welcome.

When that happened I was nine and Simone was ten.

So, you see, right from when I was a little kid things have had a habit of not turning out quite right. Sometimes they don't turn out too wrong, but either way they never go exactly as I mean them to. Mostly I get myself out of one hole and fall into another one even deeper.

Maybe it was like Harsh said. Maybe I was a thing blown in the wind. But how do you persuade the wind to stop blowing? Tell me that.

I'd hoped Harsh might've told me what to do – like when he showed me how to weight-train with no weights – how to use my own weight or my own force as the resistance to push against.

But he didn't. All he did was make me think about the old days and about how stuff in my life has never turned out quite right. And although I try to look on the bright side, like how we *were* home for Christmas and *didn't* get sent back to Burlington House, the bright side was never very bright. It was a lousy Christmas and the new place was just as bad as the old. What's more we were marked out as absconders which made things even more difficult next time.

Harsh hadn't helped at all. He'd just depressed the shit out of me. But, looking on the bright side again, he had reminded me of a simple very important fact – there was nobody on my side now. I was on my own, and I had to be even more careful.

I spent a long time getting back into the yard. I circled the whole area, spiralling inwards, making sure the streets were clean before I went home. I looked for people I knew, people who were out of place, men in parked cars, and especially for two guys sitting in a white Maestro van.

Nothing looked wrong. The Maestro van was gone. I went in. But before I could reach the Static, Mr Gambon caught me.

'What do you want?' I said. 'I'm in a hurry.'

'Why are you always in such a foul mood?' he asked, and his thin little moustache twitched. It made him look like the rat he is. 'It's Friday. I need your signature.'

Friday, I'd forgotten again. Pay day. I scrawled my name in his book and took the brown envelope. The men were beginning to clock off.

'Someone's been leaving windows open in the office block,' I told him.

'Which ones?'

'Ladies' bog. You're supposed to check.'

'That's what I like about you, Eva,' he said. 'Such a lovely personality.'

'You don't pay me for personality,' I said, and walked away before he could say anything else. I felt sharp and mean.

I found Rob lurking near the Static.

'What?' I said.

'She's gone,' he said.

'Who?'

'Eleanor.'

'Oh, her,' I said.

'She came back, picked up her gear and left with them two sammies. It looked like she knew them.'

'They're mates of hers.'

'She didn't seem the type,' he said.

'What type's that?'

'You know,' he said.

'No I don't.'

'Don't give me that,' he said. 'I can see you going round with blacks. But not her.'

'Shows how much you know,' I said. He looked really brassed off and it made me feel great.

He turned away and then he turned back. He didn't know what to do, the silly sod. I watched him. He really did look miserable.

'She coming back?' he asked, not looking at me.

'Shouldn't think so,' I said, not a care in the world. 'We're too rough for her here.'

He went away then.

I sat on the Static steps and watched him go, the big soppy wilf. What did he have to moan about? He'd had more of her than he deserved in the first place.

It was funny. I was cold, dying for a cup of tea, but I didn't want to go indoors.

I thought, I'll sit here and wait for the yard to clear. Then I'll let the dogs out. No point going in and getting comfortable before letting the dogs out.

Rob told me one thing, though. If Goldie knew those two in the Maestro it meant they were from Count Suckle's not Bermuda Smith's. And if they were from Count Suckle's it meant that they now knew I was not dead. And if they knew I wasn't dead they might want to do me over. I would if I was them.

It was dark. I sat on the steps. The men left by ones and twos. I wished they would get a move on. I wanted to lock the gate and let the dogs out. Until then anyone could come in.

I could just see the gate from where I sat, and I kept my eyes on it. I wanted to be sure everyone moving about there was going, not coming. But the light was poor and I couldn't see properly.

At last the yard cleared. I picked up the big torch and went to the gate. I'd just got the first chain and padlock on when a voice from across the road called, 'Eva? Eva Wylie.'

It was a woman's voice. I peered into the dark.

'Who is it?' I said. 'Goldie, is that you?'

But the woman who stepped out of the shadows was not Goldie. It was the lady copper I'd brushed off a couple of days past.

'Oh, it's you,' I said, and carried on locking the gate. 'What do you want?'

'A word,' she said. 'Can I come in?'

'No, I'm locking up.'

'All the same, can we talk?'

'No,' I said. 'I don't talk to the polizei.'

'I'm not police,' she said and came right up to the gate where I could see her. She wasn't in uniform, but if she wasn't polizei, I was a tomato sandwich.

I said, 'Pull the other one, copper, it plays Lavender's Blue.'

'I was a copper; you've got that right. But not any more. I went private years ago.'

They'll tell you anything and expect you to believe it, then when it's your turn they call you a liar.

I snapped the padlock on the bottom bolt and straightened up.

She said, 'You think I was part of the police raid on Bermuda Smith's club don't you?'

I didn't bother to answer.

She went on, 'In fact I'd been there for a long time.'

'I didn't see you,' I said.

'I saw you.'

'You saw fuck-all,' I said quickly. She had that copper's way of saying, 'I saw you,' which was supposed to mean she saw me up to no good.

132

'Right,' she said. 'I saw nothing. But if I was a cop I'd have seen you, and you'd be in choky right now for lifting wallets.'

She was annoying the crap out of me.

I said, 'You were too busy lifting drunks to see a crane lift a bungalow.'

'One drunk,' she said. 'Eleanor Crombie. She was going to get badly hurt down there on the floor. I was trying to get her out, and then you dived in and snatched her. In a way you did the job for me, but it meant I lost her. I've been looking for her ever since.'

I was trying so hard to remember what I told her last time she came that my head hurt. With the polizei, the trick is to keep saying the exact same thing all the time. If you say one little thing different they come after you with a pick and shovel until your story is smashed into little pieces on the ground and you can't remember your own name.

On the whole it's always best to say nothing. I said nothing.

She said, 'I'm looking for Eleanor Crombie. I'm working for her family. They think she's in trouble. They want her home.'

'What's that got to do with me?' I said. 'I told you last time I don't know where she is. I'm telling you now – I don't know where she is. And that's all I'm telling you.'

Which was God's truth, but it made me feel very sad. I turned my back on the lady copper and walked away.

'Eva,' she called. 'Eva Wylie. Don't stay here tonight.'

I stopped.

'Don't stay here,' she repeated. 'And don't fight tomorrow. There are too many people out for your guts.'

I turned to face her.

'What you talking about?'

'I told you, I'm a private investigator. I talk to people. I talked to Harry Richards.'

'Now I know you're lying,' I said. 'Harry wouldn't talk to no lady copper.'

She lost her rag completely. She said, 'Look, you silly

twommit, clean out your lugholes and listen for a change. I'm not a sodding cop.'

It was great – I'd really got her going. It was a lovely feeling, knowing I'd annoyed her as much as she'd annoyed me.

I said, 'Clean out your own lugs. I don't know where Goldie is. And I don't talk to the polizei.'

I marched away leaving her on the other side of the gate. And then I hurriedly opened the dog pen.

'Go for it,' I yelled as Ramses and Lineker came crowding out. 'Go on. Kill!'

And they went hell-for-leather straight at the gate, snarling and barking, climbing up the wire.

It was a shame, really. She didn't fall on her backside and wet her knickers the way I'd hoped. She just turned and walked away, that back of hers as straight as a telephone pole.

All the same, she left me quite charged up and ready to go into the Static. I hadn't wanted to before because I thought it would be all cold and empty and it would make me sad. But now I went in without a second thought. I went for the kettle without looking right or left and started to heat the water. I did not use the electricity – that was something Rob had fixed for Goldie. It didn't have anything to do with me.

In the end, though, with a mug of tea safely in my hand, I felt I could bring myself to look round.

Everything was the way it was before she came – cold, empty and whiffing of brine. The only thing different was in the bedroom – that still smelled of her, and the soap she liked was still in the shower. She hadn't taken it.

The other thing was on the bed in a Selfridges carrier bag. At first I didn't want to look in case it was something awful, like a message about what she really thought of me. But, after a couple of minutes I forced myself to look.

It was an enormous T-shirt with 'Big Is Beautiful' written on the front. And a cuddly stuffed tiger with an evil grin on its face and wonky whiskers.

I sat on the bed. I was in bits, I admit it. I couldn't help remembering her coming back squiffed-out, the night I was so narked with her, telling me she'd bought me a present. I can't remember what I said but I expect I told her to stuff it. I do that – say things without thinking. I wish I didn't, but I do.

She didn't leave any message, so I didn't know what the present meant. Perhaps she thought, 'Well, I bought these things with Eva in mind, and now I can't stand the thought of her so I don't want any reminders.'

Perhaps she thought, 'Well, I suppose she did help me out of a jam once.'

Perhaps she didn't think either of those things. Perhaps she simply didn't care and forgot them the way she forgot the soap.

I didn't know what she meant by leaving me a present on the bed. I stuffed both items in my emergency kit bag, and I blew my nose, and I finished my tea. It doesn't do to dwell on stuff you don't understand – take it from an expert.

There were things to decide. Decisions. Farkin' decisions. How do you make them? Mostly you don't. You fart around and get a headache, and then, when you're totally pissed with doing nothing, you do something and call it a decision. Anything will do.

I decided to leave the yard. Why? Well I'll tell you – although it's against my religion to believe anything the polizei tell me, there was a niggling feeling that the lady copper wasn't just screwing around with my head. I was looking for advice, wasn't I? Well, she gave me some, didn't she?

'Don't stay here,' she said. All right. It was a tip I was ready to take. I already had everything in an emergency kit bag.

She could stuff the rest of her advice, though. Not fight tomorrow? Not meet Rockin' Sherry-Lee Lewis, Star of the East? I mean, really! Do I look like a wimp? Does a cat act like a canary? Come on, behave.

When taking advice, always do what you want to do. That's *my* advice.

But it was cold – not cold enough to burn your face, but cold enough to see your breath – and I have to say I wasn't looking forward to sleeping out. At one time I did it every night. I didn't particularly want to, but it's a thing you get used to and after a while sleeping indoors seems almost unhealthy. If you sleep in a room you can't breathe and you feel trapped. On the other hand, you can sleep easier knowing you won't be moved on or that there's no one coming up on you in the dark.

You see, no matter how poor you are, you've always got something to lose. It's a law of nature. It may be your coat, or your bit of shelter, but if you've got it you want to keep it.

The other law of nature is that if you've got it, there's someone out there who will want it too. And if they come up on you in the dark, they'll try to take it.

The knack is not having anything you can't protect.

That's what houses are for – to protect all the stuff you don't want to carry round with you. If it was just a matter of a place to sleep and wash there would be no problem. Nobody would need much space. But people collect stuff and then they have to protect it, and the more they collect the more space they need to house it. It isn't people who need big houses. It's things.

Look at me. I was dithering on the steps of the Static. And for why? Well, if you must know, I was worried about what I was leaving behind. It wasn't much. Just some clothes, a few old pots and pans and my London Lassassin poster. But it was enough to make me dither.

Also there was my stash. I couldn't take that, not if I was sleeping out. When I slept out before, I didn't have a stash. Now I do, and let me tell you it's a worry.

I went back inside. There was no heat on, but it was warmer than outdoors. Maybe I was going soft, but suddenly it was hard to leave. Perhaps I had been happy in the Static. I couldn't remember if I had or not, but for sure it had been my home. The only place I'd ever had a right to. Mine by right.

Bleeding daft, I thought. I was only leaving for the night. I'd be back tomorrow. I had to be – there were the dogs to feed and the yard to open.

I took a last look round. Then I walked out and locked the door.

Chapter 18

I WOULD HAVE walked straight out the gate but the dogs were acting funny. They were sticking together and prowling. Normally, when they are first let out, they race round the yard, stretching their legs, sniffing out what's happened during the day. After that, Ramses takes up a central position, out of the wind, and settles. He stays very watchful all night but he doesn't waste much energy. Lineker, being younger and dafter, scurries about hunting rats and barking at cars. Sometimes he tires himself and gets to sleep before morning.

I watched them for a minute, and then I put down my kit bag and followed. They were most interested in the fence on the gate side. They ran a few steps, stopped, tested the air, then ran on. Sometimes they stood side by side, paws up on the wire as if they could get a better view on their hind legs. A better view of what?

I kept to the shadows because I didn't want to show myself. And I used the heaps of metal and tyres for cover.

I couldn't see anything wrong. It was silent and dark. There were no cars passing. All I could hear was the shuffle and rustle of Ramses and Lineker as they prowled back and forth. But all of a sudden I felt bad – like I was being watched by someone who wanted to do me damage.

I backed away from the fence, and kept the cars and machinery between me and the road until I made it back to my kit bag.

Better not leave by the gate, I thought.

There was a back way out. Nobody ever used it, but I found it when I first moved in. I was glad of it to begin with. Not that I ever used it myself, but I was glad to know it was there. It comes from sleeping in derelict houses. The first thing you do when you go into a house is to find another way out the back. The last thing you want is to be trapped in a place with only one exit. It might be the polizei coming in to clear you off, or it might be a gang of tramp-bashers, or it might be winos. Whatever. You just can't make a quick exit through the same door the enemy's coming in at. You don't have to believe me – any burglar worth his salt will tell you the same.

In this case the back door was a metal gate set in the ten foot brick wall at the very back of the yard. It doesn't really go anywhere. Beyond the wall is a space and then another brick wall. Behind that is a disused railway siding. I suppose the space used to be an alley but it got blocked off by buildings at both ends.

If I wanted to get out without being seen, that was the way I should go – through the metal gate, across the space that wasn't an alley, over the wall and through the siding.

I shouldered the kit bag and started off.

The metal gate was easy because I had all the yard keys. I let myself out of the yard and into the space beyond. And then suddenly it was awful. I was in a narrow space between two walls, two high walls. I started to sweat for no reason at all.

I looked up at the wall I had to climb and saw that the top of it was protected with broken glass stuck in concrete. It reminded me of something but I couldn't remember what. I began to feel quite ill, so I went back into the yard and sat on the ground near the gate.

It was stupid.

'This is stupid,' I said. 'Stupid, stupid, stupid.'

And then I thought, suppose there's someone on the other side of the wall? Someone waiting to catch me. Suppose Count Suckle's people, or Mr Cheng's or Bermuda Smith's or whoever they are – suppose they did a proper job of sussing out the yard? Suppose they had it surrounded?

I felt a bit better because now I had a reason for feeling so awful.

139

I left the kit bag where it was and went to call the dogs. They were still roaming around on the far side, all jittery and uneasy. When I put my hand on Lineker's collar he flinched away and I noticed that his hackles were up all along his back.

They came with me to the back gate. They didn't want to, but they came. I shooed them into the space between the two walls and watched them as they ran from one end to the other and then back to me. They didn't bark or snarl. They just looked at me, puzzled, before padding off back to the fence.

I looked at the wall. According to Ramses and Lineker it was safe. According to them there was no one on the other side. I trusted those dogs. They weren't stupid – not Ramses leastways.

'Fuck it,' I said, and went to get some tyres.

When the tyres were piled high enough I climbed up. First I balanced the kit bag on top of the wall. Then I spread my padded jacket on the glass. Then I heaved myself up and looked over.

There was nothing moving out there. As far as I could see with the torch there was just old slurry and broken bricks and rotten railway sleepers. I dropped the kit bag down. I shifted myself so that I could stand on the wall where the glass wasn't sticking up too proud. I picked up my jacket and jumped.

It was easy. If you don't know how to fall, don't take up wrestling.

As soon as I was down on the other side I felt fine, really all right. And I couldn't understand what had gone wrong before.

I picked my way slowly through the rubble. It would be plain daft to make a perfect ten foot landing and then twist an ankle on half a brick.

Half a brick. Do you know, in that old siding, there was not one solitary thing which was not broken? Broken bricks, broken glass, broken and rotting sleepers, broken pushchairs, broken supermarket trolleys. Everything was smashed and rotten.

At the bottom of the slope, near where the railway line had been, was an old shed. The door was missing, the window was broken and part of the roof had been ripped away. But, I thought, it would be a bit of shelter, just for one night.

I went in. It smelled of piss and old bonfire. I knew that smell. Once you smell it you never forget it. Sometime, not too long ago, that shed had been a doss for winos.

There were piles of damp newspaper, bits of torn cardboard and rag. There were broken bottles and crushed aluminium cans. I cleared some space in a corner, the corner which smelled least of piss. I unrolled my sleeping bag and sat on it. Then I switched the torch off and waited. I waited until my eyes got used to the dark and my ears began to sort through what they could hear.

You have to sit very still for at least ten minutes before you can hear what's going on around you.

There were rats. There are always rats. There was an owl. Even in the middle of London you can hear owls. They hunt the rats and mice. There were the deadened sounds of traffic. There were the sharp scampering sounds of small animals and beetles. There was the rattle of paper in the wind. There was me breathing. But there were no people.

I began to relax, and as soon as I relaxed I felt hungry. I had hardly eaten a thing since breakfast. It had been that sort of day. I thought about the sort of day it had been. I thought about what Harry Richards said to me. I tried not to think about what Goldie said. I tried to think about Rockin' Sherry-Lee instead. But I couldn't. One thing was certain, it had been one of the worst days in my life. And it only seemed natural that I should end it in a doss for winos.

'Eat,' I said out loud. 'Fucking eat and cheer up.' It sounded like I was talking through a loudspeaker.

I switched the torch on and opened my bag. I decided on a tin of beef and potato stew. I wouldn't make a fire because that might draw attention. I would eat the stew cold. It doesn't make much difference – tinned stew isn't very nice anyway, but if you are as hungry as I was then, you won't mind much.

141

I had the tin of stew in one hand and the torch in the other.
I was staring down into the kit bag when this horrible thought
struck me. I was flabbergasted. It seemed like the end of the
world, the last straw. I had forgotten to pack a tin opener.

Can you believe that? Can you? I couldn't. Three fucking
bolas and no tin opener!

I stood up and hurled the tin of stew through what was left
of the window. Glass shattered. I heard it bouncing off the
rubble outside. I went out after it. I picked up bits of brick and
cinder. I chucked them one after the other as far as I could
throw. I jumped up and down. I was blind with rage. I howled.
I opened my mouth and let out this great roar with so much
force it hurt my throat. I punched the wall of the shed so hard
it made my knuckles bleed. I kicked the wall until the toe of my
boot split.

What can I tell you? In prison once I knew a woman who felt
so bad she used to break windows and when there was nothing
but herself left to destroy she used to cut herself with the broken
glass. Sounds weird, does it? Well, maybe you haven't felt bad
enough to understand her.

The screws used to sit on her. They'd tie her hands and feet
with bandage, and they'd gag her to stop her biting herself. It
was a kindness really. She would've killed herself bit by bit if
no one had stopped her. At least it always looked as if she
would. She was never allowed to go far enough for anyone to
find out. Who knows, maybe she would have stopped by herself
given time.

Violence blows itself out. Mine did anyway, and I just felt
tired and cold and foolish. I was very glad there was no one
watching.

I went back in the shed and I couldn't stand the place any
more. So I packed up and left.

While I was walking away I began to think about Mr Cheng.
It was partly because I was so hungry and the first thing that
popped into my brain was a plateful of his chicken and snow
peas. But chicken and snow peas are no use in your brain when

you want them in your mouth and I started to get angry again. Because it was all Mr Cheng's fault. If it wasn't for Mr Cheng I would be at home in the Static with Goldie and I wouldn't be tramping the streets with cans of stew on my back and no tin opener. I wouldn't be cold and hungry without a friend in the world. Mr Cheng had a lot to answer for.

And let me ask you this – why were Count Suckle's boys out to get me? *Me.* They should have been out to get Mr Cheng, but they weren't. I was an easy target. I was on my own. I was a woman. And, when in doubt, men always blame a woman. But it wasn't fair. True, I hadn't exactly been an innocent bystander, but I didn't know that at the time. And Mr Cheng had tried to kill me too. His people followed me to the shebeen. They locked the kitchen door. I was just the dumb animal who carried the bomb and I wasn't any use to him after that.

The further I walked the angrier I got.

'Dumb animal,' I said, out loud. 'I'll show him dumb animal.'

A couple passing in the opposite direction stopped and stared at me.

'Who you looking at?' I said, and they hurried away.

It brought me up short. I was acting as if I was all alone in the siding, but I wasn't. I was out in the streets and I had already walked a long way. I was nearly at the river, but I hadn't noticed.

'Shit!' I said. I'd done it again. I was going somewhere without knowing how.

All right, I thought, I'll go to the Beijing Garden and I'll dumb animal Mr Cheng. I was halfway there already – white headlights coming towards me, red tail-lights running away. I followed the red. It suited my mood.

In the West End you couldn't walk straight without banging both shoulders. Everyone was going somewhere – going to eat, going to dance, going to a movie or a play. Everyone on the move. No one standing still in the cold.

No one except me. I stood and looked at the Beijing Garden. There were plastic plants in the window and paper lanterns on the light bulbs. There was silk embroidery in picture frames on the wall. There were pink tablecloths on the tables and blue and white ashtrays. I couldn't see it all from where I stood, but I knew it was there. I had been there so many times it was almost like home. Every time the door opened the smell that came out with the customers made my mouth water.

It was so familiar I could've almost walked right in and had a joke with Auntie Lo. A joke with Auntie Lo, that was a laugh. The only joke to Auntie Lo was me. 'When you getting married, Eva? Huff-huff-huff.' That Eva, she's a hoot, a real stand-up comedienne. Let's blow the shit out of her along with everyone else at Count Suckle's place. That'll be a regular side-splitter. Huff-huff-huff.

There was a party of smart people sitting at the big round table in the window. It was a table reserved for big smart parties. It made the place look successful. While I watched, one of the smart well-fed men paid the bill. The other smart well fed men and women began to look for their coats. That was good. I looked round for a brick.

Just then Mr Cheng's Astra purred round the corner and stopped outside the door. The guy driving it got out in a rush. He wasn't allowed to park there because it was a no parking zone. He dashed into the restaurant and got tangled up in the smart well-fed party coming out. They were all talking at the top of their well-fed voices.

I crossed the road. I didn't have much time. The guy had left the Astra door open but he had taken the keys. I discovered that when I got in.

I did the quickest wiring job ever.

The well-fed party drifted up the street towards theatre land still braying and whinnying.

I jammed the Astra into reverse and swerved back across the road until the nose of the car was pointing straight at the Beijing Garden's front window. I flicked the headlights to high beam, and leaned on the horn.

Faces gathered at the door and window – curious faces which changed very fast into anxious faces.

I threw the gear stick into first and revved the motor. The horn kept blaring.

They had plenty of warning. More, much more than they had given me.

I took my foot off the clutch and stamped on the gas. The Astra leapt forward. And I drove straight through the Beijing Garden front window. It hardly took a second.

And it was *lovely*.

There was the scream of the motor, the crash as I hit the glass. The way the big round table disappeared under the bonnet. The way the people shrieked and ran.

I let the motor stall. Then all I could hear was the tinkling of falling glass, and the high sounds of people in hysterics. To me it was the sound of perfect peace.

I shoved the door open and got out. I walked out of the shattered window, my feet scrunching on broken glass. Then I got on my toes and trotted away.

I was laughing.

It was better than I'd ever imagined – much better than a brick. And anyway there aren't that many loose bricks lying around the West End.

I was satisfied. Satisfaction doesn't come easy, but I had wrecked Mr Cheng's restaurant and I had wrecked his precious Astra all in one go. Call it what you like. I call it satisfaction.

'Huff-huff-huff,' I said, as I jogged through the crowds crossing Piccadilly Circus, but I didn't say it very loud. To anyone else it would've sounded like me panting.

I slowed down next to the Academy. I really was out of breath. The bag on my back was heavy. I thought about Milo of Croton running around with a calf on his back. That was the way he weight-trained. I ran around with cans of beef and potato stew on my back. If I wanted to increase the weight, I could buy more stew. Milo had to let his calf grow. It's a slow business, waiting for a calf to grow. Maybe they had a lot of patience in ancient Greece.

I walked all the way to Hyde Park Corner and looked at the

monument with the dead soldiers on it. I hadn't killed anyone this time. I hadn't even hurt anyone. I might have done. If I'd seen Mr Cheng in the restaurant, or Auntie Lo, I might've kept my foot on the gas and ploughed straight into them. But I hadn't seen them. Maybe they were there, back near the bar. Maybe they saw me. But I didn't see them. I stopped the car right after the crash. I was so thrilled with the crash and the mess and the frightened faces I didn't have to go any further. But I might have. If I'd seen Mr Cheng or Auntie Lo I might have.

That's the trouble with feeling bad. You feel bad, so you do something to make yourself feel better. And the trouble with *that* is that feeling better doesn't last long. The thing you did to feel better sometimes has a habit of making you feel worse in the long run.

I stared over the traffic circling round Hyde Park Corner, over at the statues of dead soldiers. I still felt pretty good but I wasn't laughing any more. I was wondering how I would feel at this very moment if I had seen Mr Cheng and Auntie Lo – if I had kept my foot on the gas. I wondered if I would have laughed then as I trotted away.

The awful thing, the really horrible thing was that I thought I would have laughed.

It was weird, standing there, looking at dead soldiers, thinking about what I might have thought if things had been a bit different. Looking at dead soldiers, and feeling bad about feeling so good.

That's what thinking does. It spoils things. It doesn't pay to think. It hadn't solved any of my problems either. I was still cold and hungry and I still didn't have anywhere to sleep.

I crossed Hyde Park Corner by the underpass. It didn't make any fucking sense at all. Why was I feeling bad because I *might've* hurt Mr Cheng and Auntie Lo? I hadn't even touched them. And you can bet shit to a sugar-cake they hadn't felt bad about me.

There was a busker in the underpass, probably right below the dead soldiers. She was singing something about someone she called Dear Dandelion. The voice was nice but the guitar was

146

out of tune. Maybe a cold damp underpass is a bad place for a guitar.

I stopped under one of the lights and took the pack off my back. My shoulders ached. I needed a rest.

The busker sang, 'Only needed a shoulder to cry on. Don't run away, dear Dandelion.'

I looked at her and she stopped playing. Perhaps she saw something in my face. Perhaps she thought I was going to pinch her takings.

'Go on,' I said. 'Don't mind me.'

'Nah,' she said. 'My fingers are dropping off. I was packing it in anyway.'

Like I said, the voice was nice. She pocketed the loose change, dropped the guitar into its case and hurried away. Her footsteps rang on the hard floor like church bells.

'Got to do something,' I said.

People crossing by the underpass glanced at me out of the corners of their eyes and went on their way. And suddenly I saw myself as they saw me. It wasn't nice. A hulking great creature squatting over a kit bag, talking to herself in a public place.

'Gawd!' I said. 'That ain't me.'

Because it wasn't. I was Armour Protection. I was the London Lassassin. I was going to fight Rockin' Sherry-Lee Lewis tomorrow night. I was going to be famous.

But it was me. Stuck right dead centre in the richest part of London between Knightsbridge, Mayfair and Belgravia with no tin opener and nowhere to kip. How lucky can you get?

So I pulled the zipper of the kit bag and looked inside. Looked straight at a cuddly tiger with wonky whiskers.

'Shit,' I said, staring at the tiger.

I could go to Ma's, I thought. She'd just love to see me. I bet. She'd have a bloke there by now if she'd got lucky. He would just love to see me too.

'What you think?' I asked the tiger.

The tiger leered at me but he didn't say anything.

147

Then I remembered the artist dwerb. He thought I was 'perfect'.

The tiger leered some more.

'Screw you,' I said.

Three bolas, a tiger and no tin opener. That tin opener was still a very sore point. I couldn't believe I had been so careless and it scared me. I wasn't fit to live out any more. I had lost condition. I had lost my smarts.

The artist's catalogue had worked its way to the bottom of the bag along with the solicitor's letter.

An Exhibition of Sculpture by Dave de Lysle. He had written his phone number under his name. Thoughtful chap.

I patted my pockets for money. Then I heaved the bag on my back and trekked off down to Knightsbridge tube station for a phone.

Chapter 19

I NEVER SAW anything like it in my life. The man must've been rolling in money. He had a whole house to himself and the ground floor was what he called his studio. It was filthy – all white dust and smeary stuff. Things which looked like people were all wrapped up in wet cloth and polythene so that you couldn't see more than ghostly shapes. I only caught a quick shufti through a glass door because he took me straight upstairs.

Upstairs was better – more like a proper flat with tables and chairs and things. But you'd think that a bloke who could afford a house to himself could afford new furniture. Everything looked really old. I'd bet my Ma's sofa was newer than his, and hers was second-hand.

But it was big, really big, and I was a bit gob-struck, partly by the size, and partly because there was so much to look at. There was stuff everywhere – little models of people, drawings, paintings, bits of people – arms and legs and hands. There were things on the walls, things on the floor, things on shelves and tables. Bits of stone, bits of wood. Rugs on the walls instead of on the floor.

I tell you, the man was a lunatic – everything was arse-end up.

'Well, well,' he said. 'It's very nice of you to come.'

Even that was arse-end up. I burst in on him at almost ten o'clock at night and he says, how nice. Also he looked so pillocky. His hair was sticking up like a day-old chick and he was wearing corduroy strides. Corduroy, for Gawd's sake!

'Have a drink,' he said, waving a bottle.

'Nah,' I said. He wasn't going to get me drunk in that room – no chance!

'What then?' he said.

'Cup of tea?' I said. That sounded safe enough. 'Got anything to eat?'

Just then a woman came in. She was wearing what looked like a duvet cover and she seemed surprised to see me.

'This is Eva,' he said.

'Hello, Eva,' she said.

'Eva, this is Wendy.'

'Hello,' I said.

'I think Eva could do with a cup of tea and something to eat,' he said.

'Could she?' Wendy said, and sat down in one of the old armchairs.

I grinned. This was more like it. Dave de Lysle stood there like a carrot, looking at her. She was looking at my kit bag. She caught on quicker than he did. It would be hard not to.

'Don't move, I'll get it,' he said. And he left the room looking bewildered.

She didn't move. She just looked at me with expressionless brown eyes.

After a while she said, 'Isn't it a bit late to come visiting?'

'I'm not visiting,' I said. 'Got a business proposition.'

I turned my back on her and pretended to look at some things on the table.

She said, 'Isn't it a bit late for business propositions?'

I didn't answer. I was looking at the drawing book he had out on the table. He had done a drawing of Wendy. You could see it was her by the long neck and the piled-up dark hair, but in the picture she looked younger and more peaceful. I picked up the book and turned round.

'This you?' I said.

'Of course.'

'How many years ago did he do it?'

She showed me her teeth. 'Tonight, actually,' she said.

'Oh,' I said. I looked at the drawing and looked at her. He hadn't caught the acid in her, that was for sure.

She wasn't as old as him, but she was thirty-five if she was a day. He had made her look like a girl.

'Pretty,' I said.

'Thanks,' she said.

'The picture,' I said.

'I know what you mean,' she snapped.

I grinned again and turned away.

Dave de Lysle came in with a tray. He cleared a space on the table and put it down. There was a pot of tea, milk and sugar, and there were a couple of doorstep sandwiches with ham and tomato hanging out along the sides. Tomatoes at this time of year – I ask you!

'There,' he said in a jolly voice, 'that should keep the wolf from the door.'

'Eva has a business proposition,' Wendy said. She sounded like she was warning him.

I picked up my kit bag. It was a risk, but well worth taking.

I said, 'I shouldn't have come. Your friend says it's too late. I'll be on my way.'

'For goodness sake!' he said. 'Sit down and eat up. It isn't late. Stay as long as you like.'

'Ta,' I said. But I was looking at Wendy and she was looking at me. It had really hurt to turn my back on those sandwiches and she knew it.

I sat down and he poured me a cup of tea while I started in on the food.

'Great,' I said with my mouth full. 'Thanks.'

He looked pleased. Poor wilf, I bet that Wendy ran rings round him in her spare time. I felt quite sorry for him, but not sorry enough to leave him to a good night's kip with his lady-friend.

You see, Dave de Lysle's place was safe. Nobody would come looking for me there – not even the polizei. No one on earth would think I'd fetch up in a place like this. I was amazed myself.

'I'm exhausted,' Wendy said, yawning to prove it.

I carried on munching. Even if she got me out, she wasn't going to stop me enjoying those sarnies.

'Why don't you tell us what you came for,' she said. 'Then we can all go to bed at a reasonable hour.'

'Not you,' I said. 'Him.'

'Oh-oh,' she said. '*Private* business. Why didn't you say? I'd have toddled off long ago.' She made 'private business' sound very rude. She was really getting up my nose.

'Please, Wendy,' the poor dweeg said, 'it's not like that.'

'Not like what?' She flapped her eyelids. 'Oh, not like *that*. Good heavens, David, I never thought it was.'

She looked at me and laughed. I could feel myself getting all knotted up.

That's the trouble with these superior women with superior educations – they're ever so sorry for things like crippled babies and dead seals but they don't give a toss for real live people when they turn up on their own doorsteps needing a place to doss and a bite to eat. I wanted to bop her on her snooty little nose and toss her out of the window just to show her what real life was like. But I had to mind my manners.

I finished the last sandwich and said, 'That was great, Mr de Lysle. I was really hungry.'

It was true and it didn't hurt to say so.

'Have some more tea,' he said all warm and beaming. He poured the tea and I stirred in three spoons of sugar to show how hungry I'd been.

'How about a slice of cake? Wendy, isn't there some . . . no, it's all right, I'll get it.' He bustled out again.

Wendy sat watching me. It isn't very comfortable when people just sit and watch you eat.

Dave came back with a huge chunk of something fruity and I got my laughing-gear to work on it.

Wendy said, 'Well, I can see this is going to go on for some time. Maybe *I'd* better wander off home.'

She didn't live there. That perked me up no end.

'Wendy, please!' Dave de Lysle said. 'This is the first weekend we've had in months.'

'I know,' she said. 'I thought *you* had forgotten.'

'It's just . . . ' He stopped and she didn't help him. They both looked at me.

I was going to tell them I had a business proposition again, in case they'd forgotten. But my mouth was too full of cake. Cake and 'proposition' don't go well together – not in a poncy big house they don't. I chewed as fast as I could and tried to wash it down with more tea.

Dave de Lysle said, 'I met Eva at Bermuda Smith's club. You remember, the club where we heard that good jazz. The other end of Ladbroke Grove.'

'I remember a club where you got up and played your saxophone and I couldn't get you to come down and go home.'

'That's the place,' he said cheerfully. 'It's closed now. I don't know for how long. There was an amazing scene there – a police raid, and in the middle of that someone started throwing tear gas.'

'Tear gas?' she said, startled. 'David, you should be more careful. Why do you go to those places? You are an Academician, you have a reputation. Why take these risks? If you want jazz, why not go to Ronnie Scott's?'

'I do go to Ronnie's,' he said defensively. 'But I also like to hear less established music.'

'You mean they won't let you sit in with the band at Ronnie's,' she said.

'Ouch,' he said. 'No, it isn't just that. I want to go places where the people aren't just like me. I get tired of people just like me.'

'And me?' she said, with that touch of acid.

'Of course not.'

It suddenly occurred to me that they were having a fight. Only it wasn't the kind of fight I knew anything about. They didn't shout, they didn't throw stuff, they didn't beat up on each other. But it was a fight just the same. I was really interested.

'Well, it seems to me that is precisely what you are saying,' she said. 'You want to go to places where you risk police raids and tear gas. Places where I feel uncomfortable. You want to meet people I feel uncomfortable with. There are very few times when I can get away and we can be together and you risk those too.'

'Those times would not be so few and far between if you would only make up your mind about that husband . . . '

'David!' she said quickly.

They both glanced at me, but I was pouring more tea as if it was all way over my head.

'Meanwhile, there is my work,' David de Lysle said quite loudly to cover up his slip about the husband. 'The Canadian job. Remember? I need models.'

'Oh yes, you do need models.' She sounded so sarky I was surprised he didn't wallop her.

'Yes I do,' he said. 'I showed you the drawings and maquette of the javelin thrower, didn't I?'

'At some length,' she said.

'Well I found him while I was looking for Eva. He is a light middleweight wrestler.'

'I suppose she's a wrestler too.'

'Yeah,' I said. 'I am, actually.'

That shut her up. She looked totally blown.

'She's perfect,' Dave de Lysle said. It was the second time he'd said that but I still couldn't get used to the idea.

I must have smirked or something because all of a sudden she stood up and said, 'Well if she's perfect I must be in the wrong place. I must really be in the way.' And she stormed out of the room.

'Sorry,' Dave de Lysle said to me. 'I'm most awfully sorry.' And he rushed out after her. Which was a pity. I wanted to see how he was going to get out of that one.

I tiptoed over to the door and put my ear against it but I couldn't hear anything much. People with superior educations seem to fight in whispers which is no bleeding fun at all.

I went over to the big old settee and sat down.

So, the artist dweeg and Wendy long-neck were up to a little back-seat leg-over. That was nice to know. Maybe they weren't so superior after all. It made me feel a bit less knotted.

It was warm. The food felt nice and heavy in my belly. The cushions were soft.

I heard a swoosh of wind and rain on the windowpane. But it was behind thick velvet curtains, and it seemed a long way away. I wasn't out in it so it didn't matter.

'Rain on somebody else,' I said to myself.

The next thing I knew there was music playing. I opened my eyes.

'Don't move,' Dave de Lysle said.

I couldn't see him. He was somewhere off to the side.

'Go back to sleep,' he said. 'I'm drawing.'

I closed my eyes and drifted away again. But I didn't quite go back to sleep.

And then I thought, he's drawing me. But he hasn't paid. And my eyes popped open again.

'You haven't paid,' I said.

'What?'

'Money.'

'Oh,' he said. 'Hold on a minute.'

Well, he had a whole house to himself. Money wouldn't mean much.

I sat up.

'Damn,' he said, but he kept on drawing.

It was like stealing really – him drawing me without my say-so, and me asleep and all.

'That's stealing,' I said.

'What?' He looked sort of vague and blurry.

'You said you'd pay. Where's the money?'

He stopped drawing and stared at me. It was like he was coming back into the room.

He said, 'But I gave you a ham sandwich.'

'Right,' I said. 'You did. I asked for it and you gave it me.

155

Thanks very much. I didn't pinch it off you while you were asleep.'

'Oh,' he said. 'I see.' He began to laugh.

'Funny, am I?' I got to my feet.

'No, no,' he said. 'Not funny. Logical.'

'That's me,' I said. 'Logical.' It was a funny word and I started to laugh too.

'What's the music?' I asked.

'Miles Davis. You said you had a business proposition. Let's hear it.'

A business proposition? I did say that, didn't I? I rubbed my eyes. I felt a bit strange and tired.

'Well, it's like this,' I began. But I didn't know how to go on because it seemed too complicated to explain to a stranger. So I opened the kit bag and fished the solicitor's letter out for him to see.

'It's about my sister,' I explained. 'They talk about a child. She's my sister, Simone.'

He frowned while he was reading.

'But this was written years ago,' he said when he finished.

'Yeah, but I only just got hold of it. My Ma kept it.'

'So what do you want?'

'I want to find my sister. See, I always thought, you know, she'd get in touch. I always thought one day she'd just come back. But she ain't. And I thought maybe I'd better go looking.'

He looked at me and then he read the letter again.

I said, 'I can't talk to solicitor people, can I? Well, I can talk to them but I won't get piss-pudding out of them. People like that don't like people like me.'

'You want me to talk to the solicitors?'

'Yeah.' You had to explain everything to this geezer.

He seemed to be reading the letter all over again.

I said, 'I mean, you're a really well-spoken bloke.' I thought he needed some encouragement.

'Thanks,' he said. But he sounded like he was thinking of something else.

'Did they adopt her in the end?' he asked. 'These people she was fostered to, the Redmans?'

'Dunno,' I said. And I suddenly felt very choked. 'Nobody told me nothing.'

'So she might be Simone Wylie or she might be Simone Redman.'

'She wouldn't change her name,' I said, narked. 'Look, all you got to do is talk to the fucking solicitors and get the fucking foster-parents' address off of them. Then I can go round there and sort it out.'

'Mmm,' he said. And do you know, he sounded just like Goldie when he said it.

I snatched the letter out of his hand. 'If you don't want to, open your mouth and say so,' I said. 'Just don't piss me around. It's only a bleeding telephone call.'

'Oh, I'll do it,' he said.

'You will?'

'Of course. But it might be a little more complicated than you think and I can't promise to get the information you want.'

'But you'll try?'

'Yes.'

'Swear?'

'I swear,' he said, really serious.

'All right then.' I gave him back the letter. 'You can start drawing your picture again.'

'Is that it?' he asked. 'You'll model for me if I phone the solicitor?'

'Yeah,' I said. He wasn't very quick, was he?

'When?'

'Now,' I said. 'What're you waiting for?'

'Nothing,' he said. 'What have you got on under your sweat-shirt?'

'Another sweartshirt and a couple of T-shirts and a singlet.'

'Good grief,' he said.

'Cold night,' I explained. He really was a bit slow.

157

'Strip down to the singlet,' he said. 'You'll be warm enough in here.'

'You ain't going to do anything rude?'

'Rude?' he said. 'I promise I won't do anything rude. But it's you I want to draw, not your laundry.'

So I stripped down to the singlet. And I took off my shoes and socks and track bottoms and leggings. But I kept my knickers on. I mean, how much is one bleeding telephone call worth? I ask you.

'Just stand,' he said. 'Weight on both legs. Let your arms hang.'

So I stood. I stood for over an hour. I stood facing him. I stood sideways on to him. I stood with my back to him. And let me tell you, posing for an artist sucks. Being stared at ain't my idea of a fun Friday night out, and my legs started aching after only ten minutes. I never would've thought standing still could be so tiring – but it is. And if you know an artist-dweeg who wants to do drawings of you, take my advice and tell him to cock off. It's a totally pillocky occupation, believe me.

When I was practically ready to tip over he suddenly said, 'Okay, take five. Would you like a cup of tea?'

Would I? I didn't know whether to kiss him or throttle him. I was that boneless.

When he came in with the tea I was lying on my back with my feet up on the arm of the sofa.

I said, 'How much is standard rates?' And then I said, 'No don't tell me, it can't be enough.'

He said, 'You're right. People think modelling's easy. It isn't. It's a hard job, especially if you aren't used to it.'

He poured the tea. Did I tell you he had very nice hands? Well he did. When he was drawing his hands looked sort of useful. The rest of him might look twizzockish but his hands were useful.

He stirred sugar into my cup and said, 'If I don't get any satisfaction from those solicitors, you know who you should ask?'

'Who?'

'That private detective.'

'What private detective?'

'Anna Lee,' he said.

'Never heard of her.'

'Didn't she find you? She was looking for that blonde friend of yours.'

I would've sat up but I was too weary. 'Her?' I said. 'She's polizei.'

'What?'

'She's a copper.'

'No,' he said. 'She told me she was a private detective.'

'You *believed* her?'

'Well, yes,' he said. 'That night when there was all that trouble at the club, the police were there, and when the smoke cleared they questioned everyone who was left. They questioned her along with everyone else.'

'They did?' That was a new one. Polizei grilling polizei. 'Her with the lamppost up her back?' I asked, to be sure we were talking about the same one.

'She *is* very upright, isn't she?'

'Yeah,' I said. I would have to think about it. I don't like being wrong about stuff like that.

'She came to talk to me the next day. Apparently she had seen you and me in conversation at the bar earlier on. She thought I knew you.'

'But you didn't.'

'I told her to ask Harry. He seemed to know you.'

'That was you, was it?' I was too tired to be really narked, but he had to be told. 'Look,' I said, 'you better sew your yapper up with string. You don't go round telling strangers where to find people. You don't dob off on people you don't know, or them same people might stuff your yapper full of your own feet.'

He just blinked at me. He was about as bright as a twenty-five watt light bulb.

'Don't worry,' I said. 'I couldn't stuff a chicken at the moment. Got any more tea?'

He poured and we drank in silence.

Then he said, 'All the same, she knows how to find people.'

'She didn't do too good on Goldie.'

'Not yet, maybe. But she'd know how to find someone who'd perhaps changed her name.'

'I'm telling you,' I said, 'Simone wouldn't change her name.'

'All right, all right,' he said. 'Forget I mentioned it.'

He picked up his drawing book and pencil. 'Stay still,' he said, 'just the way you are. That's magnificent.'

He stopped yapping and starting drawing again and I was ever so chuffed that he didn't make me stand up because I was really butchered and I don't think I could've stood up unless someone pinned me to the wall with a nine inch spike.

Chapter 20

WHEN I WOKE up next, there I was on the sofa with my feet up. I hadn't moved a muscle, only someone had covered me with a blanket. There was a small lamp left on in the corner and I could see without moving my head that the clock on the shelf said it was seven o'clock.

I got up and climbed into my clothes. I couldn't quite credit the fact that I'd spent all night in my underwear. And half the night with some stranger staring at me. Dave de Lysle was a very weird man but he seemed harmless enough.

I slid around very quietly and found the kitchen. There was all sorts of food in there but most of it looked like hayseed, so I cut myself another big slice of his fruit cake and shoved a banana in my pocket. Then I went out.

The milkman had already come and left a couple of bottles on the doorstep. I drank half a pint of milk to wash down the cake.

Dave de Lysle probably thought he had got the best of the bargain – loads of time to draw his pictures for one little phone call. But look at it this way – I got supper, breakfast, and a warm bed for the night, so you tell me, who was the winner? All that, for just monging around in my singlet and knickers. What a steal!

About fifty yards down the road I found a nice old Volvo estate just begging to be borrowed which took care of transport back to the yard. I ate the banana in the car and whistled along with the radio as I drove. I was whistling because I felt good. I felt good because the banana was ripe and sweet – neither hard nor mushy. And I sort of felt I was in the clear. Last night I had taken care of business with Mr Cheng, and I did not think he would turf me up with the polizei. Say what you want about blokes like Mr Cheng but they don't go whining to the polizei any more than I do.

He would know it was me. He'd know that with knobs on. And word would get round. Word would get back to Count Suckle's people. Then they would know where I stood too.

See what I mean? I was in the clear.

Also, tonight was the night. Tonight, at the old Ladywell Baths I was fighting Rockin' Sherry-Lee Lewis, Star of the East. Tonight would be the first night I fought a real star. Tonight would be magic.

Things started to go wrong as soon as I got back to the yard.

Why do they do that? Why?

Can't they leave me alone to enjoy my life? I mean, what harm would it do if I had one decent day without any fuck-ups? Other people have them, so why not me? One single solitary decent day, that's all I ask.

Did I get it? Was I born beautiful? Same answer to both questions.

I parked well away from the yard in a different street to the Cortina. It was funny but I had the Renault 12, the Fiat Panda, the Cortina and now the Volvo estate all within spitting distance of the yard, and the polizei hadn't found one of them yet. All you have to do with a borrowed motor is to park it with other motors and no one will notice it. It's trying to hide them which gets you in bother.

All the same, I was thinking I should be a bit careful and not ride my luck. I came round the corner thinking about this. And then I saw the dogs. Those poor dogs.

'Oh shit,' I said.

It was awful. The dogs were sort of hanging from the wire fence.

I didn't even want to go and look.

We were a team – Ramses, Lineker and me. We were Armour Protection.

I had to go and look.

I walked slowly towards them. I should never have left them on their own. Saving my own bacon had seemed the important thing. I should've *thought*.

But as I got closer I saw Lineker move. I ran.

He was hanging all right, but his back legs were on the ground and he had been able to save himself from choking.

Further on Ramses' great body dangled from the fence. His huge neck was rolled up in a ruff round his face.

As I approached he opened his evil yellow eyes and glared at me.

He blamed me. I could see that at a glance.

I raced to the gate, opened it and took a look round. The yard seemed to be empty and silent. Everything looked in order. It was just the two dogs hanging from the fence.

I went to Lineker first. To tell the truth, although Ramses looked worse off I was worried about what he might do to me when I cut him down.

As soon as I got to him Lineker started threshing weakly. The silly bastard was even trying to wag his stumpy tail.

'Stay still, you dopey bugger!' I growled, because he was just making things worse for himself.

His head was in a noose and the free end of the noose was tied tight to the fence. There were scraps of sacking caught between his teeth. While I was freeing him, I realised what had happened. It's a method of trapping animals which is in my own SAS Survival Handbook. I could do it myself if I wanted to.

You stand outside a fence with two sticks. On one stick you have something to attract the animal – a piece of meat or something. On the other stick you have the end of a noose. The animal puts its own head in the noose to get at the bait. Then you drag the animal towards you, the noose tightens and the animal chokes.

With guard dogs you don't even have to use meat. Guard dogs are trained to attack moving objects, so all you have to do is wave a rag or a piece of sacking to provoke the dog and you get the same result. But you don't have to choke the dog. You only have to tie him up. A nice person would cut him free afterwards. There's no need to hurt him. If he's tied up, he can't hurt you.

Lineker's throat was red raw with rope-burn. He was so weak from struggling that he dropped to the ground and lay there. I was not dealing with nice people. Whoever they were, they were not dog lovers.

I approached Ramses with caution, but he didn't move. He didn't move when I cut the rope. And then I saw that on him the bastards had used wire as well. It was buried so deep in his neck that I couldn't see it. I went to get some wirecutters and when I got back I found that Lineker had recovered enough to come over and try to lick the blood from Ramses' chest.

Ramses just stared at me. I didn't like that look at all, so I made a rough muzzle with the cut rope and slipped it over his nose. You'll think it was cruel, but I know Ramses, and the way he was looking at me – as soon as I freed him he would have torn my hand off at the wrist and used it for shredding practice.

I supported his weight and cut the wire. I let him down slowly. I couldn't let him go because I had to find the wire that was still round his neck.

'Sit!' I said.

And I talked to him while I searched in the folds of his neck.

'You stupid bastard,' I said. 'Fancy you falling for that old trick!'

He kept looking at me with those evil eyes. Lineker was too stupid to blame me, but Ramses knew better, and Ramses is an unforgiving sod. Even when he was strangled half to death I had to dominate him or he would murder me.

'You should know better,' I said. 'What do you think I feed you for, you great plonker? You're supposed to be the brains of this team.'

I got the wire off. It was only because he had enough brains to stay still that he hadn't died. The wire had almost cut his throat in half.

I led them back to their pen. Lineker went straight for his bowl and lapped up water like there was no tomorrow. Ramses wanted a drink too, but I couldn't take the muzzle off him till I'd cleaned his neck.

I went to the Static to find some cloth. And then I saw what they had done to my home. It looked like they had attacked it with an axe. The outside wasn't too bad except for the broken glass and the smashed door. But inside! Inside was like the council rubbish tip.

I squeezed my eyes tight shut and just stood there. The only way I could think was by shutting my eyes and not looking.

'The dogs,' I said to myself. 'See to them first. Then you can worry about this lot.'

I opened one eye and grabbed the first piece of rag which came to hand. Then I ran back to the dogs.

The rag was one of my own T-shirts. I wet it and got to work on Ramses' neck. The wound looked nasty and I cleaned it as best I could. I rummaged in my kit bag until I found the antiseptic cream. It was the same stuff Goldie had used on me the time I came back from Count Suckle's scraped and bruised. I spread it all over his cut neck.

'You fool,' I said to him. 'You silly old fool.'

All the time I was thinking, if this is what those bastards did to the dogs what would they have done to me if they'd caught me?

'You poor old bugger,' I said to Ramses. I ripped a bit more off the T-shirt and tied it round his neck to keep the germs out.

Then I had a go at Lineker, and the dumb animal tried to lick my face.

'Don't you ever learn?' I said. 'Look what being soft does for you.'

I put food and fresh water out for them, and when I was ready to go I slipped the muzzle off Ramses' nose. After all I'd done for him he still tried to snap my fingers off. You can't blame him though, can you? Not after what he'd been through.

He drank a little water, but he wouldn't eat. He just slunk away into his shed to hide, poor old bugger.

I trailed slowly back to the Static. I wasn't feeling too bright any more. Armour Protection had taken a terrible whacking. There was only one good thing about it – this was Saturday and there was no one in the yard to see what had happened. Some of the second-hand dealers would come in at about nine, but they stayed in their nice clean area. They hardly ever strayed into the wrecker's yard.

I stood outside the Static shaking with rage.

What shall I tell you first? Well, first, the bastards had found my stash. I can tell you where it was now. Why not? Everyone else seems to know.

My stash used to be in a hole in the ground under the steps to the Static. The steps were box-steps. They looked nice and solid, but you could move them easily. I had dug a hole and lined it with polythene. A board went over the hole and the steps went on top of that.

There had been some extra protection. The hole had been quite deep – you had to reach your arm in to get at what was inside, and while you were doing that you couldn't see where your hand was going. If you didn't know, your hand went straight into a small coil of razor-wire. And, if that wasn't enough to put you off, at the bottom, on top of my stash, were two mousetraps.

It wasn't much comfort, but there was blood on the razor-wire and both mousetraps were sprung. Some bastard, some-where, had a very sore hand.

But my stash was missing. All my savings, everything I had put by to pay for new teeth, all gone. Nothing left. Not even the little gold earring Simone gave me when we had our ears pierced. Well, *she* had her ears pierced. I gave up after one. I have never fancied punching holes in myself anyway, and I only did it to keep her company. It wasn't the pain which frightened me off. It was the horrible crunching sound as the punch went through the earlobe. Anyway Simone gave me one of her gold

166

earrings beause she lost the other and I only had one hole instead of two. My earlobe went septic in the end and the hole closed up, but I always kept the earring. Well, it was gold, wasn't it? And Simone gave it to me.

As for inside the Static – well, it took me all morning to clean up. It was such a tip that I didn't know where to start. There was nothing that wasn't broken, torn or dented. The bastards had even pissed on the sofa and crapped in my bed. They had written stuff on the walls, like DIE OF CANCER, SLAG, and worse things which I couldn't possible tell you because they were so revolting. It's funny, isn't it, when the nicest thing someone says to you is, 'Die of cancer, slag.'

I solved the problem by chucking everything out and making a bonfire.

Everything went on that bonfire, and I do mean everything. That includes my London Lassassin poster which now had extra bits of drawing and writing on it, my bed, the sofa, the curtains – everything.

What those bastards didn't take or destroy I burned.

And when I was finished the Static was just an empty shell.

I boarded up the windows and I mended the door. Then I went and broke into the paint shop – where the blokes from the yard keep the spray guns and stuff. I chose scarlet, because it went with the way I felt, and I spray painted the entire inside of the Static with scarlet car paint.

It made me feel quite dizzy. Partly that was due to the colour, and partly it was because I shouldn't have boarded up the windows first. I should've had more fresh air.

And it looked like hell – I mean really, like hell is supposed to look. But it covered up the writing on the wall like nothing else could.

Then I went to look at the dogs. Ramses still hadn't touched his food, and it worried me. If he hadn't eaten by tomorrow, I would take him to a vet.

Then I left the yard. The bonfire was still smouldering. Everything I had left was on my back. It was, in any case, everything I needed to survive. I even had a tin opener now.

I didn't tell you about that, did I? There just happened to be a spare tin opener in Dave de Lysle's kitchen and I sort of borrowed it. But it seemed a long, long time ago. Hardly worth mentioning.

Everything I had left was on my back, and it seemed to me I was right back to square one. Except one or two of the things I had weren't exactly mine. Apart from the tin opener, I still had the keys to the Cortina. So I drove straight to Sam's Gym to have a long hot shower.

When I got there, I was in a funny old mood. You'd expect that, what with the morning I'd had. I felt as if I had billiard balls all up my back and in my neck and shoulders. I felt as if my head was packed from ear to ear with high explosives. I felt as if I had sand rubbed into my skin.

So instead of having a shower straight off, I worked out. There was no one else there, and there was nothing else to do. I went from machine to machine and from weight to weight until the sweat poured. My skin leaked poison like a battery leaks acid.

After that I had my shower. After that I almost felt clean.

I lay on the bench in the ladies' changing-room. It was the same bench where Goldie had sat when I told her about Simone.

That was yesterday, but Goldie was already a stranger.

Goldie was worse than a stranger. Goldie was an enemy.

Because it was Goldie who sicked Count Suckle's people on to me.

I knew that now. I knew it because of what happened to the dogs, and most of all, I knew it because the bastards had ripped off my stash.

Because, aside from me and Ramses and Lineker, Goldie was the only other person on earth who knew about the hole under the steps. I didn't tell her about it, but I didn't hide it either. And while she was staying with me I took some money out. I took money out because she needed things. When I found her she had nothing. I even bought the soap she washed with, more fool me.

Do you like it? I do. Goldie, my friend. Goldie, my enemy.

I counted the money in my pockets and realised I had problems. The money in my pockets was my week's wages from Mr Gambon. Normally it would see me through till next Friday. But I had to buy stuff now. First of all I had to replace my fighting gear which included knee pads and boots.

In the ring, I am the one who wears black. It's like in cowboy movies – I'm the one in the black hat. I'm the baddy. Baddies always wear black – except of course if you're a mad monk or a kendo warrior in which case you wear red. Black and red are the colours of the devil, see.

I don't go in for fancy stuff. No sparkle or sequins for me. Just a plain black costume and plain black tights. But you don't want gear which sags at the bum or bags at the knee. You want quality gear, and quality costs.

If I bought all the gear including new boots and knee pads I would be stony for the rest of the week. But it had to be done. Tonight I wanted to look my best – whatever my best was.

I put on my Big Is Beautiful T-shirt – it was the only clean one left – and I went out through the gym.

There were about half a dozen weekend recreationals pumping away with the weights. And Soraya.

Soraya stood by the window wearing a pale pink and blue sari, looking like the Queen of farkin' Sheba. Just the person you want to meet when all your clobber is mucky and all you have left is a Big Is Beautiful T-shirt. Soraya makes me feel like a toad, but I suppose it's not her fault.

'Hello, Eva,' she said, in her soft sweet voice. 'Are you leaving?'

I looked round for Harsh but he was in the changing-room.

'I got to go shopping,' I said. You feel you could get Soraya dirty just by talking to her. 'Got to get gear for tonight.'

'Ah, yes,' she said. 'It is a big night for you, Eva. Harsh has told me.'

169

I couldn't imagine Harsh telling Soraya about me and Sherry-Lee Lewis. I couldn't imagine them talking about sweaty subjects.

Harsh came out of the changing-room. He said, 'Did you find your friend, Eva?'

Fancy him remembering that. I thought his mind was on higher things.

'She's gone,' I said. 'Doesn't matter no more.'

'Eva is going shopping,' Soraya said. 'Shall I come with you, Eva? Otherwise I shall just get bored waiting for Harsh.'

'Got to go to the launderette first,' I mumbled. I was hiding my bundle of dirty clothes behind my back. 'Launderettes are even more boring than waiting for Harsh.'

'This is true,' she said seriously. 'Quite true.'

'I am flattered,' Harsh said, and went away to warm up.

I said goodbye to Soraya and left quickly. Go shopping with her! I'd rather chew lizards' tails.

Shopping shits. Shopping is for little people who can fit into the coffins they call changing-rooms without bruising their elbows on the mirror. If you are my size you don't want to be that close to a mirror, believe me. But it had to be done, and I did it while my clothes were in the washing machine.

Then I had lunch. You're supposed to eat carbohydrates. At least that's what marathon runners do. You have your last meal a few hours before your fight or whatever. And it's supposed to be easy to digest and it's supposed to be the sort of food which will give you energy quickly.

I had spaghetti with meatball sauce followed by a double helping of banana split. Harsh turned me on to bananas. I believe in bananas.

The next thing you are supposed to do is lay up quietly somewhere and get your head together.

Getting your head together is a lot more difficult than eating carbohydrates. You are supposed to be totally relaxed, and you are supposed to imagine in your head everything that might happen in a fight and then you are supposed to imagine what you will do about it. Well, ha-bloody-ha.

I fight. I don't think. If you're in the ring and you've got to stop and think what you're going to do about someone charging at you off the ropes at ninety miles an hour, you'll get slaughtered. No two ways about it. Slaughtered.

You don't think. You act.

But Harsh says, 'Run through all the moves in your mind, Eva. Then when the time comes you will react more quickly.'

That's what Harsh says. And I do try, but eating bananas is easier.

Which is why I committed the sin of sins and drove the Cortina right into the yard.

Never, ever do that. You are just *asking* to be caught in possession. If you borrow a motor, put it outside someone else's house. Putting it outside your own is about as brainless as you can get without having liposuction of the head.

But what else could I do? I couldn't lay up in the Static because the paint was still wet and the fumes were enough to make a vicar drunk and disorderly.

I lay down on the back seat and covered myself with my old sleeping bag. I tried very hard to clear my mind. Have you ever tried to do that? Not think about things? Talk about the brain having a mind of its own! I must've thought about everything except running through the moves.

In the end I got up and went to look at the dogs. Ramses still hadn't eaten his food. He was lying with his head and paws close to his dish so that Lineker couldn't get it but he hadn't touched a mouthful. I took the bandage off to look at his neck. It was nasty. What was more worrying was Ramses not trying to chew lumps out of me when I touched him. He snarled and gave me a really ugly look but he didn't go for me. It was so unlike him.

'Right, my lad,' I said. 'I'm going to take your horrible carcass to the vet.'

Well, why not? I was fed up with trying not to think. I'm

always better off doing things, and I still had a couple of hours to kill before going to the Ladywell Baths.

There was a vet half a mile away and he had someone on call at weekends. I knew that because Mr Gambon had an account with him and I took Lineker there once when he got glass in his paw. The vet was an old man who wheezed and smoked a pipe. It's silly to do both, but he did. You'd think a man that age would know better. He wouldn't treat guard-dogs unless they were muzzled – so maybe he wasn't *that* silly.

I took Ramses to see him in the Cortina. Ramses didn't like the Cortina and he hated the vet but he couldn't do a thing about it because of the muzzle.

I lifted him onto the table so that the vet could see his neck.

The vet's pipe bubbled. His hair was yellow at the front from the nicotine. He puffed smoke in Ramses' face. Ramses kept his eyes on me. I had never seen him look so evil. He blamed me for everything, including the vet's pipe.

'Fine dog,' the vet muttered, 'fine muscular animal. Splendid.'

Maybe he couldn't see the look Ramses was giving me. 'Splendid' was not the word for it.

'Well, it could be worse,' he said, after poking Ramses' neck for a while. 'No major damage. No sign of infection either. This scabbing and clotting looks worse than it is. I'll give him a shot just in case, but this is a good strong animal and he's healing up already.'

'He's off his food,' I said. 'He never goes off his food. He eats like a cement mixer.'

'How did he receive this wound?' the vet asked. He took Ramses' temperature, and Ramses looked at me the way a tiger looks at a fat goat.

I told the vet a bit about the break-in at the yard.

'What a frightful thing to do to a dog,' the vet said. He read the thermometer and told me Ramses' temperature was normal.

'Is he in pain?' I asked. 'Why isn't he eating?'

172

'Well he won't be very comfortable,' he said, 'which might affect his temper. But that isn't what's causing this loss of appetite.'

'What is?'

The vet stood back and stared at Ramses who was sitting on the table. Ramses stared at me. His head was low and thrust out from his shoulder blades as if he was going to spit at me.

The vet said, 'This dog is humiliated.'

'He's a bleeding dog,' I said. I told you he was a silly old man, didn't I?

'Nevertheless, he is humiliated. He's been hurt and he's been made a fool of.'

'That happens to me all the time,' I said. 'But I don't go off my nosh.'

'He's probably better trained than you,' the vet said crossly. 'He's been trained to protect his territory. He failed. He is humiliated, and that's that.'

'All I need,' I told Ramses when we were back on the streets, 'is a sensitive bleeding guard-dog. Pull yourself together, my son.'

But I kept thinking about it.

Back at the yard, while I did my rounds, checking the wire, the padlocks, the gates, the doors and windows, I kept thinking about finding the dogs hung from the fence.

'It won't happen again,' I said out loud. 'The bastards did their stuff. There's nothing left for them to do. Except me.'

All the same I kept on worrying about leaving the dogs on their own. Which is plain sodding daft. Ramses and Lineker were supposed to protect the yard. I wasn't supposed to baby them. They were trained fighters, for chrissake.

At the very last minute, when I'd checked all my own equipment and stowed it in the Cortina, I decided to take the dogs with me.

'You dopey great dick-heads,' I said, as I shoved them onto the back seat. 'Call yourselves attack animals? All I do is worry

173

about you. Well after tonight you better worry about me. Got that? If you go soft, it's curtains for you. Got that?'

And the three of us drove together to the Ladywell Baths.

Chapter 21

THE OLD LADYWELL Baths is built of grey stone. It looks as if it would survive a nuclear attack. It used to be an important place. Now it's all run down and neglected. But the outside looks as if it'll last for ever. It looks like a prison.

It isn't a theatre, like the one in Frome, with the ring out front and all the seating in one place. No, at Ladywell Baths, the ring is in the middle and the seats go all the way round. When you enter, you walk down an aisle with the audience on either side of you, and you march towards the ring with the loudspeakers blaring out your music. It is quite a long way from the door to the ring, and the ring looks bright as a jewel. And you march down, and the people shout, and you feel important. It's like there's a bubble in your chest which keeps getting bigger and bigger until you reach the ring, and you climb up and swing yourself over the ropes. You stand in the light and you hear all those voices, and you see all those faces looking at you. And that bubble in your chest gets so big it nearly bursts.

I went in through the side entrance. I had Ramses on my right and Lineker on my left. The first thing I saw was a pay phone and I suddenly wanted to ring someone up. I wanted to ring Simone or anyone and say, Here I am. I'm going to fight Rockin' Sherry-Lee Lewis, Star of the East. Come and see.

Of course I couldn't. But thinking about Simone made me think of Dave de Lysle. So I tied the dogs to a radiator and rang him up.

'It's Eva,' I said when he answered. 'I'm fighting Rockin' Sherry-Lee Lewis, Star of the East tonight at the old Ladywell Baths. Come and see.'

'Hello Eva,' he said. 'I'd love to.'

I'd love to, did you hear that? Love to.

'But,' he went on, 'there's a bit of a problem. I went out at lunchtime today and found that someone had stolen my car. It might be difficult to get there.'

'Oh.'

I saw Mr Deeds and Harry come through from the arena. Harry was saying, 'All ready, Mr Deeds. All set.'

Mr Deeds said, 'Quite like old times, eh Harry?' And then he saw Ramses and Lineker.

Dave de Lysle was saying, 'Will Harsh be fighting too?'

'Yeah.'

Mr Deeds came bustling over. Ramses and Lineker got up and started growling. Mr Deeds stopped.

'It's a matter of getting there,' Dave de Lysle said. What a dweeg!

'Get those fuckin' dogs out of here,' said Mr Deeds.

'I can't think what anyone would've wanted with my car,' Dave de Lysle bleated. 'It's only an old Volvo estate.'

'Shit!' I said. And I put the phone down.

'I said get rid of those animals,' said Mr Deeds.

'What for?' I said. He was going to spoil everything.

'You can't bring dogs in here.'

'They're for protection, Mr Deeds. My life has been threatened.'

'What the fuck for?'

'It's true,' I said, 'isn't it Harry?'

Harry shuffled his big flat feet.

'I don't care what they're for,' Mr Deeds said. 'Get them the fuck out of here.'

'They don't like sitting in the car,' I said. 'But if you want them out why don't you take them out yourself?'

Mr Deeds looked at Ramses and he looked at me.

'Watch your step, Eva,' he said. 'You can be replaced just like *that*.' He tried to snap his fingers but his hands were sweaty. He turned away and took Harry with him into the main foyer. Harry glanced at me over his shoulder. He seemed unhappy.

176

'One up to our side,' I said.

I untied the dogs, and went to look at the arena. It didn't look like much with the house lights up. It didn't look like a magic pool of light in the middle of darkness. But it looked all right to me. The mats were down and ready. There was red, white and blue flashing round the sides of the ring and red, white and blue ropes. Like Harry said, it was all ready. It just needed the audience. It just needed the show to begin.

Down at the front, in the first row of seats, was a little group of people. I came down the aisle slowly to see who they were. The dogs were pulling me faster than I wanted to go.

One of the group turned and saw me. She waved an arm.

She said, 'You Eva Wylie?'

'Yeah,' I said from halfway up the aisle.

'Come on down, pet,' she called.

It was her!

I let the dogs pull me down further. A man with the group saw the dogs and began to move uneasily away. I came closer. There were three enormous women and the one uneasy man.

It was her, and she was even bigger than I remembered.

She had red hair down to her shoulders and a skin as white as pork fat with little sandy freckles on it.

I said, 'Hello, Miss Lewis.' Now I was standing in front of her I couldn't think what to call her.

''Lo, pet,' she said. 'Meet me mam and me sister. They always come with me. We don't often get to London so it's a bit of a treat.'

'Hello,' I said again. The dogs were straining forward and I was trying to hold them back.

Sherry-Lee Lewis's mam looked me over like I was a second-hand car. The sister said, 'Big enough for you, Sherry?'

Sherry-Lee Lewis laughed. 'She'll do,' she said.

I felt proud enough to float up to the ceiling.

The man said, 'Um, about those dogs – couldn't you tie them up somewhere?'

'You're not afraid of two little dogs, are you?' Sherry-Lee

Lewis asked. But I noticed she kept quite still and didn't wave her arms around. She knew about dogs.

She said, 'This is Benny Knight of *Takedown* Magazine. He's doing an interview. Why don't you ask Eva some questions, Benny?'

He really didn't like the dogs, but he held his little tape recorder out towards me and said, 'Well Eva, you're a relative newcomer on the wrestling scene, how does it feel to be fighting in the big league so soon in your career?'

'Great,' I said. I looked at Sherry-Lee Lewis and she smiled at me. Her teeth were pretty good. I admired them.

'How do you fancy your chances tonight?' Kenny asked.

Sherry-Lee Lewis kept on smiling.

I said, 'I am the London Lassassin. This is my patch.'

Sherry-Lee Lewis said, 'I'm the girl to make patchwork of her patch, *and* her face.' She winked at me, so I knew what I was supposed to do.

I said, 'And I'm the girl to rock Rockin' Sherry-Lee Lewis all the way back to Newcastle.'

'Good stuff,' Benny said. 'I think I'll go and get myself a drink. Maybe I'll catch you girls later.'

He backed away until he was well out of Ramses' and Lineker's reach and then he sprinted up the aisle.

Sherry-Lee Lewis laughed. It was a nice throaty laugh. She said, 'You're not going to give me any trouble tonight, are you, pet? It's a fall in the second and a knockout in the third. Right?'

'I haven't talked to Mr Deeds yet,' I said.

'Well, you talk to him, pet, and he'll tell you the same. It's a fall in the second and a knockout in the third.'

'Yeah.'

'But we'll give 'em something to look at in the meantime. Right? That's if all your size isn't just peas puddin'.'

'Does it look like peas puddin'?'

'Take it easy,' she said. 'I just want women's wrestling taken more serious, see. You got to have a bit more about you than size.'

'I got more,' I said. 'You'll see.'

'Okay. But remember – it's a fall . . . '

'In the second and a knockout in the third. I heard.'

'Mind you remember.'

She was nice and I liked her, but she didn't have to go on about it.

I hadn't seen her standing up, but I guessed she was at least six foot two. We were a good match. The first good match I'd ever had.

'What a night,' I said as I made my way up to the dressing-rooms. 'What a flaming, blazing, beautiful night.'

It has to be said that Mr Deeds is not a very important promoter. He doesn't have a huge stable of fighters like some of the other promoters do. It's a bit of a tin-pot outfit, if you must know, but it was Mr Deeds who gave me my first chance so I ought to be grateful. And I am, when I remember.

Sherry-Lee Lewis came from a bigger stable, and I suppose she was used to better conditions. She was doing Mr Deeds a favour by appearing on his bill and so she could write her own contract.

She got the biggest dressing-room – the one the heavyweights would have expected to have for themselves. I was used to being slung away in whatever corner was left – but Gruff Gordon and Pete Carver weren't. Gruff Gordon's face was a picture when he was told the star dressing-room was already occupied by the Star of the East – and her mam and her sister.

'You gave our room away to a tart?' he thundered at Mr Deeds. 'That's not on. That's a fuckin' liberty.'

'Had to,' Mr Deeds said. 'It's in her contract. It's only this once.'

'But to a tart!' Gruff Gordon said. 'I'm not standing for it.'

'Well, sit down then,' Mr Deeds said. 'It can't be changed now. And if you don't like it you know what you can do.'

He had that epileptic look he gets before a show when things are starting to go wrong.

'It's unnatural,' Gruff Gordon said. 'Tarts in the ring.'

I was watching through a crack in the door of the smallest pokiest room at Ladywell Baths. And I was pleased as punch. Heavyweights think they're so bleeding shit-hot.

'Where's that other tart?' Gruff Gordon asked.

'Eva?'

'Not fuckin' Eva,' he growled. 'The pretty one. I ain't seen her. She's late.'

'Ask Eva,' Mr Deeds said. 'But watch out, she's got two bleedin' great hounds in her room.'

'You ask her,' Gruff said. 'It's your job.' He was in a right old state.

Mr Deeds knocked on my door, and again I was ever so chuffed. Normally he comes barging straight in without a by-your-leave. If you want respect in this life, get yourself a pair of big dogs.

I let him wait a couple of minutes before opening up.

'Come in,' I said generously. But he didn't. I never thought he would – not with Ramses and Lineker prowling around behind me.

'Where's your friend, Goldie?' he asked.

'Search me.'

'She should be here by now. Gruff and Pete are depending on her.'

I said nothing. She wouldn't come, but I wasn't going to tell him that.

'I thought she was staying with you.'

'Was.'

'She's on the fuckin' bill,' he said. 'I gave her money.'

I could've said, 'more fool you,' but I didn't. I could've told him everything *I'd* given her. But I didn't. I didn't want to soil my lips.

'Well, if she turns up,' he said, 'send her along to me sharpish.'

'Yeah.'

'You're on second after the interval.'

I grinned. It was a good spot. The best I'd ever had.

'I've spoken to Miss Lewis,' he said. Miss Lewis! Get that! 'And she wants a fall in the second and a knockout in the third.'

'I know.'

'You talked to her?'

'Yeah,' I said. 'We sorted it out.'

'None of your tricks now, Eva,' he said. 'You play this one by the book. If you fuck up on this one I'll see you never work again in this business.'

I looked at him, and behind me Ramses started growling.

He said, 'Look Eva, do me a favour. Be told.'

'You told me,' I said, 'I'm the villain. She's blue-eyes. She wins by a fall in the second and a knockout in the third.'

'And those bleedin' dogs stay in the dressing-room.'

'Right.'

I closed the door. I could've danced. I had Mr Deeds sweating, and it was lovely.

'You two little beauties,' I said to Ramses and Lineker. 'You're doing me proud. You really are.'

They both stared at me, and they both looked surprised. For yard dogs they were taking it better than I thought they would. Perhaps it was because Ramses wasn't himself, but he was behaving pretty well, considering.

I started to change. I change slowly. I want everything right. And, as I put the black costume on I feel as if I am becoming the London Lassassin. As I put on the black I become bad.

I brush my hair so that it stands out around my head. Sometimes I put on some lipstick. But always I scowl at myself in the mirror. I make my neck and shoulders big, and I scowl, and I look in the mirror and I say, 'You're bad. Man, are you bad! You're so bleeding bad you should be locked up.'

And that makes me feel mean. It makes me feel like scurfing anyone who gets near me. Because I am the villain, and everyone in the audience better believe it. And I had better believe it myself.

That's only the beginning. The other thing I do is put on a dressing-gown and go out to find a place where I can watch the audience without them seeing me. I watch them coming in and I watch one of the bouts before mine. I want to see what sort of crowd we've pulled – how many, and how they are acting. Sometimes you have to work very hard to whip up a response. Sometimes you hardly have to crook your little finger and they're howling for blood.

I hate to say it, but this is where Gruff Gordon shines. This is where he's better than Harsh. Harsh is the best. Harsh is a shooter. Gruff Gordon is too old and too fat to fight his way out of an ice-cream cone. But he can whip a crowd into flames, and Harsh can't. Well maybe Harsh could if he wasn't a purist. But he is a purist and he isn't interested in anything but fighting beautifully.

That's why they put Gruff Gordon on last. He keeps bums on seats till the bitter end. He sends the crowds home happy. Every bout is a story, and every story has a happy ending. The crowd loves it. I don't like saying anything nice about Gruff because he is such a tosser, but you have to be fair. Sometimes.

So I went out to look at the crowd.

It was shaping up nicely. Lots of people were coming in, and there was that rustle and bustle you get when folk are really ready to enjoy themselves. It's important, because the crowd is like the third character in the ring. There's you, there's your opponent, and there's the crowd.

The fourth character is the referee. He is very important too.

I met the referee while I was squinting through the door at the audience. He had come for a quick squint too. I know him. He's our regular ref, and he travels with us too.

He said, 'How's it looking?' and he took my place at the door.

'Not bad,' he said before I could answer. 'It'll be a good night. I've a feeling in my water.'

The ref's water is a good sign. He's been around a lot longer than I have. He's a good ref. He knows when to look in the wrong direction. The crowd go wild at him. He's the man without a father. He's the one that needs a white stick. But he is also the one who lets a villain be a villain. In the ring he's my mate.

He said, 'You sorted it with Mr Deeds, Eva? It's a . . . '

'Fall in the second, knockout in the third. It's sorted.'

'Okay,' he said. The referee has to know what you're going to do or he can't help.

I know what you're thinking. You don't have to tell me because I've heard it all before. You think wrestling is all phoney. I can't really explain, but it is and it isn't. You're right and you're wrong. And if you don't know I can't explain. What about the movies? That's real and it's not real, but you don't complain about it do you? You want a good story. You want good actors. You want to be convinced. You've got to believe it to enjoy it. Well wrestling's like that – but it's different.

There were a lot of kids in the crowd. I like kids in a crowd. They really believe.

I first went to the wrestling when I was a little kid. It was in the days when Ma still had boyfriends who stopped around for more than the one night, and this particular boyfriend – I can't remember his name or what he looked like – took us to the wrestling one Saturday night. It was magic, and for weeks afterwards I drove Ma up the wall asking to go again. But the boyfriend pushed off and I never went again till I was older.

I suppose some kids dream of running away with the circus. Well I never went to a circus. But I did go to the wrestling once, and I used to dream about that.

And now, here I am, the London Lassassin, and I'm going to fight Rockin' Sherry-Lee Lewis, Star of the East. Who says dreams don't come true?

Chapter 22

IT BEGAN. THE magic moment, when the house lights go down. The crowd hushes. They sit in the dark, and the ring shines like a moon in the night. The MC climbs into the ring to announce the first bout – 'In the red corner . . . in the blue corner . . . ' The music starts, and two fighters come down the aisle with their trainers.

The trainers are just bouncers really. They are just people like Harry Richards who wear white jackets with Deeds Promotions written on the back. Mostly they are old fighters, like Harry. Mostly they never really leave the game, just like Harry.

I went back to my dressing-room, because now that everything had started Mr Deeds would be pronking around the door and the corridor fussing and fuming and getting up everyone's noses.

Usually I share a dressing-room with Bombshell. I'm not used to being on my own before a fight, and the time seemed to stretch.

So I stretched too. I did what Harsh always does – I kept warm and loose. But time hung, and I found I'd done all my exercises long before the first bout was over.

The dogs watched. Well, Lineker watched. The expression in Ramses' eyes was not watchful. He had an angry, short-fuse look about him, and I thought, 'The London Lassassin should look like that.' But when I looked in the mirror I found that I already did.

I wanted to go on *now*.

I didn't want to wait.

I hate waiting.

My muscles tingled and burned.

I was ready.

Why wasn't everyone else?

A fall in the second and a knockout in the third.

Well, all right. But nobody said I couldn't cream her in the meantime. Did they? Well, did they?

I jiggled around for a bit and then I went out into the corridor. It's hard to keep still when you're ready.

I could hear the crowd – not really excited yet, but heating up nicely. Flying Phil Julio, in his blue and yellow robe, was pacing up and down, waiting to go on.

I said, 'Where's Harsh?'

'In with us,' Phil said. 'It's a piss-off in our room. That Sherry-Lee Lewis bumped Gruff and Pete out of their room, so they've bumped us out of ours, so we're in with the middleweights, and it's a squash. Dad is doing his number about the dear old days and Harsh is full of Eastern promise. That guy is such a tosser. He could toss for Britain. He's sitting in the middle of the farkin' floor where everyone has to trip over him and farkin' meditating. *Meditating*. Can you credit it?'

'Yes,' I said. 'But *you* wouldn't understand.'

'In the middle of the bleedin' floor? Too right I wouldn't. He'll give himself haemorrhoids. And he'll deserve them.'

I couldn't help laughing. I shouldn't, beause Harsh is special. But Flying Phil Julio has been in this game since Danny hoiked him out of school when he was fourteen, and he doesn't have much education. You can't expect anyone that ignorant to appreciate someone like Harsh.

Just then Mr Deeds came cantering down the corridor all of a lather, saying, 'Five minutes, Phil, five. C'mon, hustle it up. Get your dad and the Wolverines. No farting around. Move it.'

'Yeah, yeah,' Phil said, and wandered away like a kid going to school.

'No respect,' Mr Deeds muttered. 'That kid's got no sodding respect.'

Then he saw me and said, 'Where's that friend of yours, Eva? She ain't shown up yet and if she don't she'll wreck everything.'

185

I was getting a bit choked with him keeping on pestering me about Goldie so I said nothing.

'I don't know about girls nowadays,' he said. 'Do them a favour and they kick you in the teeth.'

He stood there fuming and I went off to find a bog. I didn't have one in my broom cupboard. Sherry-Lee Lewis would have one in her dressing-room but I didn't feel like tapping on her door and asking if I could use it. I was going to scurf the crap out of her so I didn't want to ask for any favours. You have to mind your manners with big stars.

The trouble is, see, that the men hog all the facilities and sometimes you have to search for ages to find somewhere you can pee in private. They expect women to have cast-iron bladders even on a cold night, and that ain't fair. Maybe when I'm rich and famous I'll complain. It's no earthly good complaining when you're not rich and famous because they just tell you to put a cork in it and that narks you off even worse.

In the end I had to cross the public foyer in front of the box office to use the one the punters use. There were a few latecomers straggling in and they nudged each other and pointed. People are beginning to recognise me. They really are. And it gives me a buzz.

A woman turned away from the ticket counter. I should have recognised her with her back turned – especially with her back turned. Once a copper, always a copper – that's what I always say.

If I'd clocked her right off maybe I wouldn't have monged around trying to be recognised myself. Maybe I'd have nipped straight across the foyer. But I'm a very visible person. It's hard to nip anywhere.

'Hello,' she said, 'Your friend turned up yet?'

'Can't talk now,' I said. And I shot across the hall into the bog on the other side.

The friggin' woman showed up everywhere. Every time I turned round there she was, just like the polizei.

I finished in the bog, went back across the foyer into the

backstage side. And, would you believe it, there she was again, in the corridor outside the dressing-rooms.

'Fuck off!' I said. 'You don't come in here. Not you.'

She grinned at me, quite friendly-like, but it made my blood boil. Well I was wearing the black, wasn't I? When I'm wearing the black I'm not supposed to be nice, am I?

'Listen,' she said, 'listen to me for one short minute. Your friend Eleanor has got herself into very bad company.'

'Piss off,' I said. 'Don't you talk to me about bad company.'

'Not you,' she said. 'You never did her any harm I know of.'

'Tell *her* that. You should see what she done to me.'

'I did,' she said. 'I told you I was a detective. Didn't I warn you? Well, didn't I?'

She did warn me. I had to admit that.

'Doesn't matter,' I said. 'You're still not supposed to be here. And anyway you're wasting your time. She ain't coming. She wouldn't show her face round me no more.'

'They might make her.'

'Who?'

'Don't you understand?' she said. 'She's bending over backwards to show she's still loyal to that singer and his family and friends. Count Suckle. Remember him? Haven't you had a look at the audience? The troops are gathering.'

'What troops? What you bunnying on about?'

Just then Harry came down from the door to the arena. He looked like a worried man.

He said, 'Yo, Miss Lee.'

'Hello Mr Richards,' she said.

'You not supposed to be here,' Harry said. 'No members of the public allowed back here. You get me into trouble with the boss, Miss Lee.'

'Okay,' she said. 'Just tell Eva here who you saw in the audience. And if that golden girl shows up she could get hurt.'

She went back through the door into the foyer.

'Nosy cow,' I said.

'She not so bad, Eva,' Harry said. 'She treat an old man with

187

respect. Not like you, Eva. You got a mouth on you like a bunch of sharp knives.'

'I'm the villain, Harry.' I suddenly felt very sad. I don't know why.

'On them boards you the villain,' Harry said. 'Not outside that ring you ain't. You should learn the difference, Eva. You should listen to your friends.'

'I'm listening, Harry,' I said. I still felt very sad. Because Harry suddenly looked like an old man and he talked like an old man and he seemed like he was a long way away. Like my nan, when she died.

'Then you better watch out,' Harry said. 'There come a big bunch of Chinese folk into that audience. I don't know one from another, Eva, but you should ask yourself what you done to Mr Cheng. Chinese folk don't come wrestlin', Eva, you know that.'

'Shit!' I said, because I'd almost forgotten about driving the Astra through the Beijing Garden window. It seemed so long ago. I thought it was an eye for an eye. Account closed.

'What you do, Eva?'

'Shit,' I said again. 'I didn't do shit, Harry. I didn't do nothing the Chengs didn't do first. It isn't my war, Harry. It's between the Chengs and Count Suckle. Why does everyone have to drag me in?'

'You drag yourself in, Eva. You act tough and you talk mean when you be better off givin' the soft answer.'

'Don't go on, Harry. I ain't the villain. Where's Mr Cheng and Auntie Lo? Where's Count Suckle?'

Harry gave me a look but he didn't have an answer.

'And where was Bermuda Smith the night you had bother? He knew there was bother because *you* knew. Else why did you ask me for muscle? Answer me that, Harry. Where are the big boys? It's their war. But they ain't fighting, Harry. Oh, no. They're at home. They're staying alive. It's us gets the shaft. We're the soldiers. The dead soldiers, Harry.'

'I don't like it,' Harry said. 'Too many soldiers in that crowd I don't like.'

He went away, flip-flopping on his big flat feet.

'Tell the guys out front, Harry,' I called after him.

'I tell them,' he called back. 'That's what we here for – crowd control. You better watch out too, Eva.'

I wasn't happy any more. I had let myself get cold, and my teeth hurt.

But the crowd sounded happy. There was a lot of screaming and yelling. It sounded like the Julios and the Wolverines were working them up nicely. Which meant that the Wolverines were beating the crap out of Flying Phil. Flying Phil was the young pretty lad who got scurfed by two older bullies while his father looked on helpless. The Julios were blue-eyes who played by the rules. The Wolverines would keep Flying Phil in the middle of the ring where he couldn't tag Danny and they'd work him over till the crowd went epileptic. Then he'd make one of his miraculous escapes so that Danny could chase them around a bit, and so on.

Another time I would have gone to have a look but my teeth hurt and I was cold so I went back to the dressing-room.

Lineker was asleep under the bench, but Ramses was sitting just where I'd left him, watching the door with his angry yellow eyes. He was an inspiration to me, that dog. I patted his head and he made a lunge for my hand.

'That's my boy!' I said, feeling better. It was a good thing he still had his muzzle on.

I warmed up all over again. Time dragged. It's always like that. Maybe I should get to a gig late and not be ready so soon. But I can't keep away. It's too exciting. I want to keep every minute in a little box for late at night when I'm all alone. I want to bottle the sound and the smell and the feeling of having a bubble in my chest, because, later, when you're all alone at night there's nothing. Just nothing. This is something. This is what makes your heart bang against your ribs. And I want it.

They wanted to take it away from me. I could feel them out there – the Chengs, the Suckles, the polizei. All the Mr Deeds, the old men, the Mas and Nans – all of them. They do nothing but take things away. Maybe they had their chances once. Maybe they blew them. Who cares? But they are never going to nick this one off me. Never. It's real. Nothing else is real.

The interval came and went.

Then it was Harsh's turn.

After Harsh it would be me. And Rockin' Sherry-Lee Lewis. Us two. Out there. On the canvas which shone like a moon in the night.

I went out to watch Harsh.

Harsh is lovely to watch. He's like a song. He is all balance and rhythm. I can't understand why the crowd keeps on chatting and drinking while he's fighting. Well, yes, I can. They don't understand the finer points. That's why. They're idiots. Morons.

'Oh, yes,' they say, 'that's *real* wrestling,' and they go and get another pint from the bar, another packet of crisps for the kiddies.

I felt a movement behind me. It was Sherry-Lee Lewis.

'Who's that?' she asked.

'That's Harsh,' I said. I was proud of him. 'He's my mate. He taught me.'

'Yeah?' she said. She watched with narrowed eyes. Then she gathered her satin gown round her shoulders and turned away.

'Well, flower,' she said over her shoulder, 'he's leaving us with an awful lot of work to do.'

And she walked off. Her mam loomed out of the darkness and followed her.

Stupid mare. Well, not really. I knew what she meant, but she shouldn't have said it.

I let her go. I'd tell her how I felt about Harsh later. Where it counted.

I bounced on the balls of my toes. I couldn't keep still. There were tickly little worms running under my skin and that bubble in my chest.

I went back to the dressing-room. There was only a couple of minutes left.

From the end of the corridor I heard Mr Deeds' voice. At first he sounded pleased.

He said, 'At last.'

And then, 'You're late.'

And then, 'Oi! You can't bring them in here.'

I folded my arms across my chest and I stood outside my dressing-room door. That brazen bitch! She'd come.

Well, let her come, I thought. She didn't mean squat to me.

The first thing I saw was Mr Deeds. He looked as if he was running backwards.

Then I saw three black guys pushing him.

Then I saw Goldie.

Goldie saw me.

She pointed a finger over Mr Deeds' shoulder. She said, 'That's her!'

Everyone stopped in their tracks. I stared at Goldie, but she wouldn't look at me. Her eyes were dull. Dead animal eyes, I thought, dead animal.

Mr Deeds said, 'C'mon fellers. We can sort this out later. Complimentary tickets all round. Wha'dya say?'

One of the guys said, 'Stuff your tickets, man. It's her we want.'

Mr Deeds said, 'Okay, okay. She's yours. But after. Right? She's going on in a minute.'

I was looking at Goldie. But she couldn't look at me.

'This what you want?' I said.

She said nothing.

'*This what you want?*'

'Don't shout at me,' she said. 'You always shout at me.'

She looked at me then. It was all so wrong.

She was beautiful. Her eyes were full of tears which spilled down those thick dark eyelashes. And she had a nasty great bruise on her cheekbone.

'What they done to you, kid?' I asked.

'Nothing,' she said. 'Nothing, nothing, nothing. I'm paying your debts.'

191

Mr Deeds said, 'Look fellers, gimme a break, will you. Come back later and we'll sort all this out. Eva's fighting in a minute.'

'Yeah,' one of the guys said. 'She's fighting. Us. Outside.'

Then Harsh came down the steps from the arena. He was with his opponent, Harry and another of the trainers.

They stopped.

Harry said, 'Oh my Lord. Suckle's soldiers, Eva. Din't I tell you?'

Harsh said, 'What's happening?'

'It's Eva,' Mr Deeds said. 'There's some mistake. These gentlemen don't want her to go on.'

'That's right,' the guy said. 'She's finished. She comes with us. No fuss. No mess.'

That was when Sherry-Lee Lewis, Star of the East, appeared. She floated in her red, white and blue satin robe, up to the crowd outside my door. She was a big woman. I told you that, didn't I? Bigger than Harsh, bigger than Harry, bigger than two of the guys Goldie brought.

Then I heard my music. Did I tell you about my music? It's 'Satisfaction' with a lot of steel and brass but without the words.

That was it.

I said, 'I'm on.'

The black guy said, 'No you're not.'

And he took an open razor out of his pocket.

Bastard.

It's like I said. They all want to pinch it off me.

Sherry-Lee Lewis said, 'Want any help, pet?'

'Fuck off all of you,' I said.

I backed into my dressing-room and slammed the door. I untied Ramses and Lineker. I grabbed my bag.

I had Ramses' and Lineker's chains in one hand and my bag in the other.

The door flew open.

The three guys came shoving in. The bastard with the razor was first. Suckle's soldiers. Fucking squaddies.

Ramses leaped. He nearly pulled me arse over teatime. The bastard with the razor jumped back.

Everyone fell over themselves getting out the way. Suckle's wimps.

'Yeah!' I shouted.

Out we went – Ramses, Lineker and me. I swung the bag with the tins of stew and the bolas in it. I didn't give a toss who I hit. Anyone stupid enough to get in my way got what they deserved.

'Come on, boys,' I yelled to the dogs.

'Come on!' I yelled to Harry. 'Let's go!'

And we went. Up the stairs. Through the door. Out into the aisle.

Far below was the ring.

They were playing my music.

I could feel it all – down to the tips of my toes. The dogs, pulling my arm off. The heat. The dark. The crowd turning. Everyone straining their necks to watch me come down.

'This is mine,' I said. 'Nobody's going to take it off me. Nobody.'

'*The London Lassassin*!' yelled the MC in the ring.

The crowd started baying and booing like they always do.

'Shut yer face,' I yelled back. 'Who d'you think you are?'

'Yak-yak-yak,' went Lineker.

'Ro-ro-ro,' went Ramses.

And as we passed the crowd went bat-shit.

'Look at the dogs!' they shouted.

'She brought dogs!'

'The bitch brought her dogs! Ha-ha-ha.'

'Shut yer freakin' mouth,' I shouted. 'Yer all morons.'

'Freak,' they yelled back. 'Slag. Cow. Slut.'

'Ro-ro-ro,' went Ramses.

It was a good entrance, if I do say it myself. The best I'd ever pulled. I wanted to drag it out, slow it down. Even then, there was part of my brain saying, 'Remember this. This is the night you fought Sherry-Lee Lewis at the old Ladywell Baths.'

But the dogs were yanking my arms out of my sockets, and, too soon, I was down at the ringside with Harry panting and flip-flapping behind me.

The ref and the MC came to the ropes. They both looked amazed.

The MC said, 'What sort of stunt do you call this?'

'Out me way,' I said.

'No you don't,' the ref said. 'No dogs in my ring.'

'Give the dogs to Harry,' the MC said.

'Not me, boss,' said Harry, backing off.

'Bucket Nut!' screamed someone in the crowd. And the front rows took it up. 'Bucket Nut! Bucket Nut!'

'Cretins!' I screamed back. And I took the dogs on a parade all round the outside of the ring. I wanted everyone to see. All the Chengs, all the Suckles, all the bastards with razors, all the Goldies, everyone who wanted to stop me.

'Bucket Nut!' they screeched. 'Dirty bitch!'

'Good show,' the ref said. 'Nice work. But you *still* ain't letting those hounds loose in my ring.'

He had a point. To tell you the truth, now I'd got us down to the ringside, I didn't know what the fuck I was going to do with them either.

And then the music changed.

It was like an explosion. 'Great Balls of Fire' came crashing out of the speakers at full volume. It made me jump. It made the dogs bark louder.

The MC scampered to the middle of the ring and turned on his microphone.

'By special request,' he shouted, 'all the way from *Newcastle*, the women's heavyweight champion of the Eastern seaboard, the one, the only, Rockin' Sherry-Lee *Lewis*, Star of the East.'

Down she came. I've got to say it – she was a sight. Her red, white and blue robe billowed like a banner on a windy day. Her red hair seemed to crackle with life. Her white, white skin picked up the light and shone back like she was lit from inside.

She had two trainers – one either side, and behind her came

her mam and her sister. I've got to admit it – she looked like a sodding queen, really regal and dignified.

The crowd gave her a great hand. There would always be a big welcome for someone who was going to show the London Lassassin what's what.

She took no notice of me whatsoever. She walked straight by me, Ramses and Lineker, like we didn't exist. She swung herself up and over the ropes in one easy swing. She took over. She claimed the ring for herself.

Round she went with her arms raised, waving and saluting like she'd already won. And the crowd loved her. They stood and cheered.

What a star!

'I'm impressed,' I shouted up at her. 'What do you do for an encore? Rule Britannia?'

She came over to the ropes.

'Oh, is that you, pet?' she said. 'Didn't see you there.'

Ha-bloody-ha.

'Aren't you coming up?' she said. 'I can't stop around all night by meself.'

'You're making out all right,' I said. 'Except you could go blind, doing what you're doing. That's what the doctors say.'

'Cheeky monkey,' she said. 'Give the little doggies to me mam. She'll look after them for you.'

Now that is *class*.

'All right, Mrs Lewis?' I asked.

Mrs Lewis looked at me and she looked at the dogs. She sighed. She took the chains and went to the front row. Four men and one woman immediately got up to give her a seat. She sat.

'*Siddown*!' she bawled at Ramses and Lineker. That woman had a bark louder than the dogs. Well, she was Rockin' Sherry-Lee Lewis's mam, wasn't she – she *had* to have a bit extra.

Chapter 23

I NEVER GO through the ropes – I go over them in a somersault. It makes me look dangerous. It makes me feel ready. I landed on my toes and strolled over to the middle of the ring.

Some bloke in the crowd yelled, 'Oy, slag, my groin looks better than your face!'

'Come up here,' I yelled back. 'We'll all have a look.'

Sherry-Lee Lewis said, 'What was all that ruck backstage?'

'Personal,' I said. 'Some blokes giving me aggro.'

The ref came over to look like he was giving us official instructions.

'What's going on, Eva?' he said. 'There's a lot of strange faces in the crowd.'

'Yeah.'

'You best not chuck her out the ring tonight,' the ref said to Sherry-Lee Lewis. 'It looks like she got trouble out there.'

'All right,' she said.

'Chuck me out the ring?' I said. 'You can try.'

'Let's get started,' the ref said, and he went off to one side.

We went to our corners. I looked down at Harry and he looked up at me. Years ago he would have looked down at me and I would have looked up at him. It seemed like whenever I saw Harry these days I felt sad.

'Cheer up, Harry,' I said. 'We got a show to do.'

'Be lucky, Eva,' he said.

The bell went, and I spun round and strutted over to meet Sherry-Lee Lewis.

We both went down in a crouch. We circled a couple of times clockwise.

I watched her feet and legs. She had good legs – loads of

strength in the calf and femoral muscles. Her feet looked a bit slow.

I made a lunge and she sidestepped. Yeah, a bit slow but not that slow.

She made a lunge and I sidestepped.

We both lunged and met with hands at shoulder level. She tried to force my arms back. I tried to force hers. Nothing doing.

I tried to jerk her in towards me. She didn't budge an inch. We stayed in the grapple position.

I tried again. The idea is to drag her in and past me. As she goes past I tangle a leg and force her down. It's a simple move.

The tug I gave her would've been enough to put Bombshell in the back row of the stalls. But Bombshell is a pile of parts. Sherry-Lee Lewis is a class act.

'You'll have to do better than that, flower,' she said, coming round a bit but not very far. She circled to my right.

Then without warning she dropped on one knee and went for my right ankle. I brought my leg up, spun on the other foot and went down on her back. She rolled out from under me and we both popped up on our toes again.

'Kid's stuff,' I said.

'That's right, petal,' she said. 'I only use it on kids.'

We went in again. Hard. She got one hand on my upper arm the other arm went behind my neck. I grabbed her elbows. Our heads clashed. I could smell her deodorant.

She had the better hold and she began to drag me down. I resisted. She put on more force. I let go suddenly and sat, whipping my arms round her knees as I went down. Again she rolled as she came down and again we got up.

We were learning a lot about each other.

The ref said, 'You finished shaking hands? Pep it up a bit, girls.'

We circled again. I feinted for her arms. As she stepped back I dropped on one knee and grabbed her ankles. I pulled them towards me and she went over on her back with a crash that made the boards shake.

197

'Oooh,' went the crowd.

I flung myself on top of her. She got her knees up, caught my weight on her feet. She kicked up and I went sailing right over her in a forward roll.

'Aaah,' went the crowd.

It was well-timed. Nicely done. And it looked good.

Fighting with a stranger must be like learning to dance with a new partner. You got to be a bit confident of the other person before you slip in the fancy moves.

I ended up on my back near the ropes. She landed on my shoulders. I brought my legs up, caught her in a scissors – my knees round her head, and pulled her over me.

Now she was on her back and I was on my knees over her face. It was time for some dirty stuff. I got up and started stomping her throat. It looks vicious and it sounds terrible, but actually I hardly touch her.

'Great ugly bully!' an old lady in the crowd screamed.

I gave her the finger and kept stomping.

'Oh-oh-oh,' cried Sherry-Lee.

The good bit was we were right on the edge and she was touching the ropes. The ref rushed over and said, 'Break it up.'

I gave her a couple of extra stomps and the ref pulled me away.

'Cheat,' yelled the crowd.

'Bitch. Ugly great slag.'

'Come up here and say that again,' I yelled, leaning over the ropes.

Sherry-Lee caught me by the left arm and spun me round.

'Go on give it to her,' yelled the crowd.

'Ropes,' she said, out the corner of her mouth.

She wheeled me round and ran me at the far ropes. They hit me in the back. I let myself sink in, and then I catapulted out. She caught me again and threw me across the ring into the ropes on the other side. I was working up a good head of steam – thwonging off the ropes, wheeling and thwonging again.

When I was going fast enough I gave us an extra spin in the

middle of the ring and instead of me crashing the ropes I sent her in, face forward. While she was hanging there I clasped both hands together, leaped in the air and walloped down with a double forearm smash on the back of her neck. She fell to her knees and I kicked her in the face.

It was a bit soon to do that sort of stuff. She didn't know me well enough to trust me, and she didn't like it. But I worked fast and I didn't hurt her. All she felt was the breeze as my boot stopped a whisker away from her chin.

She was good. She arched back like I'd knocked her head off.

I hauled back for another kick. I'm good at kicking. That's what villains do. They kick you when you're down on your knees.

The crowd was screaming fit to burst.

I let fly and she went over backwards. I stood on one of her knees, picked up her other leg and started twisting her foot. The ref got down to look at her shoulders. When he was safely out the way I started biting her ankle.

She shrieked.

'Look what she's doing!' they shouted in the front row.

The ref looked. I stopped biting.

That's where me and the ref work together. I do all sorts of filthy stuff and he always has something else to look at. It makes the crowd go potty.

'Look, look, look,' they shout. He looks. I stop. He looks away. I do all the filthy stuff again.

'You're getting me leg all wet,' Sherry-Lee said, her face contorted with agony.

So I did an elbow drop just to liven things up a bit. She scrambled away like a crab.

This was supposed to be my round. If I was going to go down in the second and third I wanted the first. The trouble was she wouldn't let me have it. She let me do all the villainy – the biting and kicking, but she wouldn't let me have any of my good moves.

I got her head between my knees for a piledriver, but when I picked her up by the waist she locked her knees round my neck and wouldn't fall.

When I tried to hip-throw her she took me down too. She always had a counter move up her sleeve, and it was beginning to make me feel a bit stroppy. I was making her look awfully good but she wasn't giving me anything at all. She just whipped by me with that damn red hair grazing my cheek – like I was a novice or something.

On the other hand I was pleased to see she was beginning to sweat. And when she tried to lift me her legs trembled under the strain. If I read the signs right I was giving her a bit more exercise than she was used to.

She didn't give me anything but lip.

'Call that a pin,' she'd say when I had her in an arm lock and was just getting her rolled over. 'I seen better pins in me mam's hair.' And then she'd do a neat little escape move and I'd have to start all over again.

But I could do it – I knew I could.

I was quicker than her. I *was*. She was an old lady really. When you got in close you could see she was nearly thirty.

But she was strong. Shit – she was strong! Not just power strong, but clever strong too.

If only I could have fought someone like her regular. You don't learn dollop, farting around with the likes of Bombshell.

So that's how it went for a while. I'd tie her up – she'd escape. I'd throw her – she'd land like a cat on her tippy toes and say, 'Thanks for the lift.' No wonder I was getting a touch stroppy.

The ref must've noticed because next time we were in clinching he said, 'Go on, give the kid a break, Miss Lewis.'

Her arms were locked round my arms and back and she had a grip like a meat-grinder. Her mouth was right by my ear.

She said, 'Does baby want a break, then?'

'You can stuff your break,' I hissed.

'Baby doesn't want a break,' she said to the ref. 'Baby wants to do it the hard way.' She was really winding me up.

She tensed her legs and started jumping me up and down. Like she was bouncing me. Up and down. Like a baby. Bounce, bounce, bounce.

'Ha-ha-ha,' went the crowd.

'Ro-ro-ro,' went Ramses. I heard him clear as a bell.

I heaved, and got my right arm free. I caught Sherry-Lee Lewis by the throat just under the chin.

She kept on bounce-bounce-bouncing. She didn't believe I'd do it. But I did. I started bloody squeezing. Proper squeezing.

'Arrgh,' she gurgled. It was music to my ears.

'Ooh the bitch,' went the crowd. 'The filthy hoo-er!'

'Aarrgh-gug-gug,' went Sherry-Lee Lewis, for real.

She let go. Well she had to, didn't she? She was being choked – for real.

I could've just knocked her over, but I wanted to do something she'd remember. So I went for the body-slam. I got her under the shoulders with one hand and the small of the back with the other. I pressed her up, just like a set of Sam's bar-bells. I pressed her right above my head – clean and jerk.

I got it right. It was amazing. I got it right, and there she was, way above my head.

I swung round. I wanted everyone to see. I had Rockin' Sherry-Lee Lewis in the palms of my hands and I wanted everyone to see. I spun. If I was dizzy, imagine how she felt.

And then I slammed her down.

And I dropped on her like a ton of coal.

It was a fall. A proper fall, and a real pin. But that bastard MC rang the bell. Ding-dong – end of round one. The turd, the sodding heap of dog-do wouldn't even let me have one little fall.

She knew how to fall. She wasn't hurt. But she was shaken up, and she was a bit narked. She wouldn't let me help her to her feet.

She said, 'Don't get too cocky with me, baby. I'll spank and you won't like that.'

I put a finger in her face. I said, 'I'll have you, *baby*. I'll have you for my tea.'

201

She tossed that bleeding red hair. 'You'll have rusks and warm milk in a bottle as usual. That's what you'll have, baby.'

The ref pushed us apart. 'Break it up, girls. Great round, *great* round. Now pack it in.'

She turned her back on me and went to her corner. After the fall she just took, it was a nice swagger.

I stood in the middle of the ring like it was mine. 'Don't you turn your back on me,' I shouted at the top of my voice. 'It'll be the last thing you do, *flower*!'

'Boo,' went the crowd.

'Roo-ro-ro,' went Ramses, like he was booing me too.

'Nice work,' said the ref. 'Now fuck off back to your corner.'

In this game it's sometimes hard to tell what's real and what isn't.

Harry climbed up into my corner and gave me a towel.

'Don't get ideas, Eva,' he said. 'I been watchin' and I can see you gettin' ideas.'

'No ideas, Harry,' I said. 'I know my place.'

'One thing you don't know, Eva, that's your place. Save your strength. You goin' to need it soon.'

Then I remembered. You wouldn't think I could forget, would you. But I'd been concentrating, and all that shit with the Chengs, and the bastards with the razor, and Goldie had gone clean out of my head.

'Where are they, Harry?' I asked. I tried to squint up into the crowd, but you can't see more than the first couple of rows because the lights get in your eyes and all the rest is a dark heaving mass.

'They all around you, Eva,' Harry said. 'Maybe you better fight slow. You safer up here than you is down there.'

I looked over at Sherry-Lee Lewis. She was leaning back with her arms outstretched against the corner post. She seemed completely relaxed, but when she looked at me her eyes narrowed. I looked at her mam, and she looked at me with the exact same expression. Even Ramses looked at me like I was dog meat.

'I don't know about that, Harry,' I said. 'It don't look too safe up here either.'

'How you do it, Eva?' Harry asked sadly. 'You make enemies everywhere. Why you do it? It ain't a good life with only enemies wishing you evil.'

I wiped the sweat off my face and hands. I didn't know what to say, he made me feel so sad.

'I'm a villain, Harry.'

'So why you not a good villain?' Harry said. 'It ain't God's wish you be a bad villain.'

'I'm just me, Harry. It ain't me. It's all these other bastards. I got to be bad or I'll be trod on.'

I thought about the bastard with the razor. And I thought about how Ramses sprang up at him when he came through my dressing-room door.

'That dog knows something,' I thought. The bastard with the razor was the one who hung Ramses up by his neck. Lineker too. Only Lineker was too dumb to remember and want revenge. But I wasn't. And Ramses wasn't. Ramses wouldn't even forgive me for letting it happen. Me. Me who fed him and took him to the vet.

Ramses would rather die than forgive and forget. And so would I.

While I was thinking about this, the bell rang for the second round, and someone in the middle of the hall shouted, 'I hope she kills you, you ugly great drong. If she don't, I will.'

'You and who's army?' I yelled back, because suddenly, even with the crowd, I didn't know what was real and what wasn't.

And then Sherry-Lee Lewis hit me in the back. She'd come out of her corner like a ball off a bat and hit me square in the back sending me half way across the ropes. She knocked the breath out of me. Crash, whoosh.

She yanked me off the ropes by my hair and the seat of my pants and slammed me into the corner post.

She grabbed me by the arm, ran me to the centre of the ring

and flicked me over using my arm like the handle of a whip. I went cartwheeling.

It's a great move if you time it right. She kept hold of my wrist just a second too long and she nearly tore my arm off. I couldn't get my feet down in time so I landed hard on my back. She came in as fast as an inter-city train and threw my legs over my head. She folded me up like an empty shirt and nailed my shoulders to the boards.

Ten seconds. It was as quick as that.

'One . . . ' yelled the ref.

'Bury her,' yelled the crowd. 'Bucket Nut, Bucket Nut.'

Ten seconds! What the fuck did she think she was playing at? Well, I knew what she was playing at. She was teaching baby a lesson. And she'd done it in style. The bitch.

But ten seconds! I heaved one shoulder an inch off the canvas.

She banged me down square.

'One . . . ' yelled the ref again.

I had nowhere to go. I was tied up like a kipper with her full weight on me. I could hardly draw breath let alone escape.

But ten bleeding seconds! It was so awful I could hardly believe it.

'Two . . . ' said the ref. 'You sure about this, Miss Lewis? It's a bit quick.'

'Sure I'm sure,' Sherry-Lee Lewis said. She wasn't even breathing heavy.

'Make her suffer,' screamed the crowd.

'Three!' shouted the ref.

Sherry-Lee Lewis got off.

I rolled over and crawled to my knees. Ten seconds was all it took. She held out her hand. I looked at her hand. It was so white and the nails were all pink and shiny. I thought about it.

'Don't even think it,' she said, and helped me up.

'I've seen better things than you in me boyfriend's condom,' some woman yelled. They were really celebrating in the front rows.

'Classy fans you've got, pet,' Sherry-Lee said. 'Cheer up.

You're going to be good. Really good. Don't try to make a fool of me and we'll get along just fine.'

'Okay, okay,' the ref said. 'You showed her, Miss Lewis. Now can we get on? We got a gig to do.'

'There now, there now, Eva,' Harry said. 'Wasn't nothin' you could do about it. Don't waste yourself frettin'. You gotta be a pro like old Harry.'

He was right. But ten manky seconds. At the Ladywell Baths. In front of all those people. I felt so little and wobbly I could've sat down and died.

And the crowd was screaming itself silly.

'What you going to do about *that*, Bucket Nut? Can't take it! Yooo-waaay, boo!'

But she said I was going to be good. Really good. Maybe she meant it.

I looked down at Ramses with his bit of white bandage round his neck. It must've hurt him, what with his choke-chain and all, but he was ignoring it.

'I wouldn't take it from anyone but her, Harry,' I said.

'You wouldn't have to,' he said.

'You're a nice old bird, Harry,' I said.

And then we began again. We began crouching and circling like the first time. Only now I knew what she could do, and I knew what she weighed and how much power she had.

She knew things about me too, and after a bit I saw she wasn't going to take any more liberties. She was just going to do the job. And I thought, all right, I'll do the job too.

She pulled some magic moves, and now she wasn't trying to mash me down so she timed them perfectly, and I never got hurt once. And this time she went with some of my moves so there was a bit more give and take.

After a while I forgot about my back and my teeth and I got into the act. And I did some lovely dirty stuff, kicking her in the guts and looking like I was splitting her legs apart – the stuff that makes the crowd go blind with rage.

She worked the crowd too. It was an education to see how

205

she worked on their sympathy and how she presented herself as noble but suffering.

It takes a really good heroine to make a really bad villain.

True, but don't forget the villain. The badder I was the nobler she looked.

I know we were doing good. You only had to listen to the crowd.

It was about the time the ref and the MC start looking at their watches. Time to wind up. Time for me to take the upper hand.

'When you're ready,' the ref said. Because he has to watch the time in case we go on too long.

And I started really scurfing her. I threw her to all four corners of the ring, and I smashed her face and I put the boot in her ribs, and I knee-dropped on her tits and I did every filthy trick I could think of.

I flattened her in the middle of the ring and then I climbed up the corner post. I was going to do a flying slam. One last spectacular stunt before she turned the fight around.

I bunched myself up to take the leap.

And then someone in the crowd threw a bottle.

It missed me, but it shattered on the canvas. Shining shards of broken glass spread around just where I was going to land. Well, I was going to land on Sherry-Lee Lewis, but I had to take my own weight on my hands and knees or I would've broken her back.

I was all bunched ready to jump, feet balanced on the ropes on either side of the post. But I couldn't jump.

'Hold up, hold up,' said the ref. 'Glass.'

Sherry-Lee rolled away and stood up.

It was like a signal. More bottles fell into the ring. One hit me in the back. It didn't hurt, but I dropped down onto the canvas. Up on the ropes I was like an Aunt Sally in a fairground.

There was a sort of roar and heave in the crowd. People from the back were surging forwards over the backs of the seats and down the aisles. People in the front were pressing towards the ring to get out the way. Women and kids were screaming.

'What the fuck's going on?' Sherry-Lee said.

'This is dangerous,' the ref said, trying to kick the glass away. 'Shit, I knew something was up. This is down to you, Eva. Isn't it?'

There was stuff flying in from all directions and it was all coming at me.

'Get out,' I shouted to Sherry-Lee and the ref. 'They'll let you go.'

'Fuck it,' Sherry-Lee said. 'Keep fighting. Come and get me.'

So I went for her. It was all part of the mess.

'Cut her,' Sherry-Lee said to the ref. 'Pick up some of that glass and cut her.'

'What?' said the ref.

'Cut her! Do it quick.'

We grappled in the middle, dancing out the way of the bottles and bricks. And then she hauled off and hit me with a series of forearm smashes to the face.

The crowd was screaming. I didn't know what they were screaming at. I don't think they knew either. Half of it was at us in the ring – Sherry-Lee coming in with such force. Half of it was because of the surge and mayhem and glass out there.

'Protect your head,' Sherry-Lee said.

I got both arms up. Which was a bit late because I'd just been cracked by a can of 7-up.

The ref stepped in, all official, to look at my face. I felt his hands on my head but I never felt the cut. He was so quick I never felt it. And anyway that was about the time I took a brick on the back of my knee.

'Go down,' yelled Sherry-Lee, and she hit me one more time.

So I went down, ker-rash.

'Stop the fight!' the ref screamed. 'Stop the fight!'

He stood over me on one side. Sherry-Lee stood over me on the other. I could feel blood and sweat pouring down my face.

The bell went and kept on going. Ding-dong, ding-dong, ding-dong.

A sort of hush fell over the crowd. Everything went quiet.

Things stopped raining in on me. Blood poured from my scalp and eyebrow – drip, drip, drip onto the canvas. I lay doggo.

Then I heard Sherry-Lee Lewis shout, 'Is there a doctor out there?'

And the ref took it up – 'A doctor. There's been a serious injury. We need medical help immediately. A doctor *please*.'

'Ro-ro-ro,' went Ramses.

'Yak-yak-yak,' went Lineker.

The crowd was shifting and whispering.

Then the MC got himself together on the loudspeaker. About time too.

'Ladies and gentlemen,' he said. 'Please calm down and take your seats in an orderly manner. There are children in the audience. Please return to your seats quietly and calmly.' He paused, and then said, 'Doctor Foster to the ringside, please. Doctor Foster to the ringside.'

In case you don't know, Doctor Foster is a code word. It means there's trouble and all the Deeds Promotion people hustle into action and sort things out.

I don't know because I couldn't see, stuck there in the middle of the ring playing dead, but everything had been so shambolic I shouldn't think there was even one person backstage who didn't know there had been a ruck. So what the Doctor Foster's message was all about, I've no idea.

I lay there pole-axed, dripping blood. It's wonderful how much gore you can squeeze out of a little scalp wound. And Sherry-Lee Lewis came back to do her Florence Nightingale act. A really concerned, terrific woman. She smeared the blood all over my face and neck.

'You're a star,' I said. 'Bleeding mastermind, you are.'

'Shut up and be dead.'

'How's your mam and the dogs?'

'Shut up!' she said. 'They'll see your lips move.'

She tried to help me sit up so that everyone could see the blood.

'Oooh,' went the crowd. 'Oh my God! Look at that.'

I flopped back down again. Murdered. Horribly murdered.

'Me mam's okay,' said Sherry-Lee Lewis. 'It's a good thing she had your dogs, petal. She's not so quick on her pins these days, but with those two barkers no one laid a finger on her. Let's get a little blood on your tits – that always goes down well.'

'The cavalry's coming,' the ref said. 'They're sorting the crowd out now, but there's still some fighting at the back.'

I felt the stage shake as people climbed up through the ropes.

'Jesus!' Mr Deeds said. 'It was a great show, Miss Lewis, but you didn't have to slaughter her.'

'Didn't I?' Sherry-Lee asked. 'Where were you? In the crapper counting the take?'

'Now, now,' the ref said. 'It's all right, George. No harm done. We had to stop the fight and Miss Lewis did it the quick way.'

'She's a star,' I said.

'Shut up!'

'We got to get her out of here,' the ref said. 'This mess was no accident. There's bastards out there want to hurt her.'

'Well I hope you don't think I'll carry her,' Mr Deeds said.

'Where's Harry?' I asked.

'Shut up!'

'There's a bunch of Chinese blokes and some blacks beating the hell out of each other up at the back,' Mr Deeds said. 'If we can't cool things down the police'll turn up and clear the hall.' He sounded like he was shitting coconuts.

'Let's go,' Sherry-Lee said. 'I'm getting cold out here.'

'What about Eva?'

'She can get up now,' she said. 'I'll help her. Give me a towel.'

She heaved me up to a sitting position. I leaned against her like a corpse. She had a dab with the towel.

'Ain't she wonderful?' said someone in the crowd. 'You wouldn't think she'd want to touch that ugly hulk after what she done to her.'

It seemed like even my near death was making the Star of the East look good.

She bent my head between my legs, like I was fainting and she was reviving me. Actually she was rubbing my hairline to make sure the blood kept running free.

'Upsa-daisy, kiddo,' she said.

I staggered to my feet leaning heavily on her. I quite enjoyed all the gasps and murmurs as everyone saw my bloody face.

We reeled and fell towards the ropes. And then the applause broke out – wave after wave of it. Most of it was for the noble Sherry-Lee, but some of it was sympathy for me. I know it was.

The MC was milking it on the loudspeaker – 'Let's hear it for the winner by a fall and a knockout – the magnificent, the one and only *Rockin'* Sherry-Lee Lewis, Star of the East, Women's Heavyweight *Champion* of the Eastern Seaboard . . . and a big hand for the loser, *Eva* Wylie, the *London* Lassassin. We will be taking Eva to the hospital as soon as possible so would you folk kindly clear the aisles. Clear the aisles as quickly as possible, please. This is a medical emergency. I'm sure we will all wish Eva a speedy recovery from her terrible injuries. A big hand *please* for our two gallant contestants. Best of luck, girls . . . '

It was quite hard to see because of the blood in my eyes, but it was clear from the noise and the tension that something a bit heavy was still going on at the back. And we would have to walk through it to get out of the hall.

'Gimme my dogs,' I whispered.

'Shut up! Me mam can handle them. She's going first.'

'Tell her to take the muzzles off.'

'Shut up!'

'Take the muzzles off.'

'Shit,' said Sherry-Lee. 'Mam, can you get those muzzles off?'

'If you say so, pet,' Mam said. She was wheezing and puffing trying to hold Ramses and Lineker back. She had the dogs by their chains and the enormous silent sister had her mother by the belt. We followed them. I had one arm round Sherry-Lee's neck, she had one arm round my waist, supporting me.

I died and fainted past the front rows and up the aisle steps. As we passed the crowd got to their feet and clapped. It was magic. Well, near magic, because they were probably standing up to get a better view of the carnage. But all the same I got more applause than I'd ever got in my whole life before.

I almost wanted to stay and count the people clapping, so that when I was all alone at night sometime I could say to myself, 'Never mind, when you fought Rockin' Sherry-Lee Lewis at the old Ladywell Baths nine hundred and thirty-four people put their hands together for you.' It's nice to have a number like that to fall back on in the middle of the night.

Up near the back, we stopped. We had to. The backstage exit was blocked by fighting men. They were going at it with fists, with knives and with bottles.

It looked like it was some of the Chengs against some of Count Suckle's men. But I only recognised a couple of blokes from the Beijing Garden and the bastard with the razor who came in with Goldie. It was hard to recognise anyone because mixed up in the middle were Deeds Promotion bouncers and a load of erks from the crowd. The bouncers weren't bouncing. They were just belting anyone who got close, including each other.

The only people not involved were the wrestlers who wouldn't fight anyone but themselves, and then only if they got paid for it. Quite right too, if you ask me. That's the difference between pros and amateurs.

Sherry-Lee's mam couldn't go on. Lineker wanted to go in one direction, Ramses the other, and they'd dragged her arms out like Jesus at Easter.

'Gimme my bag,' I said.

'Shut up.'

'It don't matter now,' I said. 'The punters can't see us back here. Gimme my bag.'

Someone slung the bag at my feet.

'What you going to do now?' Sherry-Lee said.

I didn't say anything. She'd hijacked my entrance. She'd hijacked the whole night. She'd hijacked my injuries. Well, she was the Star, wasn't she, but I was buggered if I'd let her hijack my exit too. Not all of it.

I opened my bag.

The bastards threw things at me, didn't they? They fucked up my fight. Why shouldn't I fuck up theirs?

I grabbed tins of stew and soup and I started hurling them into the ruck. And I started shouting.

'Bugger off you load of turd-tops,' I yelled at the top of my voice.

Tins of stew and soup bounced off their noddles and got trampled underfoot.

'Out me way. Out me *way*, bastards.'

I grabbed for the bolas but they'd got all tangled up and that made me narked. So I chucked the lot at the person nearest me and he went crashing into the back row of the stalls. I could see his feet kicking wildly, all wound round with bolas.

'She crazy,' someone said. 'She mad in the head.'

I let out a tremendous roar and I snatched Ramses' chain out of Sherry-Lee's mam's hand.

I wanted him to clear a path to the exit but he had ideas of his own. He was like a half a ton of pure hate and he steamed into the fight snapping and snarling, saliva dripping off his jaws.

What he didn't bite I bashed with a tin of Campbell's Big Soup. I lashed out at anything in my way.

'She's off her head,' they said. 'She's insane!' I could smell my own blood as it rolled down my face.

We cleared a path all right, but it led straight to the bastard with the razor. Because Ramses was a clever dog who knew his enemies. You can learn a lot from a dog. I was very glad I was behind him, not in front.

I saw him as he slashed at the bastard's right hand. I saw the hand drop the razor. I saw Ramses' jaws crunch down on bones and sinew. And I saw the blood spurt.

It was good to see someone else bleed for a change but I didn't like the scream. The guy screamed, and it sounded horrible, because he was frightened.

I couldn't blame him. When I saw Ramses work on that hand, work for a proper grip, I got a bit frightened myself. I hauled back on the chain.

'Enough!' I shouted.

The guy ripped his hand out of Ramses' jaws and ran. He stumbled and staggered away behind the stalls and Ramses nearly pulled me over trying to go after him.

'*No!*' I screamed.

'Ro-ro-ro,' went Ramses.

'No!' I yelled at Ramses. 'Enough.'

When he turned I saw he had blood and saliva flowing from his open mouth. He looked quite insane.

I turned him and we went back to the exit. No one stopped us. I was glad because I'd had enough. I couldn't wait to get backstage and put Ramses' muzzle on before he remembered he hated me too. That's the trouble with dogs, they're like amateurs – they don't know when to stop.

Chapter 24

'YOU'RE MAD,' MR Deeds said. 'You're stark staring bonkers. That dog ought to be put down. Go and wash your face. I can't think with you looking like that. You ought to wash that dog's face too. That's human blood he's got round his mouth. That dog has tasted human blood and he ought to be put down.'

'I haven't got a basin in my room,' I said. 'You put me in a broom cupboard and there's no bleedin' water.'

'Come to mine, flower,' Sherry-Lee Lewis said. So I went. She was still the big star, but I didn't mind taking favours off her now. We were more equal than we used to be.

Everyone was out in the corridor watching – the Julios, the Wolverines, Harsh, Gruff and Pete. Gruff and Pete couldn't go on until the ring had been cleaned up and the audience were back in their seats. They were well narked off.

'Get rid of her, boss,' Gruff said. 'She's nothing but bother.'

'And you're nothing but a waste of good skin,' I said.

'Tarts in the ring are a crime against nature.'

'Is that right?' Sherry-Lee Lewis said. She stared hard at his belly. Her mam and the silent sister stared hard too.

'Only joking, girls,' Gruff said, tying the cord tight round his robe.

'Was that a joke?' Sherry-Lee asked her mam. 'I heard someone farting, but I didn't hear no joke. Did you?'

'Ladies! Please,' Mr Deeds said. 'We've all got a little overheated.'

'Where's Harry?' I said.

But no one knew, so I trailed the three enormous Lewises to Sherry-Lee's dressing-room and had a shower.

I was glad I didn't have to push off home covered in sweat and blood, but in the shower I felt as if I was losing some of my skin as well. I almost saw it drain away down the plughole with the dirty water. It's like I stop being me when I take off the black costume, and then I wash off the hard shell when I take a shower. I don't know. I was tired and maybe the water was too hot. But anyway, by the time I got out I was feeling quite sorry for myself.

I was thinking that I didn't have a proper home to go to, and I didn't have any money for a nice big dinner. Which I wanted because I'd used up a lot of energy in the ring. Boo-hoo, poor baby.

What made it worse was the Lewises who were very nice to me – nicer than they had to be.

When I dried myself off I found they had spread this huge picnic out around the dressing-room. There was cooked chicken, and ham, and hard boiled eggs and tinned salmon and potato salad, and bread and butter, and fruit cake, and chocolate biscuits, and tea out of thermos flasks.

'Just a quick snack before the drive home,' Sherry-Lee's mam said.

'Mam won't pay London prices,' Sherry-Lee said.

The silent sister handed me a paper plate with some of everything on it, and I tucked in just like one of the family.

Mr Deeds came in with Sherry-Lee's purse and she made him stand there while she counted it. I didn't see how much she got because she turned her back.

'Can I have my money too?' I asked.

'You can have yours on Tuesday like always when I've done the books,' he said.

'I had expenses,' I said. 'I'm stony.'

Any other time he'd have said, 'Tough shit, you know the score.' But with the three big Lewises and Ramses and Lineker all giving him hard looks he handed me twenty quid.

'On account,' he said. 'I'm writing it down so don't complain you're short twenty quid on Tuesday.'

When he left, Sherry-Lee said, 'you should watch fellers like him, petal. One Tuesday, sometime, he'll turn up missing. I should know, I had a husband like him once.'

'So did I,' said her mam.

The silent sister said nothing.

'What about your family?' Mrs Lewis said. 'Doesn't your mam come to the fights?'

'Oh Ma,' I said. 'She was busy tonight or she would've come.'

Because whatever I think about Ma in private I never let her down in front of strangers. Well, you don't, do you? And she has had a hard life so I can't blame her really.

'I bet she's right proud of you,' Mrs Lewis said.

She was a nice woman, Mrs Lewis, but she didn't know piddle-pie-po about Ma.

I left soon after that because I was tired and because the yard had been unprotected for too long. I wanted to see Harry, but he wasn't around.

I don't know why I wanted to see him, really I don't. It was just that he had been in my corner that night and it seemed wrong to leave without saying goodbye. Hot water makes you go soft. That was it.

I didn't see Harsh either. He'd already gone by the time I left. Which was a pity because I wanted to know if he'd seen any of my fight, and if so I wanted to know what he thought. But he wasn't there so I couldn't ask.

One good thing happened when I got back to the yard.

Ramses ate his dinner.

I decided to feed the dogs early because they'd had a tough old day. So I mixed up their horrible nosh and put it down for them. And Ramses wolfed his up, shrurp, slurp, chomp, just like nothing had happened and he'd never been off his feed.

So that made me feel better – even if I did have to sleep on the hard floor in my old sleeping bag, and the Static smelled of car paint and gave me bad dreams.

Chapter 25

WHEN I WOKE up my head hurt like a hot fat blister. It felt as if yellow pus was ready to burst out of my ears, which was funny because I'd been dreaming about Ma. In the dream she was sitting on my shoulders and drilling a hole in my head.

It was dark and I thought it was still the middle of the night. But then I remembered about boarding up the door and windows. So I got up and opened the door.

It was broad daylight. But it was Sunday and I hate Sundays. I hate dreams and I hate Sundays. That's two things I hate and those were the two things happening – Ma drilling a hole in my head on a Sunday. How lucky can you get?

The Static was bright red but I was black and blue – bruised all over from crashing around with Sherry-Lee Lewis. I wondered how she looked this morning. Bruises would show up something awful on that white skin. I wished I could see her. It might have made me feel better.

I was hungry. I looked in my bag, but I'd chucked every last tin of stew into the crowd the night before. That's the trouble with me – I don't think ahead. If I'd thought ahead I would've saved a can of stew for breakfast instead of using it as a weapon. I hoped that last can of stew gave someone a bad dose of concussion.

That's human nature, isn't it? When you feel bad you want someone else to feel worse. Well, it's my nature anyway. Maybe Harry's right. Maybe I'm not a very nice person. But look at Harry. He may be a nice old bird, but nice didn't get him very far. He had to cover it up with a mask when he was fighting.

You can stuff nice. That's *my* opinion for what it's worth.

Still, Mr Deeds paid me last night. I decided to go to Hanif's to buy tea and milk and something to eat. But no sooner had I decided to go out than that poxy dream gave me an idea. I fetched a half inch drill from the shed and then I drilled holes in the boarding over the doors and windows. The holes were big enough to let in some light and fresh air but they were too high up to let anyone spy on me without standing on a ladder. Even bad dreams are good for something.

While I was at it I disconnected the electricity. Who needs it? I don't. You soft central-heated buggers might, but I don't. Creature comforts make you weak and wobbly. You're so used to comfort you curl up and die when it's taken away. Not me. I'm prepared.

It's like Sunday – everyone tucked away in their squishy little homes with their squishy little families hiding from the world. No wonder they all moan come Monday when they have to get out and hustle again. They're not prepared for the hustle, see. Sunday squishes you all up.

Hanif has the right idea. Hanif stays open on Sunday. It's just another work day for him.

I had just about made up my mind to go and see him when I heard the dogs. The dogs have the run of the yard all day on a Sunday because there's no one working there.

I heard them making a big fuss out by the gate. So I picked up a tyre wrench and went out there to see what was happening. I really hoped it wouldn't be more trouble, because although I was prepared I'd had enough trouble that week.

But when I got there I saw a white Peugeot outside the gate, and that lady copper was leaning against the door.

'You again,' I said. 'What you want now?'

'Not much,' she said. 'I thought you might like to hear about your friend, Eleanor.'

'You thought wrong,' I said. 'She's no friend of mine.'

She said nothing for a bit. I just stood there. I could've just walked away, but she was company – of a sort.

'Well?' I said after a while. 'If you've got something to say, say it.'

'I saw most of your fight last night.'

'So?'

'It was good stuff.'

'Yeah?'

She bit her thumb. 'I'm going down the Cut for a pie and mash. Want to come?'

'Nah,' I said. 'No dosh.' I wasn't going to tell her about what Mr Deeds gave me, was I?

'I'm buying,' she said.

'I'm coming,' I said.

So we went over to the Cut and had pie and mash.

'I was wondering,' she said, when we were sitting down, eating.

'What?' I said.

'I'm in security work.'

'So?'

'Sometimes we need a bit of extra muscle.'

'What for?'

'This and that,' she said. 'Personal protection. Someone to watch the door. Sometimes we have properties which need an eye kept on them.'

'Yeah?'

'I could put you on my books.'

'Work for you?'

'Now and then,' she said.

'Money?'

'Usual rates,' she said.

'Cash?'

'If you like.'

'In advance?'

She grinned at me. She wasn't as dumb as she looked.

'All right,' I said. 'You can put me on your books.'

She gave me her card and I put it in my pocket.

I was glad I had the chance of more work, because I was finished with the Chengs. Even if they decided to live and let live I'd never work for them again. Ever.

But the funny thing was that although I hated Auntie Lo now, I sort of missed her too. I missed her fancy shoes and her huff-huff laugh and her silly jokes. She was someone to talk to now and then. I used to think of her like she was my real Auntie. Which was stupid when you think of the way she treated me. She was too clever by half.

The lady copper was better than nothing, but what I needed was to work for someone I could handle. Someone who was rich and stupider than me. That made me think of the artist dweeg. Have you ever seen a bloke who always looks one step behind? Well, Dave de Lysle looked like that, and it made him just about perfect for me.

We went on eating, the lady copper and me. They do a good pie and mash down the Cut. After the pie I had treacle tart and custard.

'All right,' I said when my pudding was half finished. 'If you got to tell me, tell me.'

'What?'

'Goldie,' I said.

She held up her cup in both hands like she was warming her fingers. She wasn't eating pudding, just drinking tea.

'She's back home with her family,' she said. 'I got her out when things turned nasty at the Ladywell Baths.'

'Did she want to go?'

The lady copper grinned at me. 'I didn't kidnap her,' she said. 'She'd had enough. She's a nice, middle-class girl and things got too rough for her. Her father's paying for her to go to Italy. But first they're putting her in a clinic.'

'What for?'

'Clean up.'

'Why?'

'She was already doing cocaine and crack. She was just starting on heroin when you met her.'

'She told me she only took it to stop that poncy singer having it.'

'The things they say,' she said.

I finished my treacle tart.

My head felt less like a blister now. All I needed was a breath of fresh air and a chunk of pie in my belly.

The lady copper said, 'Want to see her?'

'Who?'

'Your friend. Goldie.'

'Fuck off,' I said. 'I told you. She's no friend of mine.'

'Thought it might help.'

'Help what?'

She gave me a real vinegary smile – a proper polizei grin – and said nothing.

'Help what?' I said again, narked.

'Keep your hair on,' she said. 'She's feeling guilty. Unfinished business. That sort of stuff. I thought you might know.'

'Know what?' I said. 'You a social worker or something?'

She just sat, drinking her tea. She didn't even look insulted.

'Feeling guilty,' I said. 'I should sodding well hope so. You should see what she owes me. Never mind she's a treacherous clap-ridden cow. Never mind she turned me over and her diseased mates hung my dogs and ripped off my stash and shat on my bed. Never mind all that. Baby feels guilty. What a long weak stream of stale piss.'

'Mmm,' she said. 'Feeling better?'

'Up yours,' I said. But I didn't turn the table over and stomp out. I hadn't finished my tea.

'Did you lend her any money?' she asked.

'Hundreds.'

'Oh yeah?' she said with the sour grin on her talking-box. 'Be reasonable and I'll talk to her father for you.'

'Yeah?'

'I'm seeing him tomorrow to close the account.'

'He won't cough up for the likes of me.'

'He's settling all her debts.'

'I won't hold my breath,' I said.

'You're one of life's natural optimists, aren't you?' she said, and drained her mug.

'That's a fact,' I said. And I felt quite pleased, because it's true. When you think about everything that happened to me in the past few days you've got to admire the way I was still in there hustling with a smile on my face. I do, anyway.

She took me back to the yard. When we got there she said, 'See this car?'

'Yeah,' I said.

'White Peugeot,' she said.

'Yeah?'

'Licence plate?'

'What?'

'Read the licence plate.'

'Why?'

'Well,' she said. 'I just want you to know that if my motor ever goes missing, this is the first place I'll come and look.'

And she drove off. Just like a farkin' copper. They always want you to know how smart they are. They make me puke.

Work for her? Oh, I'd work for her all right, and I'd steal her blind. Just you see if I don't!

I'd put one over on her already. I mean, who paid for the pie and mash? Tell me that. And me with money in my pocket. I didn't pay, did I? So who do you reckon was smarter?

All the same, as soon as that little white Peugeot had buzzed off round the corner I remembered it was Sunday again. I didn't exactly want her back but she had been someone to talk to. Now there was nothing to do and nowhere to go. Sam's Gym would be full to bursting with recreationals and there'd be no space for someone serious like me. Just a load of secretaries in their little pink headbands and floppy socks trying not to sweat too much. Secretary types don't like sweat. On a Sunday the gym reeks of deodorant and hair spray. It's enough to make your eyes water. The blokes aren't much better. I'll swear some of them shave their legs. I know they shave their chests. They don't want to be strong. They want to be pretty.

I thought about Goldie and the way she looked in those green leotards I bought for her.

'You can stuff pretty in the same place you stuffed nice,' I said out loud, and Ramses showed me his big yellow teeth.

I thought I'd better look at his neck but he backed off snarling and wouldn't let me get near him. That dog does not have a forgiving nature.

I did not want to think about Goldie. It was the sort of day when she would have washed her hair. She was always washing that hair. Then we might have sat by the fire and watched telly.

It was a good thing I kicked her out when I did or I'd have ended up as soft as she was.

Sundays stink worse than Gruff Gordon's jockstrap. Sundays are for the dead and dying. When I finally croak I bet it'll be on a Sunday.

Chapter 26

THE NEXT DAY was Monday and I was glad. The crusher
screamed and the metal groaned and the men shouted the
way they always do. The world came to life after dead Sunday.
It was quite a relief and I slept my first decent sleep in ages. No
dreams, thank you very much.

It was about two in the afternoon when I opened my eyes and
saw white spots on the red wall. The sun was shooting through
the holes I'd drilled in the window. I got up. I stretched. I did
forty press-ups and ditto squats. Then I washed and dressed.

Leaving the yard was tricky because through the holes in the
door I saw Rob with a face as long as a limousine and I knew
he'd pester me about Goldie. Lovesick blokes are a pain in the
tit so I sneaked out while he was looking the other way. I
had plans and I didn't want his mournfulness to spoil my day.
Mournfulness is catching and I'd only just shaken off some of
my own.

The sun was bright but not hot. It was chill enough to freeze
the spit in your mouth. I had a bacon and egg sandwich in the
caff on Mandala Street and it warmed me up no end. Then I
had a good look round to make sure. You've got to be careful
when you've got as many enemies as me. Where they came from
I'll never know. After all, none of what happened was my fault.
Well, *was* it?

I thought I'd begin with my good deed for the day. I thought
I'd do Dave de Lysle a favour. I wasn't going squishy. Not me.
It's good management. Take a tip from me – if you are going
to use a bloke, soften him up first.

So, like I said, I had a good look round and then I started the
old grey Volvo and drove smartly off north of the river. Dave

de Lysle would be so pleased to see his motor back he'd be putty in my hands. Not that he was difficult to manage anyway. I was just feeling extra kind.

But on the way there I started thinking about my fight with Sherry-Lee Lewis. It was hard not to. It was the best fight I ever fought in my entire life. Just thinking about it made my blood fizz. Dave de Lysle didn't see my fight. That's how keen he was. You'd think the least a rich dweeg like him could do was get a cab down to the old Ladywell Baths when he couldn't find his clapped-out old banger. But no. Some blokes are born dweegs. You can't educate them.

Well, it was his loss. But it was my loss too. I wanted to talk to someone about that fight. I wanted just one person to say, 'Nice one, Eva.'

It almost made me want to go on driving north till I got to Newcastle. I could talk to Sherry-Lee Lewis. She knew. She was there. She even said, 'If that Mr Deeds of yours gives you any aggravation, come up north.'

Yes, she did. And she said, 'A big girl like you can always make a living in my home town.'

What do you think of that? That shows respect. North was the place to go.

But there wasn't enough gas in the tank. The fuel gauge was nearly on zero. So I went to find Harry instead. Not to Bermuda Smith's cellar – I'm not an idiot. I went to the place Harry goes to play dominoes. I thought if he wasn't there, one of the old men he plays with might know where he was. But he was there. He was sitting in the window looking all lopsided.

When I went in and looked at him properly I saw that one of his eyes was completely closed and he had to twist his neck round to squint at his dominoes. It looked like a bird had laid a black egg in his eye-socket.

'Ho!' he said when he looked up and saw me there. 'What you doin', Eva?'

'Came to see you, Harry.'

'What you want with me, girl?' he said. 'More trouble? What you done now?'

'Nothing,' I said. 'No trouble. Why? Are those bastards still looking for me?'

'Better lie low, Eva,' he said. 'Better let the big men fight it out without you. You and me, Eva, we small fry.'

The old guy he was playing with sniggered. He set down a domino, slapping his palm flat on top of it – whack. 'Small fry!' he said, giggling. 'Someone close your other eye, man? You gone blind or what?'

Harry said, 'Go home, girl. You ain't important to the big men no more, but you not welcome in their territory neither. Din't you hear?'

'Hear what, Harry?'

'Negotiations,' Harry said. 'Mr Cheng and Count Suckle, they both go to Heathrow airport. No soldiers but plenty security. Nobody's territory, see.'

'What happened, Harry?'

'Everyone say Mr Cheng keeps Bermuda Smith's Cellar Bar. Mr Cheng is one very smart gentleman, Eva. Bermuda Smith going to open up again so maybe I get my job back.'

'Bully for you, Harry,' I said. I was choked. No one was going to give me *my* old job back.

'You stay missing, Eva,' Harry said. 'Biggest mistake I ever made, asking you to help out.'

'Fuck you too, Harry,' I said. 'I only came to be sociable.'

He stared at me out of his one good eye.

'Don't be what you ain't,' he said. 'You goin' to be a good fighter, Eva, but don't try bein' sociable. You get me killed one day. Go home. Be safe.'

Well, sod him! I went to see Dave de Lysle instead.

When he opened the door he was wearing an apron. It wasn't a lady's apron. It was a big white canvassy thing with splatters of gunge on it, but it was an apron all the same. I ask you! What sort of bloke opens his front door in an apron? I'd have blushed for him if I'd been the blushing kind.

'Eva!' he said. 'What a surprise. Come in, come in.'

Say what you like about dwerbs who open doors in aprons – at least he knew how to be sociable, not like some I could mention.

'I've got some plaster going off,' he said. 'Just let me finish and then we'll go up and put the kettle on.'

I thought he was doing a proper plaster job, like a wall or something, but he wasn't. He was smearing the stuff on a big ball thing which was attached by an iron bar to a board.

'A portrait,' he said.

'What of?' I said. 'A giant white bollock?'

'No, no,' he said. 'I'm making a mould. Under all this plaster there's a clay head.' And he kept on daubing plaster all over it. Scupture doesn't look like a very skilled job to me.

His work room was covered in grey dust and you couldn't see what anything was. All the big shapes were covered with wet sheets and polythene. It was quite boring really. Maybe one day when I'm feeling helpful I'll offer to spray-paint his walls red like the Static. Red's a good colour. It's got a bit of life in it – not like all the white and grey in Dave de Lysle's room.

To please him, I said, 'I thought you lost your old grey Volvo.'

'I did,' he said. 'Otherwise I would've come to your fight. I was really sorry to have missed it.'

I could've said, 'What about taking a taxi, dwerb? How hard is that?'

But I didn't. I said, 'There's an old grey Volvo out in the road a few doors down from your house.'

'No!' he said, sounding all amazed.

'Take a look,' I said, enjoying myself. 'You can probably see it from the window.'

He set down his plaster bowl which was just about empty anyway, and went to the window.

He craned his neck. He said. 'That's it all right. How the hell did it get there? What rotten luck.'

'Why?' I asked, beginning to feel a bit choked.

'I was going to get a new car out of the insurance company.'

He looked upset and bewildered. 'Damn,' he said. 'I *wanted* a new car.'

Well, really! You try to do some blokes a favour and what do you get? A boot in the teeth – that's what you get.

He turned away from the window, all disgusted. He went over to a big stone sink in the corner and started washing his hands.

'Someone must have brought it back,' he muttered. 'Why would anyone do a thing like that? How very odd.'

He dried his hands on his apron. Then he took the apron off and slung it on the floor.

'Never mind,' he said, and smiled, looking like his normal self again. 'Let's get a cup of tea and cheer ourselves up.'

I followed him to the kitchen. He filled the kettle.

'Sit down,' he said. 'Make yourself comfortable.'

He pulled a big glass jar out of a cupboard. The jar was full of biscuits.

'Help yourself,' he said. And I did.

He made the tea.

'So,' he said, when we were sitting on opposite sides of the table, each with a big mug of tea and the biscuit jar in the middle. 'So what brings you to my door this afternoon?'

He had forgotten! Bleeding Dweeg de Dwerb had fucking forgotten. I was glad I'd brought his rotten motor back. I was well chuffed he couldn't have a new one.

'What's the matter?' he said.

'You've forgotten,' I said.

'Forgotten what?'

'My sister,' I said. 'You promised you'd ring the solicitor. I took my clothes off and you did your drawing. But you've forgotten.'

'Don't *shout*,' he said. 'For God's sake! You don't have to chew the carpet. I'll do it now. Just sit down and . . . Where's that letter?' And he dithered around like a fart in a trouser leg. Well what would you expect from a bloke in an apron? I was just about ready to ram his teapot down his corduroys when he found the letter.

I followed him into the sitting-room where the phone was but he said, 'Sit in the kitchen, Eva.'

'No,' I said, 'you'll let those poncy blobs of goat's dribble walk all over you.'

'Thanks,' he said.

'You will.'

'I won't,' he said. 'But it's good to know you think so highly of me.' He stared at me. And I thought maybe I'd better be a bit more careful of his feelings. I'd forgotten about him being an artist and all that crap. People say artists are very sensitive about their feelings, and who knows, maybe they're right. I never met one before.

'All right,' I said. 'But I know what I'm talking about. I had a solicitor once and he never listened to a word I said. I had to chuck his briefcase out the window before he'd even look me straight in the eye.'

'Did you?' he asked, looking very interested.

''Course I did.' Well I did. But it didn't do me a blind bit of good. At the end of the day I was still on remand and that shite-hawk went home to his tea without a care in the world.

'Lawyers are nearly as bad as social workers,' I told him, because he didn't know very much and he needed some friendly advice.

'They play silly buggers with other people's lives,' I said. 'They cock up, but it's no skin off *their* noses. They just go home to their gin and tonics and forget all about you and the dog-dung they got you into.'

I wanted him to know how important it was.

'See,' I said, 'it's my sister. I haven't seen her since she was twelve and I was eleven. And the why of us not seeing each other is all down to solicitors and social workers. They don't understand family feeling. They put you in places where it's convenient for *them*. Never mind you were perfectly happy where you was before they came along sticking their noses in.'

I was feeling all hot and sore inside and my teeth started to hurt. I dug in my pocket and came up with the photo I stole off Ma who didn't deserve it.

'There,' I said. 'That's her. That's Simone two days before the last time I saw her. That's two days before the Place of Safety Order. And who did that? Solicitors and social workers did that. That's who.'

He looked at the photo long and hard. I let him look because he had to see why it mattered.

'All right,' he said. 'I'll be very, very careful. I understand.'

'You don't,' I said. 'And it doesn't matter. I just want you to believe me.' Which was true.

'I do believe you,' he said. 'But I still want you to go back to the kitchen. I can't think with you looming over me. You'll put me off. I might have to lie a little, you see.'

'Lie a lot,' I said, feeling a bit better. 'Lie your head off. You have my blessing.'

'Thanks,' he said. 'But go and finish your tea.'

So I went, and I thought about him lying to a bunch of solicitors on the telephone. For me. It almost made him a pal. And I looked at the photo and I thought of all the times I'd lied for Simone and she'd lied for me. There's a bond between people who lie for each other.

The funny thing was that people believed Simone when she lied, but they hardly ever believed me even when I told the truest truth.

Dave de Lysle said he believed me. And I believed him when he said that. But it doesn't do to believe too much, especially from blokes. So I went and put my ear to the door.

Good big houses have good thick doors. I had my ears out on stalks trying to catch what he was saying but I couldn't, and I remembered how I couldn't earwig him and his long-necked lady friend having a fight. Thick doors are a big disappointment. In Ma's flat I'd have heard every word. In Ma's flat they'd have heard every word three doors along. It's like everything else – secrets cost money.

He took his time.

Actually I don't know why I say that. He didn't take his time – he took mine. I mean, who was doing the waiting? Me. That's who. I'm glad I've acquired a relaxed mental attitude – otherwise I might've started breaking his blue and white china, he took so long. Which would have been a pity because it was nice china and it reminded me of blue eyes.

But he came back after a while. He came back frowning and tapping his teeth with a pencil. He came back with a piece of paper in his hand, but he didn't give it to me.

'Well?' I said. 'What happened?'

'You'll go through the floor if you jump around like that,' he said. 'Sit down. Please. I've got something for you but I don't think you'll like it.'

'What?' I said. 'What? Spit it out.'

'It isn't much. Are you going to sit down and listen quietly?'

I sat down, and he said, 'You wanted Simone's family address . . .'

'What d'you mean, "family"?' I said. '*I'm* Simone's family.'

'All right, all right,' he said. 'Please sit down.'

'Foster family,' I said. 'Get it right.'

'Eva,' he said. 'Take a deep breath. Listen calmly. Simone was adopted. She's Simone Redman now.'

'No she ain't,' I said. 'She's Simone Wylie, just like me. She'd never change her name.'

'She was adopted, Eva,' he said. 'Please sit down.'

I sat down with a bump. 'They lied to you, those lawyers,' I said.

He said, 'I don't think so, Eva.'

'They lied,' I said. 'And I'll prove it to you.'

'How?'

'Did you get an address off them?'

He held up a piece of paper.

'Well, come on then,' I said.

'Where?'

'Where it says on that bit of paper,' I told him. 'We'll go there and I'll prove it to you. My sister would never let herself get adopted and she'd never in a million years change her name.'

'Perhaps she didn't have much say in the matter.'

'No!'

'You're upset, Eva,' he said. 'I do understand. But shouting and jumping up and down won't help.'

'I'm not upset,' I said. 'Those cat-piddle lawyers lied to you and you believed them. I can prove it to you. Come on.'

I snatched the paper out of his hand. But the light had gone funny and I couldn't read what he'd written.

'What's it say here?' I asked. 'Your writing's all straggly.'

He handed me a tea towel.

'Blow your nose,' he said. 'I'll make a fresh pot of tea.'

'You can stuff your tea,' I said. 'I'm going to see Simone. I've waited long enough.'

'You can't just march in there unannounced.'

'When did they pass that law through Parliament?'

'Eva,' he said, 'Eva, have you asked yourself why, in all these years, Simone has never come to find *you*?'

'What are you saying?' I said. '*What are you saying?*'

'I'm not saying anything, Eva. I'm only asking.'

'What other lies they been telling you?' I asked. 'It's nothing but lies.'

Because, quite suddenly, I remembered something. I remembered something about the time I usually don't remember. I remembered something about the time I went to Braintree in Essex to rescue Simone from the Redmans. The time they wouldn't let me see her.

I remember I went there and it was a Saturday. Mr Redman was at home. He opened the door to me. Mrs Redman came from somewhere in the house and stood beside him. They didn't want me to come in. They said Simone was at her ballet lesson. And it was lies, all lies. Simone and me wouldn't touch anything soppy like ballet with a ten foot pole.

They didn't want me inside their house. But I was only a little kid of eleven or so, and I hadn't met Harsh yet, so I hadn't acquired a relaxed mental attitude. I pushed past them and I ran to the bottom of the stairs calling Simone's name. Because I knew they were telling me lies about the ballet lessons and everything.

I would have run up the stairs, but Mr Redman caught me and pulled me back. He said something. Something about how Simone had a new life now and a fresh start and how I mustn't upset her.

Me! Upset Simone! He was lying to me and I was so angry I started kicking and punching him. And I remember him fighting me and yelling at his wife to call the police.

Well, the polizei came. But not before I'd given Mr Redman a very hard time. Because, even then, I knew a bit about fighting. I remember he had a bloody nose and mouth, and all the little china whatsits in the hall and living-room had got broken. I don't remember actually breaking them, but there was glass and china all over the floor. And Mrs Redman had a nasty gash on one of her knees. And her face was all red and swollen up.

The polizei came. And I'm not sure how it happened but they got me so I couldn't move. I couldn't move an inch. I felt like a helpless little baby. Me!

And Mrs Redman said, 'Take her away. Take her away. She's mad. Insane. She's violent. She always has been. My daughter must be protected from her.'

My daughter must be protected from her.

Can you imagine that?

The lies they told about me!

I was screaming at the polizei about the lies and about rescuing Simone. But they didn't listen to me. They never do.

They carried me backwards out of the house.

But this is the part I remember now, which normally I don't remember . . .

'Eva!' Dave de Lysle said. 'Eva, what's the matter?'

'Nothing,' I said. 'I was just thinking, that's all.'

'I'll get you a drink,' he said.

He brought me a glass tumbler with something in it.

'Slowly,' he said.

So I drank it slowly. It didn't taste very nice but it warmed me up inside and I stopped shivering.

We sat there, all quiet. Him on his side of the table and me on mine with the big jar of biscuits in between.

'Better?' he said, after a bit.

'I'm all right,' I said. Except I was feeling tired. Which was funny because I hadn't done any proper exercise since the fight.

'You gave me quite a scare,' he said. 'I thought for a minute you were going to beat me up and throw me out of the window.'

'Me?' I said, surprised. 'Hurt you? What you ever done to me?'

'Nothing, he said. 'But I thought you were angry.'

'Me?' I said. 'Angry?'

'About me advising you to think twice about going to see the Redmans.'

What a funny bloke. I wasn't angry. I was once, but that was years ago.

'I am thinking twice,' I said. 'And maybe you're right.'

'Good,' he said. 'Rushing off without thinking might do you more harm than good.'

'You sound like Harsh,' I said. Which surprised me because I've got a lot of respect for Harsh whereas Dave de Lysle is only an artist.

'Take care when applying force,' I said. Which is what Harsh always says. Harsh says, 'Force applied without thought may harm only you.'

He's talking about wrestling, in case you didn't know. But, although it might sound like a load of crumble, I thought about it in connection to the Redmans.

Because the part I remembered about going to rescue Simone from the Redmans – the part I usually don't remember – was about when I left.

The polizei were dragging me out backwards and I couldn't move and I couldn't run and I couldn't save myself. And the last thing I saw as they dragged me out was Simone at the top of the stairs.

She *was* there.

I knew she was there all along. I knew the Redmans had been lying to me. I knew they'd locked her up so she couldn't see me. But she got free and there she was at the top of the stairs. I was so happy to see her. She would explain. She would tell them, and they would believe her. People always believed Simone.

'Simone!' I said. 'Tell them. *Tell them.*'

But she never got a chance to tell them because Mrs Redman rushed up the stairs. She said, 'Never mind, darling. We're here. You're safe now.' And she put her arms round Simone. It made me boil over. What *right* had she?

I expected Simone to push the poxy old cow down the stairs. But she never.

I couldn't understand it.

And the worst thing was that Simone was wearing a frilly little dancing dress and soppy little dancing shoes. And they'd put her hair up in a daft little knot on the top of her head. They had turned her into a stranger.

And then Mr Redman slammed the door and that was that. I can't remember what happened next.

This, then, was what I was thinking about.

You see, I'm not an angry little kid anymore. I am Eva Wylie, the London Lassassin. And next time I go to visit the Redmans I want them to respect me. Next time I go there I want to be Heavyweight Champion, and I want to have money in my pocket. Proper money, so that I can take Simone away properly.

I mean, we aren't little kids on the run. Not now.

I'm grown up. And the next time I rescue Simone I want it to work. I want her to know I'm someone to look up to. Someone to respect. Someone who can take care of her family.

So I looked at Dave de Lysle sitting there in his big kitchen, like he was permanently one step behind as usual. And I thought he was a good place to start. Because of course I needed cash and those bastards had ripped off my stash. I needed to get my teeth fixed and I needed cash for Simone.

So I said, 'You want me to pose for you now?'

'Now?' he said.

'Now,' I said.

'All right,' he said.

'Proper money this time?' I asked.

'All right.'

'In advance?' I said.

'If you want,' he said.

There are some people just begging to be taken advantage of, aren't there? And I'd be a fool not to, wouldn't I?